The
Virgin's
Knot

The Virgin's Knot

HOLLY PAYNE

DUTTON

DUTTON
Published by the Penguin Group
Penguin Putnam Inc., 375 Hudson Street, New York, New York 10014, U.S.A.
Penguin Books Ltd, 80 Strand, London WC2R 0RL, England
Penguin Books Australia Ltd, Ringwood, Victoria, Australia
Penguin Books Canada Ltd, 10 Alcorn Avenue, Toronto, Ontario, Canada M4V 3B2
Penguin Books (N.Z.) Ltd, 182–190 Wairau Road, Auckland 10, New Zealand

Penguin Books Ltd, Registered Offices: Harmondsworth, Middlesex, England

Published by Dutton, a member of Penguin Putnam Inc.

First printing, July 2002
10 9 8 7 6 5 4 3 2 1

Grateful acknowledgment is made for permission to reprint the following:

An excerpt from "Were These the Hands?" from SELECTED POEMS OF FAZIL
HÜSNÜ DAGLARCA, translated by Talât Sait Halman, copyright 1969 by University
of Pittsburgh Press. Reprinted by permission of the University of Pittsburgh Press.

Text from the song "Bakmiyor çesmi siya." Issued by Traditional Crossroads, CD
4280 Women of Istanbul.

Poems from THE ESSENTIAL RUMI translated by Coleman Barks. Copyright
Coleman Barks. Reprinted with permission.

REGISTERED TRADEMARK—MARCA REGISTRADA

LIBRARY OF CONGRESS CATALOGING-IN-PUBLICATION DATA

Payne, Holly.
    The virgin's knot / Holly Payne.
        p. cm.
    ISBN 0-525-94657-8 (alk. paper)
        1. Rug and carpet industry—Fiction. 2. Women weavers—Fiction. 3. Rugs,
Prayer—Fiction. 4. Virginity—Fiction. 5. Turkey—Fiction. I. Title.

PS3616.A97 V57 2002
813'.6—dc21   2002016093

Printed in the United States of America
Set in Sabon

PUBLISHER'S NOTE
This is a work of fiction. Names, characters, places, and incidents either are the products
of the author's imagination or are used fictitiously, and any resemblance to actual persons,
living or dead, business establishments, events, or locales is entirely coincidental.

To my mother,
for teaching me to love words

and Sam Scribner,
with gratitude for your wings

ACKNOWLEDGMENTS

I would like to thank those of you who guided me either here or in Turkey while I wrote this book. I could never have finished without your knowledge, faith, and friendship.

My parents, Joan and Ellis Payne.

Jale and Perry Robertson of Blue Odyssey Tours; Bill McDonald and his inspiring collection at Return to Tradition, San Francisco; Serife Atlihan of Marmara University, Istanbul; Mehmet and Muammer Uçar, family of Ipek Yolu; Hari and Gerdi of Orientalia; Kalkan, Vedat Karadag, George Fine, Carol Delaney of Stanford University; the DOBAG weavers of Ayvacik and Yuntag. Thank you for opening your hearts and homes to me.

James Ragan and Sid Stebel of the USC Master of Professional Writing Program, Los Angeles.

Adrienne, Bob, and Maureen Hall. And those magical mountains that offer shelter and inspiration.

Patrick Lango, Lydia Rheinfrank, Deanne Koehn, Julie Oxendale, David Defries, KC Waters, Tara James Gibb, Craig Adair, Cristy Lipscomb Duckworth, Kristan Sargeant, Greta Rose, Jango Sircus, Amy Todd, Lysa Selfon Puma, Brian Edgar, Uncle Matthew Henry, Scott Stender, Colleen Lenihan, Steve Gratwick, Jane Dill,

Rich Peilish, Erik Noland, Dianne Lipscomb, Borge and Gordon Neset, John Cooke, Jeremy Schmidt, Win Blevins, and the 1998 Jackson Hole Writer's Conference.

Team Hardcore. You know who you are. Thank you for believing in me, on and off my bike.

And finally, James and Katie Dalessandro for introducing me to Peter Miller, our agent, friend, angel who found Laurie Chittenden at Dutton. Words do no justice to your talents.

The
Virgin's
Knot

Sometimes there are places in the world we have never been but the minute we step into them we are forever changed. We have native towns, houses where we grew up and return to now and then, but somehow, something overtakes us when we set foot in our homeland. Some call it the karmic debt land and we know it better than the places with which we are most familiar. A crooked tree, a bend in the road, the way a mountain whispers. We need no road signs here because we already know the way, and everything at once becomes home. I have felt such things in Turkey.

—HLP

Prologue

A long time ago in ancient Anatolia there lived a peasant farmer named Gordius who ruled an ancient city of the Lydian Empire. One day when Gordius was plowing his fields, a flock of birds gathered around his oxen. The image startled Gordius, and he knew it must be an omen. He set out to consult the augurs in a nearby town, where he met a beautiful maiden who told him the birds were a sign of his royal destiny there. Realizing the value of this peasant before her, the maiden offered herself to Gordius as his queen.

Gordius then drove his oxcart to the temple, where he was immediately greeted by the people as their ruler. An oracle had informed them that the first man to arrive at their temple would be their king, and they accepted the peasant farmer with great reverence. To show how grateful he was for his new power, the farmer decided to enshrine his oxcart to the temple by attaching the yoke to the shaft with a long, elaborately knotted strap, the legendary Gordion knot.

The elaborate knot had no visible end and was considered impossible to unravel. Legend had it that whoever succeeded in unraveling the knot would be the next ruler of Asia Minor. When

Alexander the Great arrived to set up his winter quarters in Gordion in 334 B.C., he set out to fulfill the prophesy and climbed the citadel to Gordion's oxcart. Although he knew that a knot must unravel itself, Alexander failed to loosen it and instead, sliced through it with his own sword.

I

June 1953
Southwestern Turkey

Nurdane moved between the looms, inspecting knots. The room was cool and smelled of burnt cedar. The floor, damp, freshly washed. The chairs and desks had been pushed against the walls, where skeins of colored wool hung like wigs from the hooks and half-carved reed flutes lay propped in the windows. The lodge was normally used as a music school for boys, but on Saturday afternoons the headmaster allowed her to teach the village girls weaving, the only formal education they would ever know.

She stopped in front of a larger loom shared by two sisters and moved her fingers slowly over the pile of wool. She wiggled her pinky between the strings to search for gaps, poking her finger through the weft. She had found a large hole, the size of a coin. She raised her eyebrows in disapproval.

The young girls sitting at the loom stiffened, slowly lifting their small chins to meet her gaze. They watched her lips part, waiting for a smile, begging her approval with their dark eyes. But she withheld, careful not to mislead them with a false sense of accomplishment. She found their workmanship satisfactory. They had woven a prayer rug filled with scatter motifs, stylized representations of familiar objects. A deer, flowers, sheep, water, the concerns of daily life in the village. It was not a difficult pattern, a modern prayer rug of no great beauty or merit. The center, or field, consisted of a plain red mihrab, or prayer niche, surrounded by a green border of angular flowers. The motifs, like all motifs in Turkish rugs, were based on geometric units. Called *nakis*, embroidery, the motifs had functioned as a language among the women of the weaving communities. Passed from mother to daughter, the geometric symbols were the basis of communication among the Anatolian women kept illiterate under Islam. Birds for the soul; stars for eternity and marriage; eyes, hooks, and amulets to protect against evil; roses for happiness; running water for a long life; swastikas and dragons to protect the tree of life; apple blossoms for fertility; pinwheels, symbols of heaven, fortune, and hands for protection.

To weave was to write and to write was to be understood. Using any one symbol or a combination of several, a Muslim woman was safe to express herself, channeling her creativity into a body that would survive her long after the Prophet had stripped her of her tribal solidarity. The sum of symbols, too, insured the Turkish woman with the only possession she could own. In possessing the rugs, women owned a part of themselves that no fundamental law could ever compromise.

Like any good grammar instructor, Nurdane looked for errors in the compositions she read, her unflinching eye slashing mistakes. She had reminded her students that the choice of symbols was not the point of weaving, despite how poignant or obscure the themes they conveyed. She wondered if the two sisters had ever listened. The goal of every weaver, she reminded them, was to tie knots so strong they could hold the dead.

She picked up a beater, a wooden comb, from the floor, and handed it to the youngest sister.

Tighter, she instructed.

Tighter?

The girl panicked and dropped the comb. Her sister snatched it from the floor.

I know how to make them tighter, she said.

Nurdane dropped her hand on the older girl's shoulder. She spoke calmly.

I know. So let *her* try.

The older girl sighed and reluctantly passed the wooden comb to her sister's trembling hands. She was younger than the rest and bony, wearing her elbows like weapons on bent arms. Her nails were dirty and her hair fell out of her headscarf in multiple braids, like a bride's. She looked vulnerable beside the others, anxious, too, and yet she had about her a determination that Nurdane recognized as her own. She could see the pride in the arch of the young weaver's back while the others sat slumped and defeated at the loom. The girl looked up at Nurdane with expectant eyes.

What do you want me to do?

Pack it harder.

The girl inserted the long, forklike slats of the beater between the weft and pulled down on the pile. Her tiny muscles bulged from her forearm.

Again.

But it's already tight.

Nurdane shook her head and poked her finger through the weft again. The hole smaller, but still there.

Is it?

The girl lowered her gaze to the floor and shook her head, ashamed. She spoke quietly, humbled.

It's hard.

I know. It takes time.

The girl shifted her eyes to balls of wool scattered about the floor.

You were better than any of us at our age.

I had a lot of time to learn. You must be patient.

The girl swallowed, her eyes glazed like large round tiles in the light.

You were better than our mothers. Better than our grandmothers, she insisted. How did you ever learn to tie them so well?

Nurdane stepped behind the loom and stood in front of the window, a silhouette in the backlight.

Put your hand over your heart. All of you.

Nurdane panned the room from one loom to the next until all the girls had followed her instruction.

Now close your eyes.

The girls shifted, the wooden benches creaking beneath their weight.

And listen.

The room fell silent. Only the tinkling of goat bells came in through the window. Nurdane continued.

Imagine the rug has a heart. It has a rhythm, a beat. Your job as a weaver is to breathe life into the knots. Feelings. Emotions. When you're sad, the knots will be sad too. When you're happy, they will sing. When you are confused or lonely or excited or scared, the knots will hold it all. They will remember everything about you so you don't forget who you are.

Nurdane paused for the caw of a raven, the flap of wings. Then silence again. She whispered.

Every weaver records a part of herself in each knot.

She watched their faces twitch, the nervous bite of their lips. Some had opened their eyes to peek at the others, then shut them quickly when they caught Nurdane watching. She continued.

Now imagine your heart with a hole.

Gasps from the girls.

What do you hear?

Nothing.

Right. Nothing. A broken heart can't beat. You see, if the rug has a hole because the knots are loose, the rug won't sing. And we like songs—because they tell us stories.

She watched the girls nod, small smiles stretched across their faces as they remembered bits of folktales too ancient to unravel at the loom. Perhaps when they were older, better weavers, they would find a place for their stories in the rugs.

Nurdane stepped out from behind the loom and crossed the

lodge. The slow squeak of her braces broke the silence. She stopped at the door.

You can work now.

The girls rubbed their eyes, trying to focus again in the harsh light that fell in triangles across the room as the morning sun shifted over the village. The air was warm and dry, sweet with sage.

Nurdane stood at the door and ran her hands along the old Arabic carved in the wood, prayers she could not read.

Let me hear the songs.

The girls began to pluck the weft like the strings on a harp. They worked up their speed, each relying on the other to keep the pace until they synchronized the twanging of fingers into a soft, hypnotic percussion.

Nurdane stepped outside and followed a stone pathway to a group of elderly women and their married daughters, who sat cross-legged, spinning wool under the shade of a fig tree. Three of the eldest and most experienced weavers were building a warp, the foundation of every carpet. They used no formal measuring device to build the apparatus, estimating the length of the warp with a long plank, which they laid across the ground, and two adjustable posts, driven into the earth with stakes. The warp was prepared as one of the women walked from one pole to the other, wrapping yarn continuously around the posts, where the other women sat, crouched on their heels, inserting twine between each thread, ensuring the sequence of the warp. The process would take about five hours, so they worked quickly, speaking little, concentrating. Together with the spinners, they formed a colorful sight. Their bright, baggy trousers, blouses, and vests were a mismatch of prints and patterns leaving no empty space for the eye to rest. Most of their heads were wrapped in two cotton scarves, a white one covering their hair, tied behind the nape of their brown necks. The other, either a pastel or elaborate floral design folded into a flat band, then tied around the forehead, framing their faces like a crown.

Nurdane joined the spinners, lowering herself to the ground slowly, awkwardly, beneath the braces. The wind lifted her skirt, revealing her legs. The muscles were severely atrophied, the skin purple and green, her knees imprinted from the metal rim. Her upper body was completely disproportional to her lower body. Her arms were healthy, long, and slender, the muscles tight and cut over her shoulders, defined by years at the loom.

The women did not stare at her legs, their eyes locked on the spindle passing into Nurdane's bare feet, bare humps and bulbs, too misshapen for shoes. The soles had grown thick and yellow with calluses, and the toes curled like talons and reminded them of raptor's claws. Nurdane took the spindle, anchoring the pointed end between her toes, and spun in silence. The women did not disturb her when she was teaching and kept their questions to themselves. They worked quietly, listening to the thwap of combs pounding the knots tighter on the loom. Toothless smiles among them. They were content to hear the labor of others after spending a lifetime tying their own knots, sowing, weeding, harvesting crops in the fields. Their hands had become gnarled, their fingers bony and twisted like the ancient roots of an olive tree. Most suffered from arthritis, but they insisted on spinning. They insisted in putting a part of themselves into the rugs for as long as they could.

Nurdane could feel them watching her work, studying the turn of her fingers, the way her left hand fed the wool into the spindle while her right rotated it clockwise, making a Z-twist with the yarn. Her speed, twice theirs. Her movement effortless, seemingly involuntary. Spinning ran deep through her blood, passed down from her mother and grandmother and the women of Anatolia. She had never seen her mother weave, nor had she ever seen her mother, dead after childbirth. June twenty-first, the solstice, at once a celebration of life, had also become a reminder of death.

It was her father who taught her to weave, borrowing from his wife's techniques. He taught Nurdane to manipulate the flywheel, as she did now, by tilting the spindle every few seconds, to either slow down or speed up according to the dictates of her fingers.

Faster now. The cadence chased the song from her lips. Songs of the nomad. The drop spindle was old technology, the most practical, too, for the nomadic life from which she came. She stopped only when the spindle was full and heavy with wool, and only then did she pause to massage the cramp in her hand.

You've been working a lot.

She nodded, shifted her eyes to meet the crinkled faces of the older women. They were filled with concern now and pressed her for answers.

I'm catching up, Nurdane said.

Quickly?

Fast enough.

How many knots are tied?

I haven't counted yet, she said, cutting off their questions. The women lowered their heads, ashamed. Nurdane guarded her secrets well. The women knew better than to beg for answers from her, but the nervous twitch of their hands, the way their fingers picked at the wool, gave them away. The women wanted to know more.

When will the rug be finished?

A rug is never truly finished. Is it?

She looked up and locked eyes with them. Her quick answers frustrated them. She removed the wool from the spindle and began to spin again, interrupted by the hand of a short, squat woman pressing on her shoulder.

Don't forget who you make the rugs for.

Nurdane lifted her eyes and searched the woman's weathered face. Two silver braids dangled over the woman's milky eyes, challenging her not to look away too soon.

A bride waits for you.

They always do.

The old woman shook her head and leaned closer. She pressed her cheek against Nurdane's and lowered her voice. This one is different, she said. Her life depends on you.

The men came in droves to the orchard to offer bids as the shadow of the minaret stretched longer through the trees. Cherry blossoms covered the ground where Nurdane's father sat cross-legged, listening to the village men plead for her rug, a chance to buy the virgin's knots for their daughters' dowry. He did not stand to greet them, nor look up at them, fixing his eyes on the ground to study the advancing feet, the display of shoes he would never own.

The men always wore shoes for the occasion, leaving the usual rubber galoshes on the racks outside their homes. Most were like him, too poor to afford shoes with the pittance they earned making charcoal, selling trout and wheat. The shoes they had managed to buy over the years were used and too small, making them walk funny, waddling with their toes scrunched inside the leather. Or too big. Dusty halos around their ankles as they shuffled across the road, then stood shifting, ill at ease in Ali's presence.

He rolled cigarettes on his thigh, one by one, lining them inside a small tin can perched on his knee. He did not speak and turned his eyes on the ground, roving the cherry pits as if he were reading. He was a thinking man, always deep in concentration. He possessed the cold, classic features of an Ottoman aristocrat. His nose was long, his cheekbones sloped elegantly down his face, and beneath the stubble on his chin were scars and their secrets. His eyes were steel gray, tired, darkened, it seemed, from the demons of sleep or a darker betrayal. On his bottom lip he wore a constant cut from chewing it too long when he worried.

He held a cigarette between his teeth and managed to smoke it without ever taking it from his mouth, exhaling only when he met the gaze of the men as if the smoke were meant to screen them. He noticed several of the men had been crying, the quick flick of their hand against dirty cheeks stained where the tears had dried. Some turned their faces into the shade to hide their eyes, pleading for salvation, believing Nurdane's rugs could answer the prayers that Allah could not.

He did not trust them. Few understood the true worth of his daughter's work. Most were bent on superstitions, the babies conceived on her prayer rugs, the animals healed, the crops saved. The diseases cured. The lives made prosperous.

Only a rare man considered the miracle of the knots themselves, the fact that his daughter could tie them in her condition. The polio had reduced her activity to the loom, where her hands took the place of her feet. Through her fingers she traveled to places where her legs could never take her. The loom, her tiny universe. The upper side heaven. The bottom earth. The left and right sides, both east and west. The ways of the spirit, good and evil. She had learned to inhabit that world with a passion, grateful for the life it gave her beyond the stillness.

To set a price on her rugs was futile, but Ali did so year after year. It frustrated him to spend so much time with the brides' fathers, and their stories left him tired and irritable. But he continued to entertain their desperation, perpetuating their belief in the powers of the virgin's knots.

The men stood with their hands behind their backs, feeding prayer beads through their fingers, one by one, like gears on a clock. They were nervous and chatted quietly about the coming weddings, the slaughter of lambs, the prospects they had for their daughters' futures. Their pants were ironed and their shirts were clean, starched to impress him. In Homeric times, the father of the bride organized a competition among her perspective suitors, or he set himself against them like the story of Oinomaos and his son-in-law Pelop, who competed in a chariot race to win the heart of his daughter, Hippodameia.

In a way, Ali felt like Oinomaos now, setting himself against the perspective bidders. Nothing had changed this time except for his own plan for Nurdane's rug. The men did not know this, and he felt foolish, even dishonorable, allowing the bidding to drag on through the day. He was bored and drew Arabic letters in the ground with a stick, testing himself with verses, laws from the Koran. *Allah changes not what is in people until they change what is in themselves.* He blamed nobody but himself for his suffering and did not expect Allah to help him now. He had waited too long to make his decision. He thought about it now, dragging the stick through the dirt, hoping she would forgive him.

The late afternoon sun burned through the trees and made him eager to end the bidding. His stomach growled. His throat was dry. He had not eaten since dawn and felt light-headed in the heat. He had been there all morning, and the offerings only half filled the threadbare kilim at his feet. Incense and candles, live goats and chickens, antique coins and wooden bowls carved from Asian sandalwood, even a brand-new magazine featuring Rita Hayworth had been offered in exchange for the rug.

What is this?

He took the magazine and waved it at the man before him, cowering in the funnel of light coming through the trees.

Rita Hayworth.

Ali stared at her, his pale eyes soaking in the light.

Who is she?

A star. From America. She's Muslim. Married Ali Khan in 'forty-nine.

A star.

Yes. A movie star.

Ali sucked on the cigarette, then exhaled slowly. The slow, shrewd look in his eyes silenced the men.

The only stars we know are those Allah puts in the sky, he barked, hurling the magazine at the man so hard, the cover tore on a stone, ripping Rita's face in two.

You're not from this village. Are you?

The man shrugged.

No. But I've heard about your daughter's rugs.

From who?

The shepherds. They tell us. Everyone knows, Ali.

The man stared at him quizzically, uncertain if this was news.

Ali pushed himself off the ground, towering above the others. He dragged his eyes over the stranger, studying him. His thin arms. Oiled hair. The shoes that fit.

How did you find us?

The man looked around at the other fathers, who had suddenly fallen silent, eyes thrown at the kilim where Ali had been sitting.

Tell me.

The man shrugged. Ali continued.

This village is not easy to find. Especially before summer. The roads are impossible.

He tossed his cigarette at the man's shoe.

Somebody told you. Didn't they?

The man shot a look at Ali.

No. The shepherds did.

When have you ever talked to a shepherd?

The man stepped back from the cigarette and Ali stamped out the ash with his bare heel. He picked up the torn picture of Rita Hayworth.

Is this a joke?

The man shook his head.

It's a collector's item, he persisted. It will be worth something.

What is it worth today? Nothing more than the dead tree it came from, Ali said, wadding up the movie star's face into a ball, hurling it through the trees.

The man stepped back in line and did not take his eyes off the ground until Ali finished speaking.

You come here wanting the virgin's knots. You bring me incense and candles, but don't be fools. These things can never compensate for Allah's work.

Allah's work? asked one of the younger men.

Yes.

But your daughter makes the rugs.

Allah makes them through her. You see?

Ali touched his heart with his hand, then extended it outward, proffering a response. He had rehearsed this for years and the words rolled off his tongue, no longer contrived. He believed a man could convince himself of anything, over time.

It's true, then, said the stranger, stepping out of the shade. About her hands.

Ali took another cigarette from the front pocket of his vest and caressed it between his thumb and forefinger. He then jammed it between his lips and spoke quickly.

She's been blessed.

She'll never marry, will she?

He paused before speaking and shifted uncomfortably.

It was not Allah's will.

His voice had suddenly grown thin and glassy, and he turned from the men and stepped into the dappled light.

Allah yazmis. Allah has written it.

Where?

In her hands.

Ali pointed to the kilim, flicking his wrist at the array of offerings.

Take it with you. It means nothing to me.

The men looked at him, eyes shifting slowly.

Then how will you decide who gets the rug?

I won't.

He panned each of their faces, studying them, wishing to remember the crestfallen stares. His own face softened in the light when he made his announcement. His eyes apologetic, yet without regret.

The bid, he said, was accepted long ago.

I t's you, isn't it? You bought the rug.
  The soldier said nothing, peered up from his hand of cards,
yellowing in the cigarette smoke that screened the teahouse at
night. Lanterns hung from wooden beams and breathed soot onto
the ceiling.

He could feel the eyes of the men on him, not so much for the
strategy he employed in his hand, but for the prospect of what lay
in his pockets. He seemed too young to have enough money for
one of Nurdane's rugs. He was twenty at most, nine months into
his compulsory military service, but home for the month of his
wedding. His cheeks were full. His skin smooth and beardless. He
was merely a child, still hoarding sugar cubes for tea. The tinkling
of his spoon against the glass seemed to draw more attention. He
spoke defensively.

Why would I want a rug?
For Ayse. For your wedding night.
I can't buy dowries. I'm a groom.
For her mother. A widow can't afford it.
The men shook their heads, cigarettes dangling from their lips.
I'm no different. I have no money to buy such a piece.
The soldier's voice was raspy from years of smoke, as if some-
one had rubbed his throat with steel wool. One of the other men
playing backgammon spoke from across the room.
Ali respects soldiers. Maybe he's doing you a favor.
The soldier laughed.
A favor?
I'm serious. He makes exceptions.
Ali makes only rules.

You're right. He doesn't sell to liars.

Excuse me?

The soldier turned to a young man who sat in the corner of the teahouse hunched over a pile of books. The flicker of a candle on his face.

Ali knows a man who values the rugs.

What do you know about value, Mehmet? You haven't taken your nose out of those books since you got here. Come to think of it, you never stop hiding behind all those words. I hope you know that books won't keep you from the army for long.

Mehmet lifted his eyes slowly.

I have work to do.

What work?

Studying.

The soldier began to laugh, the infectious, insidious howl between old village rivals that his friends, the young men at the table, patronized.

You're a student again?

A professor in the fall.

Professor?! Ahh.

Mehmet nodded.

You claim to work?

Very hard.

The work of an intellect is no work at all. Show me your hands.

The young men were laughing so hard now that they choked on the smoke. Mehmet dropped a leather shoelace to mark his page, then closed the book. He rose slowly from the table, his face shrouded in cigarette smoke. He stood with his arms in the air and turned his hands palms-up. His hazel eyes narrowed to slits through the glasses he wore. He was a muscular young man, barrel-chested and proud. His head skimmed the ceiling when he walked.

The library's in Antalya. I think you lost your way.

My patience.

Mehmet, go home. There's no need for trouble tonight.

The young man turned to one of the elders sitting in a pile of wood chips. He was carving a spoon from sandalwood and waved his knife admonishingly at the young intellect. Mehmet ignored him and studied the soldier through the smoky haze.

You consider yourself a proper groom?

Of course.

So you've tried.

The soldier cocked his head quizzically.

I don't have to. I'll make Ayse an honest woman.

She's honest already. It is Ayse who will make you an honest man.

The soldier's friends began to laugh, and he turned to them, silencing them with a cold stare.

How am I dishonest?

You don't love her.

Love?! Oh, Mehmet. When did you become such a fool?

He wandered over to Mehmet's table and waved the book in the air. It was a volume of Nazim Hikmet poetry, the pages folded and marked with cigarette papers.

Put it down.

It's been banned, Mehmet. It's against the law.

Not here it's not.

That's because nobody can read the laws. I could have you arrested.

The soldier continued to wave the book in the air until Mehmet grabbed it from his hands and stomped once on the floor. By now the teahouse had grown quiet, the skid of dice across backgammon boards, the shuffle of cards.

You don't know what love is.

I'll learn.

You can't. Love does not obey laws.

Mehmet lay the book on the table and took a deep breath before he spoke. His words soft despite his rage.

What color are her eyes?

I don't know.

And her lips in the morning?

I've never seen them.

Her hair in the afternoon? In the late sun. What precious metals do you see in the highlights?

The soldier balked, stepping back. His jaw clenched.

Go back to the library.

Have her lips taken you willingly?

If you want to play, Mehmet, play the winner. But you'll have to wait your turn.

The soldier turned at once from Mehmet, but Mehmet stepped closer to him, on his heels.

I don't gamble with paper. It tears too easily.

He leaned toward the soldier, pressed his mouth against the man's sunburned ear where the skin was peeling in thin white flakes.

Do you know what she smells like in the morning?

The soldier stepped away from him, swatted his ear with his fingers as if a fly had landed there. Then he placed his hand on his gun.

Take Hikmet home. We have no use for him here.

Mehmet nodded, then took the soldier's hand in his and pressed his palm against the small red circle, stained with henna, the mark of a groom.

Rain, he said.

What?

She smells like rain.

Nurdane sat at the loom, wearing a miner's helmet, and worked through the night. The oil lamp cast a dull glow across the weft and warp, where her fingers moved quickly, plucking the strings. She was tired from teaching and her thoughts were heavy, pressed by the old woman's words. She wondered about the warning, about which bride needed the dowry so desperately.

She moved her lips, mumbling, not the song from the loom but the mathematical formula she used to ensure symmetry in the rug's design. She could rely only on her memory once the rug was wound onto the lower beam and hidden from her view. Her concentration was critical.

It was hot inside the hut and she stuck her hand through the warp and pushed the curtain back from the window for air. Her forehead glistened in the light, her dark hair matted beneath her headscarf. She could sit for hours at the loom and work without tiring, eyebrows puckered in concentration. But her back had grown stiff and her lungs hurt, lodged with the woolen fibers she had breathed through the dust. She paused to drink *ayran* from the bota tied around her waist. She held the mixture of yogurt and water in her mouth and swallowed slowly, throwing her head back as the thick liquid cooled her throat.

Her dog lay sprawled at her feet and looked up every now and then with large, expectant eyes, as if he were waiting for her to finish. He was a retired sheepdog, a Kangal, who no longer wore the rusted spiked collar that protected his neck from wolf attacks. His fur looked silver in the dim light, his tired eyes red. She called him Attila. The hypnotic nature of the weaving lured him to sleep, and whenever Nurdane began a new row of knots, the dog's head grew heavy and dropped like a large stone between his paws before he drifted off to sleep.

The call to prayer took them both out of their concentration. Nurdane shifted her eyes to the window and watched the muezzin circle the minaret. Dark shadows twisted around the white tower as the old man shuffled slowly around the balcony, head lifted to the sky. She wondered if he sang to Allah or to the sliver of moon.

She turned back to the loom, cut the last knot, then laid the knife in her lap. She closed her eyes and took a deep breath, trying to decide if she had any more strength to work. Thirty thousand more knots. She had fallen behind since the spring snow. It had been too cold to work in the hut and the warp strings had frozen. The inclement weather had set her back, but she was determined to make up for it by the end of the week.

A low growl from the dog. She opened her eyes to find him standing, baring his teeth at the shadow of the curtain moving back and forth over the floor. She clicked her tongue twice and silenced him. He sat at attention, watching her roll her baggy trousers and slide the braces over her legs. Bruises covered her shins and she was careful not to pinch the skin when she snapped the metal into place. She buttoned up her vest and dragged her body across the stone floor to the door, then grabbing the knob with her hands, pulled herself into a standing position.

She was light-headed, almost dizzy from the exertion, balancing herself between the frame of the door. An intense heat surged through her body, entering by way of her toes. It quickly spread through her feet, up her legs, deep into her hip sockets. It was as if the cool stone floor had turned to hot coals, and she lifted her feet off it, alternating one with the other, trying to find relief.

In a few seconds it would be gone. The sensation was common for her condition, but she held her breath and dug her nails into the door frame to keep herself from screaming. The wood was scarred with tiny slits, her fingers bearing the splinters from more than one occasion. The phantom burns entered her without warning, and she prayed they would vanish as quickly. Attila sat still, ears pricked, following her strained breath as she moved the pain through her body and out through her nose like the doctor had instructed.

Then nothing. It was over. She lowered her foot to the floor and wiped her forehead with the back of her wrist. The doctor had warned her of postpolio syndrome, the sudden hot flashes, the restless nights, the frequent nightmares. And the aches. The backaches, the muscle spasms and atrophy, the shortness of breath, the crippling arthritis. At twenty-two, she felt like an old woman and wondered how much longer she could endure the pain.

She unlatched the lock on the door of the hut and opened it to the night. The sky was clear, bejeweled with stars. The minaret, a white finger in the moonlight. Most of the villagers were asleep, and she could hear their snores coming through the windows. She closed the door to the hut and walked slowly, each step calculated, bearing more weight on her left leg than her right, compensating. The left was stronger, more defined. She had never fully understood her condition, the paralysis that slowly went away since she was five, each year a progression in her healing. She could remember running but her legs could not. In her mind, she saw herself jumping and swimming, swinging off hemp ropes tied to the cypress arched over the river. Now her movements were retarded by the braces brought to her from the doctor in Antalya. Her father had told her she would never walk again. The doctor told her that she would walk with the braces. Her mother, dead, could offer no words to comfort her, too assuage her loss, and so she had no choice but to accept it.

She followed a narrow goat-path that snaked its way down the hill to the village. Wildflowers covered the trail and poked through pockets of snow still left from winter. Attila ran ahead of her, tromping through the mud. He stopped every few feet to wait, then bounded after a rabbit, disappearing into her father's orchard.

Attila?

She clapped once.

Come back, Attila.

She could scarcely hear above the creaking of the braces and pressed her ear against the wind, hoping to hear the dog's panting. He was restless tonight and she did not know why. His constant begging to be let out of the hut, his refusal to enter. She had to pull him by his collar to get him through the door, and even then he had not taken his eyes off it, as if he were waiting for an unexpected arrival. Wild boars roamed the area and she did not want him running alone at night. A black bear, too, had been spotted by the shepherds, and the villagers were warned to keep their dogs chained until the bears moved farther down the mountain in search of berries.

Attila?

She spoke louder, straining her voice. When she did not hear him, she entered the orchard alone and moved among the shadows and trees, twigs snapping beneath her feet. She saw a woman smoking a cigarette, her back draped by a shawl, standing under one of her father's ladders. The woman turned abruptly when Nurdane approached.

Emine!

I'm sorry, she said. I didn't mean to scare you.

Moonlight flooded her face. Her skin was pockmarked and scars radiated over her cheeks as if she had been shot. Her bottom lip was swollen from bee stings. She was the village beekeeper.

What are you doing here?

Emine lowered her head, ashamed.

I wanted to give you something for your trouble.

It's midnight.

I know.

Emine stood and brushed her skirt off, then pulled out of her apron a bouquet of red and white poppies. Their silken heads had been crushed and they had already withered in the heat.

You've been working so hard.

Nurdane lowered her gaze when Emine handed her the flowers.

I've been watching you since dusk, Emine said, and stepped closer. When will the rug be done?

When Allah wills it.

Nurdane stepped back. The woman was too close. It made her nervous.

My daughter . . . She's not well.

What?

She watched Emine's hands rub each other, nervous.

She's been sick.

Nurdane cocked her head.

Ayse?

She never eats anymore. She's been losing weight.

Nurdane lifted her head slightly, enough for the woman to see her face, to see that the news concerned her. But she did not offer her eyes and locked them on the moth-eaten holes in her vest.

I didn't know.

We're waiting for the doctor.

He's coming soon. To bring me new braces. As soon as the roads clear.

Nurdane's voice was filled with hope, and she watched Emine's lips part in a smile, eyes fixed on the moonlit corridor dividing the orchard.

If he can't cure her, I know what will.

But you don't know what's wrong.

It doesn't matter. I know what will help her.

Emine forced the words out of her wheezing lungs and continued.

Your rug. That's all she needs.

Nurdane, doubtful, looked up at Emine. The woman tossed her cigarette on the ground.

Do you know my son?

Nurdane nodded.

Do you know his voice?

No. He never speaks.

That's what we believed. Until last week. It was Friday. After the noon prayer. We went for lunch at my sister's. My son saw your rug there.

Fatma?

Yes. Her dowry.

Nurdane cocked her head, remembering. The rug was one of her favorites. A series of trees with a water border. Emine continued, speaking quickly.

My son walked over to the rug and sat in the middle with his legs crossed, staring. Sat there all afternoon. Didn't take his hands off it. When we tried to call him for dinner, he said no. It's the first word he's ever spoken.

The woman's eyes grew wet and glistened in the moonlight. She smiled.

We tried to get him to move, but he kept pulling away from us. He wouldn't leave. Stubborn boy. I tell you, took after his father. *Gypsy* blood. You know. He put up such a fuss, my sister agreed to watch him for as long as he wanted to stay. She figured a few hours. He stayed three days. When we came to pick him up, we found him in the backyard, staring at the mountain, singing a folk song my husband used to sing to him as a baby. We thought our son had never heard it.

Emine stepped back and lit another cigarette. A cold wind rushed through the trees and shook the cherry blossoms like confetti.

You don't know the power you have.

They're only rugs, Nurdane said, moving into the shadow so the woman could not see her face. Her brows scrunched in confusion.

There are miracles in your rugs.

Miracles?

Yes, Emine insisted, running her hand along the cherry bark. Don't tell me they can't cure my daughter.

Nurdane sat on the veranda, waiting for Attila's return, and drank tea in the dark. Her legs throbbed and she unbuckled the braces to massage her calves. The pale skin shimmered in the moonlight, her kneecaps dented like old coins. They looked so strange to her. The unnatural divots in her shin where the bone had grown too thin. And the discoloring. The pale green and violet spread down her muscle like the faded colors in a prayer rug. In its own peculiar way, the combination pleased her. The colors pretty and rare. She laughed softly at the irony and lifted her hair off the back of her neck to let the cool air soothe her.

She could not get Emine's story out of her mind. Her head throbbed, remembering. It was hard to believe her rug had given her son a voice. Perhaps the weather. Maybe Allah's will. Definitely a coincidence but not a miracle. She did not believe in miracles.

She wanted to help Ayse if she could. Befriend her. Invite her for tea and talk. Comfort her through the illness and let her know it would soon pass like the pain she knew too well. But she was not sure how her rug could help Ayse. She was not sure the knots could cure anything. She had never believed in their miracle despite the stories she had been told. Emine's was not the first. She had heard of sick animals. The withered plants. So many lives had been resurrected on the rugs. She did not know how or why.

The phenomenon of miracles deluded her. They did not make sense. There were no miracles in her world. A series of losses, yes. A few exchanges, bargains with Allah. A life for a life, her mother's for her own. Her talent for her legs—weaving for walking. It was always a plea bargain between her and her father, her father and Allah. Miracles were as real to her as the mythic images of minarets that pierced the sky over Istanbul, a fabled site in a fabled city she would never visit. She had seen a postcard once of Antalya. The yacht harbor and the clock tower where the doctor lived by the sea. He promised she would see it one day. He promised the city boasted exotic flowers and foods and dresses that matched those in her dreams. He promised her, too, that she would walk again without the braces. But she hadn't yet, nor did she believe she would. She was too old for fables, too tired by myths. She did not believe in miracles. If her rugs had helped so many, why hadn't they made her stronger? Why hadn't they helped her to walk again?

A sudden wind picked up and bent the trees backward. Nurdane tucked the ends of her headscarf behind her ears to keep from being whipped by the beaded tassels. A raindrop splattered her forehead and she took the braces under her arms and dragged herself into the house before the storm broke over the village.

She left her braces outside and closed the door. It was warm inside and humid. Rain curtained the windows and fogged the glass. She took her crutches and crossed the room to a series of camel bags that hung from the wall. They were stuffed with flour, sugar, spices, dried herbs. The last hung by a thread, weighted down by a large leather-bound book that had poked a small hole through the bottom. She took it out and set it on the ground. The pages were waterlogged and cracked when she turned them. She could not read but she recognized the pattern of the text. A series of names and numbers. Three columns per page. The book was a ledger that chronicled the rugs she had made, which bride had received them, when, and how many knots had been tied in each. She ran her finger down the page, trying to read the names. She paused at the first, Emine, the first bride who had ever received her rug. She remembered the others. *Roza. Cennet. Saddet. Fatma. Zehra. Bahriye. Faide. Jale. Hamiyet. Sefaya.* Her friends, former students, weavers, and wives. They were women now and led lives she would never know. Each girl had learned to write her name and sign the ledger on her wedding day to officiate the passing of the virgin's knots.

Nurdane had never really thought much about who had received her rugs or why. Not every girl in the village owned one. In most cases, the father of the bride had to win the bid, and it had never been Nurdane's place to decide. Her father awarded the rugs and she had always trusted his judgment. It was not that he excluded her from the decision, she had never really asked to be a part of it. But she wondered if she could now, for Ayse. Her father was a reasonable man, respected and judicious. He seemed capable of making an exception. She remembered he had broken the fast at Ramadan once because he was sick. He said Allah would understand. Certain rules were meant to be broken, he said, to make sure Allah still listened.

Nurdane closed the ledger slowly and ran her hand over the cover. A fragment of her first tapestry. Her father had cut a small square from the flat-weave kilim she made the winter after the polio had struck. The fabric was stiff, but the colors had not faded. The natural dyes had passed through the years without compromise. She inspected the textile as she would her students' work, her brows arched, eyes wary, searching for error. She found none. The piece was flawless.

A crack of thunder. She lifted her eyes and stared out the window as lightning split the sky above the mosque. She expected Attila at any moment and turned to put the ledger back in the camel bag, when her shoulder brushed it off the wall, exposing an odd indentation in the plaster. She ran her fingers around the perforation and felt the edge of a loose cinder block that had been whitewashed to match the wall.

She pressed her hand against the block and pushed it back a few centimeters, then wedging her pinky between the space, jiggled the block forward, and lifted it out. She reached her hand into the darkness and felt a lumpy bag of coins, a few beeswax candles, and a flat, rectangular box wrapped with string.

She took out the box and shook it gently. It was covered with postage stamps and dust and she wiped it clean with the back of her wrist. She could not read the markings. The letters meant nothing to her. A series of lines. Ataturk's new alphabet. She lowered herself to the floor on a pile of bolsters. She could see the box had already been opened and retied with a piece of string. She pulled the strings and let them fall across her lap, then lifted the lid. Layers of tissue paper, a tape measure. Beyond that, a kind of clothing pattern. She pulled out the paper and spread it on the floor, matching the blue-chalk lines. A floor-length dress. The sleeves were long, the collar high. She wondered if it was a gift.

It's a mistake.

She startled and shifted her eyes along the floor to the doorway. Wool slippers. Her father. She lifted her eyes to meet his. He stared at her curiously, his eyes wide. Like a spooked goat, she thought.

Why aren't you asleep?

Attila's run off. I'm waiting for him.

Ali shook his head and shuffled across the floor.

Full moon, he said. He'll be back.

He quickly crouched to the pattern and folded it, his fingers trembling. In his haste, he accidentally tore the edge of the paper.

Bok.

Shit. He pinched the skin on the bridge of his nose. Rubbed his eyes.

What is it?

A mistake. I told you. The postman made a mistake.

He raised his voice and she moved back from him, pulled her hands against her stomach.

The pattern, Nurdane said softly. Is it a dress?

Ali raised his eyes to meet hers and nodded, then quickly tucked the pattern inside the box. He picked up the hemp and tied the box shut, then, standing toward the wall, ran his fingers along the edge of the recess, inspecting it. After a moment, he slid the box inside, lifted the cinder block off the floor, and covered the hole. He caught his eye on the fallen camel bag.

What did you want?

He spoke to her as if she were a child.

I was checking the ledger.

For what?

To remember who received the rugs. But I found the hole instead. Is that where you keep the bids?

He turned slowly to face her, his hands behind his back. Head lowered, thinking quickly.

For valuable things. Yes.

I never knew it was there.

He watched her eyes narrow. She sat up straight, squaring her shoulders, suspicious. She looked around the room. She expected piles of beeswax candles, homemade soaps, carved tools and bowls, but there was nothing.

Did you start to collect the bids today?

Ali said nothing, taking the ledger from the floor. He stuffed it inside the camel bag and hung it on the wall, careful to cover the cinder block. He turned toward her, his eyes glazed. He did not drink, but he looked exhausted, weighted with worry. He scratched the back of his neck and spoke with a strained voice.

I've made my decision, Nurdane.

Already?

He nodded, moved away from the wall, and grabbed a small broom, sweeping the dust off the stones.

How do you know after one day?

He paused and locked eyes with her, reading the concern on her face. He stiffened and gripped the broomstick harder.

Allah's will, he said. Sometimes the decision is made for me.

I don't understand.

It's not important that you do.

Nurdane dragged her finger along the tassels of her headscarf. She knew better than to ask who the bride was. Ali made sure everyone in the village, including Nurdane, did not know the identity of the bride until her wedding day. He said all great secrets were the nature of Allah and he advised her not to question them. But she could feel her heart beating as the question crawled up her throat. She gathered the ends of her skirt in her fists.

Does Allah make exceptions?

Ali swept around her feet.

Sometimes.

Would you ever let me decide?

Ali stopped and looked down on her. He could see her mother looking out through Nurdane's large blue eyes, wide and expectant, full of questions.

You?

I've never had a chance.

You've never asked.

I'm asking now.

Ali's forehead glistened in the candlelight and he wiped it with the back of his sleeve. He shifted his eyes, considering.

You want to choose the bride?

She nodded.

Just this time.

A li met Emine in the teahouse the next morning. They sat in the corner by the window, lifting their feet every now and then for small boys dragging mops across the floor. Rain had flooded the building and most of the men gathered there had rolled their pants over their ankles to wade through the water. The wind had ripped off parts of the roof and a group of young men sat on the rafters, nailing scraps of metal over the holes, stealing glimpses of Emine, the only woman they had ever seen in the teahouse.

Ali poured her more tea, but his hands shook, spilling it. *Allah,*

Allah, he said, and pounded his fist against the table, flipping both of their glasses. Emine reached across and took Ali's hand.

It's okay, my friend.

She offered a smile, but Ali shook his head. He ran his fingers through his hair and took a cigarette from his pocket and shoved it between his lips.

It's not okay, he said.

What's a little more water? We should be grateful there's no drought.

It's June. Wait until August.

Ali lit his cigarette and bounced his leg nervously under the table. He shifted uncomfortably, considering his words, searching the palms of his hands as if he could find the answers there. The hammering only aggravating him more.

Emine rolled a cigarette and looked up.

What is it? You haven't said a word all morning.

Ali took a deep breath and blew the smoke out slowly. Emine watched him for any signs of hope.

I want to help Ayse. I really do, Ali said, and studied the bee-keeper's face. Her wide eyes, naive yet cunning. She ran her hands over the gloves in her lap, the leather sticky with honey. She worked hard. Ali respected that. He wanted to make things better. Find a way to help the woman's daughter. Ali saw himself in Emine, the widow, and yet he could find no words to comfort her.

It's a shame to hear of her illness, Ali continued. But there's nothing I can do that Allah hasn't already done.

Oh.

Emine's face fell flat. She shifted her eyes along the floorboards, where the rain formed tiny pools in the slats.

Nurdane talked to you.

Yes. Last night.

I didn't mean to scare her.

I never said you did.

Emine leaned forward, pressed her elbows into the table, and lowered her voice, obliging Ali's hard stare.

She's our only hope for Ayse.

Maybe, Ali sighed, unconvinced. He seemed bored and breathed a smoke ring into the barrel of light coming through the roof.

Have you prayed?

Emine shook her head.

Allah's not listening.

Allah's always listening. But sometimes he doesn't want to hear.

Emine stiffened.

What good does that do my daughter?

Gives her time.

For what?

To heal on her own without Allah's help.

Ali studied the woman's fingers, nails chewed to the cuticle.

You're a smart woman, Emine. A survivor. But don't be such a fool to mistake superstition for medicine.

Emine cocked her head. The comment offended her and she pointed a blackened finger at Ali.

It's not superstition.

Ali chuckled.

Please, Emine. Don't embarrass yourself.

I'm telling you the truth! My son talks now because of Nurdane's rug!

She had raised her voice above the idle chatter in the teahouse.

You can change your decision, Ali.

Ali pushed the teaspoon across the table with his thumb and watched his fingerprint vanish.

It's too late.

It's not! Tell me another bride who needs the rug more than Ayse. Show me another girl who's as sick.

Ali breathed the smoke out of his nose but did not move, his eyes locked on Emine, silencing her.

My daughter.

Who?

Nurdane.

This has nothing to do with her.

It has everything to do with Nurdane, Ali said, and lowered his voice. Then he grabbed Emine's shoulder so hard, the woman winced. He pushed her into her seat and moved so close to her face he could see the reflection of the boys and their mops in her eyes.

Stay away from my daughter until the wedding is over. She has a fragile heart. Your story affected her. She can't sleep. She can't work. All she thinks about is helping Ayse. What am I to say? Who am I to tell my own daughter that she cannot help somebody? That is all Allah ever asks of us. To help each other. But how dare you plant the idea in her head that she's responsible for somebody else's health? Somebody else's happiness? Don't tell her there are miracles in her rugs when you have no proof.

Emine looked up.

Since when did we ever need proof?

Silence. Only the swash of mops across the floor.

I thought you were more clever than that, Ali. Why do you think everyone makes such sacrifices to bid on your daughter's rugs? Most of us have willingly given our life savings. Men have starved so their daughters have a chance. But you wouldn't understand their sacrifice.

The hammering stopped. A flap of sheet metal dangled from the roof. Ali felt the men watching him. He swallowed hard and stole a glimpse of a small boy who stood frozen with a mop in his hand.

You don't know the value of Nurdane's work.

Ali stiffened. The words stung him and he felt his eyes fill with water.

Everybody knows. Even my son's not afraid to say it, now that he can speak.

What? Ali asked, rising a few inches from his chair.

Emine roved the blank faces of the men watching her.

Go ahead. Tell me, Ali demanded, locking eyes with the men in the teahouse.

Tell me what everybody says when I'm not around.

Emine crossed her arms over her chest and took a deep breath.

My son says your daughter is a poet.

Ali shook his head slowly and pushed his chair back from the table. He stood. A small smile spread across his face, then his lips flattened immediately and he fixed his eyes on Emine with a stare intent on snapping a neck.

Tell your son he's mistaken, he said, spitting his cigarette on the wet floor. He stood from the table and splashed his way to the door, turning one last time before he stepped outside.

Tell your son that Allah is the only poet.

The boys wanted a reward for finding Attila. They wanted to see the rug for finding the dog, but Nurdane told them no. They followed her through the village, past the mosque, along a gravel road behind the washhouse where women hauled laundry to the ancient pipes of an aqueduct, but stopped to watch the weaver and the boys pass.

Nurdane preferred to walk alone, but the boys followed her on their rusted bicycles that clanged and clacked and squashed mud beneath their tires. Most of the bikes were too big, and their bare feet dangled from the pedals when they coasted. But they were poor and the ride was good and they did not complain. They rode slowly, keeping pace with her. She could feel their dark eyes watching her legs buckle. She tried to control her limp by taking long strides, lunging into the mud to keep her balance. The braces dug into her shins and slid around the damp skin, pinching behind her knees where the hinges were. Her muscles had gotten weaker, and she had to stop every now and then to slide the braces up her thighs, the metal hot beneath her trousers.

Does it ever stop hurting?

She stopped and the boys braked, sliding on the mud. Muammer, the postman's son, stared up at her, his eyes like two large pieces of coal pressed deep into his face. He ran his tiny hands nervously along the bristles of his shaven head.

What? she asked.

Muammer pinched his lips together, shifted his eyes, then pointed to her legs and spoke.

Your legs.

She stood up and acknowledged his question by looking into the boy's eyes. He immediately withdrew his glance, throwing it on the ground, shamed by his curiosity.

After a while, you forget, she said.

Muammer scratched his head.

The pain?

She shook her head.

What it felt like before it.

Muammer drummed his lip with a dirty thumb and stared at her, thinking.

Would you like to ride?

He dismounted and offered his bike. She smiled.

Is it much farther?

He pointed to a shallow depression on the slope.

Down there.

I think I can make it.

You sure?

She nodded.

Yes. Thank you, she said, hearing a familiar howl. The high-pitched cry of Attila.

That's him, Muammer said.

The dog howled again. From the distance, he sounded like a wolf. Nurdane winced, listening to the pain in his voice. A dull groan followed his cry.

How long has he been gone?

Too long, she said, immediately mounting the boy's bike. She sped down the hill, negotiating her way over a series of thickets

and roots that spread over the slope. She followed the dog's bark-
ing, short, successive yelps leading her closer through the trees.

She skidded around a pit of ashes left over from a campfire.
They were gray and hot, still smoldering, traces of burning oak in
the air. She looked around for the sign of a shepherd, looked for
the trail of his staff in the mud. Nothing but bootprints and scattered cigarette papers. A pop, then hissing. She looked down. The
back tire was quickly shrinking. She got off the bike and pulled the
tip of a razor blade from the back tire. Muammer ran up behind
her, the other boys following.

Careful. There might be more.

What is it?

She lay the razor blade on the palm of her hand and showed
him, but he shook his head and pointed to the campfire.

It wasn't here this morning.

She shifted her eyes from the razor blade to the boy's face.

Somebody's been here, he insisted.

When did you find Attila?

After the first call to prayer.

She looked up at the sun, at the trees. There were no shadows.
It had to be at least noon.

Maybe a shepherd had a late breakfast.

Muammer shook his head.

Not today. They're at my uncle's. Helping to shear.

She bent her fingers over the razor and looked past the boys,
through the wind-shorn oak trees that disappeared into the folds of
the canyon. The village ended here and nobody really spent a great
deal of time by the west cliff. A shepherd had been blown over once
and was found sprawled in the branches of a pine tree like an ancient god she'd seen in picture books. The villagers knew not to
tempt this side of the village and left it alone. The campfire aroused
her suspicions. Maybe the dog had sensed something, his constant
pawing at the door of the hut. She had thought it was the wind.

Nurdane crouched down and drew a deep line through the mud
with her finger. The ground was more solid than runny, claylike.

She split apart the clump with her hands, inserted the razor, then repacked the mud on top. She stood and gave the bike back to Muammer. He took it without looking at her, his gaze fixed on the little mound.

It doesn't seem right?

What?

To bury a razor. What if somebody steps on it?

She turned to him, considering.

Only the person that left it in the first place would come back to look for it. You boys know better now.

Somebody's going to get hurt, he said, and looked up at her, his eyes full of portent.

They wanted that. Can't you see?

Muammer.

Shhh. They're still here, he said, and looked around, squinting.

One of the boys nudged Muammer on the back.

You're weird.

But Muammer crossed his arms and silenced the boy with a defiant stare.

They're coming back.

A sudden wind rushed through the trees and blew a small nest out of the leaves. The eggs cracked immediately and the yolks bled onto the ground. Muammer nodded, as if the act itself confirmed his suspicions.

I'm sorry about the tire. I'll get you a new one.

The boy shook his head.

I want to see the rug.

Nurdane sighed.

My father doesn't even see it until it's finished.

Never?

Not once.

He stared up at her, incredulous. She nodded.

It's bad luck, she said.

Muammer eyed the mound.

Like finding a razor blade.

Then you understand, she said. Don't ask me again.

She moved quickly in the direction of Attila's next whimper. She made her way through the trees and found him lying on his side, matted and entangled by a wire trap. His back paw and tail were caught between the metal jaws. She recognized the device. Villagers set them to catch the wild boars and wolves of Pisidia. Not sheepdogs. Attila had seen the traps before. He had led countless flocks away from them and had never been caught himself.

Attila, what happened to you?

She crouched beside him and put her hand on his silver muzzle. He lay on his side and thwapped his tail against the grasses, happy to see her despite the pain. His mouth was swollen, the pink flaps of skin inflamed, pricked with what appeared to be multiple bee stings. His breath was labored and his eyes were glazed and dilated even in the sun. She lifted his swollen lip and ran her finger along the gum. More stingers. And something sticky. She touched her finger to her tongue and tasted honey.

You little thief!

She wanted to laugh. Attila had run off and found himself trouble. The beekeeper's hives, perhaps. A random nest in the trees. But that was on the opposite side of the village. How he had fallen into the trap she did not know. It didn't make sense. He was smart. He knew better.

The boys crowded around him and offered sugar cubes from their pockets. But the dog stared at them listlessly. Nurdane ran her hand gently over his chest. The fur was warm and wet, like carded wool dunked in a bath. She wrapped her fingers around his front paws to comfort him, but she found a thorn lodged between one of the pads and he winced. She plucked it out and studied it in the light. A rose. The pink petals crushed beneath his paw. She looked up, scanning the grasses. There were no flowers here. Thistles and thorns and weeds, yes. An occasional poppy between the rocky outcrops, but no roses. The villagers grew them in their gardens, sheltered from the elements behind the courtyard walls. She had seen a wild rose by the banks of the river, where the water was plentiful and the sun strong. But not here in the volcanic ash soil. The conditions were too harsh and uncompromising.

Where have you been, Attila?

He pricked his ears at her voice. Thwapped his tail once, twice. She touched her finger to his nose. It was still cool and wet. He was not sick, only injured, and she was thankful for that. Under any other circumstances she would have been amused, too, by his insistent play despite his age. But there was something sinister about the situation, and she did not believe it was entirely an accident. Her sheepdog in a wolf trap. She looked up at the boys.

Have you seen any strangers?

They scrunched their faces, thinking. They knew everyone in the village. There were fifty-four families. They knew the dogs by name, the sheep by their bleats, the men who grumbled in their sleep and the women who sang before the sun roused the muezzin. They knew the doctor from Antalya, the name of the traveling-merchant's cat, the census taker, and the undertaker. There were no strangers in Mavisu. They shook their heads.

No one?

When Allah comes, I'll tell you, said Muammer.

He was serious. He stood with squared shoulders, his chest puffed with pride.

Thank you. Please do, she said.

Never know which direction he'll be coming from. You have to keep your eyes out. He could be the wind.

She nodded and offered him a small smile. She appreciated his imagination and often thought of teaching him how to weave, but it was not for a boy to know.

She pulled off her headscarf and folded it into a triangle, rolling it lengthwise, threading it through the trap to lift the wire and free Attila's back paw. His tail had been caught, too, and she brushed it out of the way, seeing dry blood where the trap had slashed him. He backed himself away from the trap and she snapped it shut. He started and tried to jump away, but he could only stagger forward, limping on his back leg. He brushed up against her, nudging her to move on, and for a moment she had to laugh at the tragedy. She didn't know who looked worse, the dog limping or herself.

We'll carry him, Muammer offered, laying his bike on the ground.

She considered. The dog weighed one hundred pounds, almost twice their weight. The boys looked at her with eager eyes, supplicants despite the effort. The dog panted, eyeing both sides, waiting for a decision. Nurdane nodded and the boys quickly abandoned their bikes and carried the dog up the hill and back down the road toward the village.

Nurdane insisted they stop at the first house, a cramped cement-block dwelling where her uncle lived. They found him in the backyard, pounding sheets of copper into sheep bells. The man wore grease marks under his eyes to protect him from the glare. It was hot. Sweat crawled along his jaw, and he wiped it with his torn sleeve. Seeing Attila, he dropped his hammer and rushed over to the boys, taking the dog in his arms. He laid him on the stones by a small outdoor oven where loaves of bread had been set out to cool. The smell of yeast in the air.

What happened?

He turned and looked up at Nurdane.

He was stung.

Muammer stepped up behind her.

Somebody set a trap for him.

The bellmaker cocked his head.

A trap?

There's been a campfire. We saw footprints.

What?

Bootprints, really. Cigarettes, too. The ashes are still hot and—

Muammer! Please.

The boy sighed and stepped back, head down, shoulders slumped.

It's going to be too late.

Too late? the bellmaker asked.

The boy nodded.

Somebody's going to step on the blade.

What blade? What's he talking about?

Nurdane raised her finger at the boy when he opened his mouth.

I found a razor blade. It popped his tire. He's upset with me.

Muammer drew his lips together and tilted his head, catching her eyes in the harsh light.

Not with you. *For* you, he mumbled. Somebody's going to get hurt.

Go to the mosque, Muammer. Talk to Allah about it.

I already did.

He was angry with her and turned abruptly, motioning his friends to follow him to the gate. He held on to the iron post and looked back at Nurdane, sorry she did not heed his warning better. He pivoted on his heel and walked down the driveway, flicking gravel with his toes.

Muammer sat on the steps of the mosque and buried his face in his knees. He could taste salt and dirt on his skin. He spit on the ground. Once, twice. A third time for Nurdane. Why didn't she listen? Adults never wanted to know the truth. Nobody paid attention to the signs until it was too late. And it was always too late.

Your hands are dirty.

Muammer lifted his chin off his knees and looked up at an old man wearing baggy wool trousers and a knit skullcap. He pulled a small glass bottle filled with an orange liquid from his pocket. Muammer cupped his hands as the old man poured the lemon cologne over his fingers, studying him in the harsh light. The boy's eyes were bloodshot. Nose red, cheeks ruddy. He could see the network of veins in his neck as if he'd been crying for some time.

You must be patient, boy.

Muammer scowled.

For what?

Allah can't answer everyone's prayers at once.

I didn't ask him to.

Then why the long face?

Muammer watched a group of women cross the road, piles of fodder hauled on their backs. They reminded him of moving bushes and trees, as if the forest were walking away from itself.

You've lived in Mavisu your whole life, right?

The man shook his head.

Half. We wandered the mountain before Ataturk.

Muammer nodded.

But you know the village well.

The old man waved his hand.

Like the lines here.

Well . . . the boy scratched his neck.

What?

How often have you been to the west cliff?

The old man stood up, his eyes wide.

Many times. But never since the shepherd was killed. The winds get angry there. I don't know any sane man who's gone there since.

Only if they didn't know about the winds.

I suppose.

That's what I thought.

The old man pulled on the edge of his beard.

So what's this got to do with your tears?

Everything, Muammer said, and stood.

He walked up the steps, following the swell of prayers from the mosque. The door was open slightly for the heat and he could see the men in their positions on the prayer rugs, bowing, standing, kneeling in the Islamic postures, reciting ancient suras of thanksgiving and praise. Squares of light fell through the windows and rested on the heads of the pious deep in prayer. Their voices drifted toward the great onion dome as if the mosque itself had breathed the word of God.

Alahut akbar. La ilaha illa Allah.

Muammer stood by a small stone pipe that jutted out of the wall and washed his feet, drying them on a clean cloth laid over the threshold. He entered slowly, pausing to hear the women behind the curtain. He could see them when the cross-breeze blew back the cloth. They sat hunched on the ground, their mouths covered by the ends of their headscarves. They intrigued him, these voices behind the dark sheet. He was not sure they were the distraction everyone believed them to be.

He tiptoed past them and took his place behind a group of soldiers. He could see the reflection of the glass bulbs in their shiny black boots and something else. A slow movement along the carpets. He kneeled and looked over his right and left shoulders to welcome the protective angels, catching in the corner of his eye a group of three men. They were bearded and dirty and he did not recognize them, kneeling, not reciting prayers. They bowed their heads as if they were praying, but their lips were still. Their dark eyes darted right then left, then stopped on a man in the far right corner of the mosque. Muammer recognized him as the village shopkeeper. He pressed olives into oil. Muammer had helped him collect bottles and clean them for a ride on one of his horses. He was a devout Muslim, who seemed to spend more time in the mosque than he did in his own shop.

The man stood, dug into his pocket, and pulled something out. Muammer could not see from the distance. The men blocked his view. He could see only the shopkeeper's shoulder, his angular silhouette when he faced east. He held a curious object, a small black bag, then kneeled again, pressing his forehead to the floor.

Muammer watched him carefully, his snakelike movements pushing the bag through his legs, passing it to the first of the three strange men who passed it in the same manner to the next man. The third man stuffed the bag into the hollow of a small rolled-up prayer rug, then walked out of the mosque, passing Muammer, who stood hidden behind the curtain, his finger pressed over his lips begging the women for silence.

Nurdane spread crushed garlic and parsley around Attila's swollen mouth, packing the mixture with her fingers. He kept his head still on the hot stone, his wet nose pressed against her leg, his breath hot. She covered him with her headscarf, then doused him with a watering can to keep him cool. Water spilled by his mouth, but he was too tired to lift his head and drink. So listless and sedate. The only sign of movement, his eyes, darting nervously in the direction of his attackers.

Mavisu had always been unjaded in the presence of strangers. Nothing could intimidate it, the warlike spirit of its people, an internecine intrigue to historians. Mavisu loved its freedom as much as the other cities of ancient Pisidia, factioned and territorial. The villagers defended their independence fiercely and more than once contemplated a mass suicide like the legendary Xanthos of Lycia; however, they had preserved their independence, staving off foreign rule until five hundred years before Christ. Alexander the Great failed to conquer Mavisu after taking great pains to navigate through the folds of the mountains, the southern passes blocked by the warriors of Termessos. After the Romans defeated Antiochos III, they gave their allies the city of Pergamon and the Greek island of Rhodes, tossing in Pisidia to the Pergamons. Having little direct contact with the king of Pergamon several hundred kilometers westward, the people of Pisidia took to piracy and fortified their economy, minting a coin in the first century B.C. Still, Mavisu remained hidden, high in the Taurus, and even the Crusaders failed to locate it. Too many travelers mistook its scattered hamlets for shepherds' huts and passed through the village without knowing they had even encountered it.

The villagers chose isolation and it served them well. They were safe in the folds and cracks of ancient rock too high for the timid to scale. But in their innocence, they migrated to a way of life that eventually betrayed them. They shared a history of movement and resisted Ataturk's goal to settle them. They accepted his alphabet only in exchange for the electricity he promised in the mid-1920s, the power lines threading them to a world they did not know, to a way of life they were made to believe they needed. They wanted only to pass the time with their flocks, to sit together under a new moon and feel Allah was just beyond the stars if they reached high enough, if they believed in the bounty of their own space. They entertained an irony in their isolation; in wanting ultimately to be left alone, they created an unprecedented solidarity.

The people of Mavisu adapted to change but did not subscribe to the prophecy of progress. They found comfort only in the consistency of their superstitions, in the curative powers of folk remedies too old to refute. And so they drank pigeon egg on an empty stomach for forty days to treat asthma, heated black cabbage leaves to take away pain. Animal bile and henna wraps cured headaches. Milk and honey for the stomach. The villagers were alchemists with their poultices, tinctures, and salves. They could cure nearly any ailment but they did not have a remedy for the wrongs of men.

Do you think it was an accident?

She looked up at her uncle, who sat hunched over the dog's hind legs, pulling thorns from his paw with tweezers.

I'm sure he just got lost.

He doesn't get lost.

Nurdane stroked the dog's ears. They were warm and sticky with honey.

He can hardly see, Nurdane.

I know. It's just that . . .

She rested her knee on her chin and watched a small lizard scuttle across the stones.

What?

It's silly.

What is it?

I felt somebody . . . watching me work.

Last night?

She looked up and nodded, her eyes wide.

The bellmaker laughed, reaching out to her, gently cupping her cheek. She looked so fragile to him.

You're working too hard. Soon, you'll start to hear things. Let me get you some tea.

He got up and entered the house, passing his son Mehmet, who emerged with a tray of tea glasses and sliced cucumbers.

Mehmet?

He set the tray on the steps and ran toward her, lifting her off the ground like he did when they were children. Her hair was loose and fell around her shoulders, streaked copper in the sun. He spun her three times, then set her down on the ground. She grabbed his arm, dizzy, trying to steady herself. She brushed her hair away from her face and slapped her hands on her hips, delighted by his presence.

I thought you were still studying.

He nodded.

I came back for . . .

He glanced at his father, picking up the tray and carrying it toward them.

I came back for you, Mehmet said quickly. To see my favorite cousin. Celebrate your birthday.

You're staying for the month?

He nodded.

We have a lot of catching up. I want to swim. Will you go with me tomorrow?

She smiled. Her fondest memories, playing with Mehmet. He knew her as she wanted to remember herself best, before the polio, moving freely, unaided by the braces. Neither ridiculed nor pitied. Only a girl who could walk like the others.

Does my father know you're here?

Backgammon tonight. It's been set.

She raised an eyebrow.

You don't count anymore, do you?

Most certainly not! Professionals don't count the spaces. We commit them to memory.

He imitated Ali's graven tone, then flashed a smile. He was full of energy and had about him a vitality that the other villagers lacked. His shirt was stained with watermelon juice. A few seeds stuck to his pocket.

You like Antalya?

He pounded his chest and howled.

You wouldn't believe how many books are there. More than Pergamon. More than Ephesus. Stacks and stacks. It makes you dizzy staring at them. The most depressing thing is that I won't get to read a quarter of them in my life.

She smiled politely. She could not read and did not understand his love of books, but she shared his enthusiasm. He kneeled before her, taking her hands in his own, and recited a few verses from his favorite poem.

Were these the hands that used to leap
Out of fables into dreams, were these the hands?
Full of yearning, full of life,
Were these the hands that clutched the pictures and fell asleep?

Gone from those lines for good
Are aspects that the fortune-teller read as happiness,
Where the jackknife had slashed
While carving whistles out of willow wood.

They abandoned all the cherished, flighty
Toys and smashed their tiny bottles, too.
Yet, in the face of everything,
Were these the hands that opened up to God Almighty!

She met his eyes.

Did you write it?

Mehmet shook his head and smiled.

I wish. Daglarca did.

Daglarca?

Fazil Husnu Daglarca.

It's beautiful.

Mehmet nodded.

If I could write even half as well as he, I'd die a happy man.

Will you teach me?

To write?

To understand hands like Daglarca, she said, shifting her eyes to the hill, where her hut sat alone in the shadow of passing clouds.

She left Attila at Mehmet's to sleep, then climbed to the aqueduct, where she found Ayse, alone, scrubbing clothes. It was late in the afternoon and the oak trees cast dappled shadows on the stones. The leaves silver in the light.

Nurdane did not expect to find the girl working. She was sick. At least that's what her mother had told Nurdane. But here she was, rubbing the clothes against limestone without a care, singing. Her voice light and airy. There was a dreamlike quality about it, transporting her from the mundane task into another world.

She smiled. She was a beautiful girl with high cheekbones and heart-shaped lips. Balkan blood, too. She was different from the other girls Nurdane knew. Calmer, more mature. Quiet. She looked like them. Slender, small-boned, slight in stature, a mix of Asian and Caucasian. Several tribes in one. But her eyes were those of an older woman, wiser for the things she had seen, and sharper, too, for the things she had lost. Her father had died of consumption the winter before she had been born, leaving her mother and two brothers alone in the village. Theirs was a household of rumor and rage. Ayse was the only unmarried girl from Mavisu who had been to Antalya. The circumstances of her travel fueled gossip circles every time she left the village. Both the men and women believed Ayse had been taught to read, and in their own proud way were both appalled and pleased by her advantage.

Her arms were long and firm, and she wore a coil of metal around them like a snake, the silver white against her olive skin. Her muscles contracted into little mounds the harder she worked. Sweat crawled along her cheek but she did not stop to wipe it, continuing her song with a longing for something she could not have, a pain Nurdane recognized as her own. Verses about love and loyalty and the grief of separateness.

Nurdane waited for the girl to finish, then moved beside her, washing her own headscarf. They worked in silence, only the splash of water over the rocks and the constant drip from the pipe jutting from the aqueduct. They had shared this comfort of silence since they were young girls, bonded by a common loss that they had never named or discussed or felt obliged to remember too clearly, exchanging their pain only through lyrics.

Please, keep singing.

Ayse turned to Nurdane and offered a smile.

You like it?

It's beautiful, Nurdane said, pushing up her sleeves, dunking her headscarf into the stone trough filled with water.

She's the most beautiful woman I've ever seen.

Who?

Sabite Tür Gulerman.

Sabite?

She's a famous singer. Studied classical music. She moved from Ankara to Istanbul last year and performed as a soloist with Istanbul Radio.

Nurdane twisted her headscarf and squeezed out the water.

You know her?

I met her once.

She came to Mavisu?

Ayse smiled, her eyes filled with both amusement and pity for the weaver's ignorance.

In Antalya. I saw her perform. She sings the most difficult classical pieces. She wears her hair like this . . .

She ran her hand flush against her head, then moved her fingers up and down, indicating a curl.

What about her headscarf?

Ayse whispered, parlaying the secret.

She doesn't wear one.

In public?

In public.

Nurdane exchanged an incredulous look with Ayse, but the girl giggled as if it were common. She took the wet headscarf from Nurdane and hung it on a branch to dry.

Is this what you've come to wash?

Nurdane nodded and studied the girl's face in the light. She hadn't noticed before but her eyes were bloodshot and circled by dark rings.

It's not my day to wash.

Then why are you here?

Your mother talked to me last night.

Ayse grabbed another soiled shirt from her basket and lay it on the stone.

What did she say?

She said you're ill.

Is that why you came?

I came to see how you're feeling.

Tell her I'm fine, Ayse snapped.

Her voice had suddenly grown tighter and Nurdane detected a sudden defiance, wondering if the question had offended the girl. Ayse opened the pipe and flooded the stone slab with water. She rubbed a chunk of olive oil soap over the shirt, then beat it with a wooden paddle. Foam oozed out of the cloth. Little rainbow bubbles in the light.

Your mother's very concerned about you.

Ayse looked up.

What else did she say?

You're not eating.

I'm not hungry for what she feeds me. Lies, you know?

Nurdane pulled her hair over to her left shoulder, her eyes glancing down at the paddle in Ayse's hand, her forearms thinner than she remembered them.

She said you've lost weight.

Ayse shifted her eyes to meet the weaver's.

My heart is heavy, she said.

But you're getting married. You should be happy.

Ayse poked at the soap bubbles.

I want to choose the man who will make me a woman.

Ayse slid down the stone basin and sat with her back against it, pulling her knees to her chest. She picked acorns off the ground and tossed them at a lizard darting through a cluster of poppies. She did not speak until Nurdane sat beside her, shoulder to shoulder, the late afternoon sun in their eyes.

You're lucky, Nurdane.

Lucky?

You don't have to get married.

I think about it.

Ayse turned to her.

You do?

Nurdane nodded.

I wonder what it would be like. What kind of man.

Nurdane smiled, her cheeks drilled with dimples, then quickly covered her mouth, a customary gesture for Islamic women. Ayse turned from her, watching an old man lead his donkey down the road, its back laden with broken twigs.

It's a big mess, she said.

The donkey? Nurdane asked.

The marriage arrangements. For what? Nobody is really happy in the end.

Nurdane studied her. She looked hurt, punctured by the accusation.

Your mother wants you to be happy. She's concerned about your illness.

A broken heart is the worst sickness there is.

Ayse looked out into the distance, where Nurdane's hut sat alone on the hill. Silence, then the flapping of a raven's wings overhead, its wicked caw carried by the wind.

Can you keep a secret?

Nurdane nodded.

Yes. Of course.

I don't want to marry the soldier.

Why?

I don't love him.

Nurdane turned to her, seeing the conviction she held in her face.

You must, she insisted.

I can't.

You will learn how.

Ayse shook her head and wiped the tear sliding down her chin. Her lips trembled when she spoke.

I can't, Nurdane. I love another.

Ali polished the samovar with the back of his sleeve, then filled the brazier with charcoal and set a match to it. He packed a brass teapot with mint leaves and filled it with water, placing it over the fountain to brew. He could see Mehmet's figure distorted in the brass as he paced the room.

Have a seat.

When the tea is ready.

Now, Ali insisted. You're making me dizzy.

Mehmet sighed, lowering himself to a small pillow on the floor across from Ali, who sat cross-legged, his back against the wall where the camel bags were hung. Ali took out his glasses and arranged the backgammon board, solid walnut with black and white checkers, polished obsidian and boar's bone.

You ready?, Ali asked.

I'm ready.

You sure?

Yes. I'm sure.

You're nervous.

I'm not.

Your fingers are shaking.

They're excited.

Nervous.

Ali shot a glance at his nephew in the half light of an oil lamp burning on the floor. Mehmet shared the same sloping forehead and high cheekbones of Nurdane. They had often been mistaken as siblings. The young man possessed the large deerlike eyes of her mother, his aunt. They were shrewd, intelligent eyes. The eyes of a professor, not those of a gambler. Ali took the cigarette from behind his ear and stuck it between his lips.

Since when did you become a risk taker?

Mehmet lifted his eyes.

Since I left the village.

I see, Ali said, and struck a match.

This a money game, Mehmet?

Mehmet shook his head, setting his thumbs on the edge of the board, pulling it toward him to even the distance between him and his opponent. He did not want to give Ali any more advantage than he already had.

I don't want to play for money.

Cigarettes? From Antalya? A cigar perhaps?

Scotch.

Scotch? Ali whispered.

Whisky. Scotch whisky.

Yes. I know what it is.

Ali's face flattened. He sat up tall and stiffened, as if the words had pushed him farther against the wall.

I don't drink, Mehmet. Never have. I don't plan on starting now.

Mehmet flashed a smile.

I'm kidding.

It's not funny.

It is. A Muslim drinking Scotch. Think about it.

Ali scowled. He wanted to laugh with his nephew, but he still assumed a parental role.

You're not drinking now that you're . . . a poet?

Mehmet shook his head and laughed. He was having fun with his uncle, testing his authority.

The writers are always drunks.

I'm a professor, Uncle Ali. Almost.

Ali waved his hand dismissively.

Same thing. You sit alone and think a lot. That would drive any man to the bottle.

I'm not a drinker.

But you think. Be careful.

Ali exhaled through his nose.

You never tried a sip? he asked.

No.

Never?

Believe me, Ali. I have too many things I want to do more than get drunk with a bunch of miserable fishermen. Because they're the real drunks, you know, the fishermen. And the sailors. I see them stumble around the piers. One guy fell in last week. Never came up for air. Probably drowned himself first with the bottle. I saw it floating on the surface. The label was peeled back. Ouzo, of course. The drunks aren't only poets, Ali. They're Greeks too.

Yeah, well, Ali grumbled, the hell does that tell you?

He cracked a smile and Mehmet wiped his forehead with the back of his hand, relieved the man had not lost his sense of humor entirely. He was tense. He could see that. The way his eyes darted from point to point on the board as if he were already playing the game without a single checker moved. He was preoccupied with something, his eyes pressed with worry. He entertained a certain formality that Mehmet did not recognize, as if the meeting were more business than family. And it was, to a point. They both knew it.

You know the Egyptians played only for money.

Mehmet shook his head.

I didn't know that.

They even locked the dice in little boxes to keep the players from cheating.

That right?

But sometimes that didn't work.

No?

The hustlers loaded the dice. Filled certain sides with lead or gold to make it heavy. To make certain numbers appear more frequently. Double sixes. That sort of thing.

Ali took the teakettle from the samovar and set it on the floor.

You must know, Mehmet. Backgammon is about paradoxes and probabilities. Risk, really. The stakes are high.

He looked up and locked eyes with Mehmet.

I know, Ali. It's a dice game. The ancients used to predict the future rolling dice.

We're not going to predict the future tonight.

Maybe we will, Mehmet suggested.

Only Allah predicts the future. So I hope you're not wasting my time, trying to learn an opening move or something that will make you a hero among those college students.

Mehmet was offended. He crossed his arms over his chest.

No, Ali. I wouldn't do that. I'm serious about this.

So am I. You're not a good player.

I've gotten better.

You still count?

No.

Good, said Ali with the slightest hint of approval.

Besides, I thought backgammon was about luck anyway.

Ali narrowed his eyes to slits.

You're mistaken. Luck is just that—the inevitable reward of the skillful.

I'm skillful, Mehmet insisted.

We'll see.

Ali poured the tea into small tulip glasses etched with gold paint. He used them only for special occasions; and although he refused to surrender to superstition, Ali believed the glasses guaranteed good luck to those who drank from them. That he should offer one to Mehmet was his way of proving he believed skill, above anything, would be the final determinate in backgammon. He handed one of the dice to Mehmet, took the other for himself.

So it's not money or Scotch or luck. Remind me again what we're playing for?

He spoke sarcastically and Mehmet could hear he was getting agitated with the delay. He took a deep breath, then lifted his eyes to meet his uncle's.

A favor.

A favor?

Mehmet nodded.

I've never played for a favor.

Would you make an exception?

Depends.

If I win, you have to do what I ask.

What is it that you want?

Mehmet drank his tea. It was too hot and burned his tongue.

What is it that I can do for you that your father can't?

My father doesn't know about this.

Ali set his tea glass down.

What?

Mehmet swallowed and stiffened. His hands left prints on his pants.

No matter who wins tonight, you have to promise that my father never hears a word about this. Nobody in the village can know.

Ali leaned across the board and took the boy's face in his, tilted it to the light, and looked deep into his eyes.

You in trouble?

Mehmet raised his eyebrow and cracked a smile.

Love is always trouble.

Ali let go of his face.

What has this got to do with love?

I want to marry Ayse.

Ali's mouth dropped open and the cigarette fell to the stone floor. Mehmet took it and handed it back, but Ali refused. The smoke rising between them.

Her wedding's already been arranged.

That's why I came back now. I need you to ask her mother for me. Before it's too late.

Don't you understand? It's prearranged.

Mehmet rolled his eyes.

Please, Ali.

Ali looked back over his shoulder to make sure they were still alone, despite the fact that Nurdane had long since left to work on the rug.

Does Ayse know about this?

We've known a long time.

Ali pinched the skin on the bridge of his nose. He shook his head and clicked his tongue, disapproving.

Is she . . .

He made a round gesture with his hand around his stomach. Mehmet shook his head.

Of course not, Ali. I'm a man of honor.

Ali said nothing. He sat stiffly with his thin legs crossed like the wings of a butterfly. His head pushed back against the wall. A dark smudge of oil marked the space as if he had always done his thinking from this position.

I can't play Allah.

I'm not asking you. I want you to change a tradition.

Ali threw his glance down upon the samovar.

The arrangement is more than a tradition. It's a matter of economics. Genetics. It is not a dance for dancing's sake.

I pity the dancer.

Why?

Did you love your wife?

Ali nodded.

Very much. From the moment I saw her.

Then it wasn't arranged. It was fated, wasn't it?

Love cannot save you from your fate, if that's what you think.

Ali handed Mehmet his tea glass, but Mehmet pushed his hand away and locked eyes on his face.

You fell in love once. Just like me.

We were nomads. The rules were different then.

Fate is the rule. There is no other.

Don't be a dreamer, Mehmet. You'll die an unhappy man.

What do you know about dreams?

They end in the morning, Ali said.

Mehmet sat back and crossed his arms over his chest.

Do you want me to leave?

We haven't even started.

I need your help, Ali. But I won't beg.

Ali shifted his eyes across the floor to a basket filled with skeins of red-dyed wool. His head throbbed.

You're asking me to tempt Allah.

Tell me one man who doesn't.

Ali sighed. He rubbed his eyebrow with the back of his thumb. Mehmet continued. His face was flushed and his skin glistened in the light.

If Nurdane could marry somebody, if she were healthy enough, would you let her choose the man who would make her a woman? Or would you arrange the marriage yourself? Not based on what she wanted, but what you think she needed?

Ali scratched his chin and refilled his tea glass. He took the dice, handing one to Mehmet, then tossed his onto the board and started the game.

Nurdane sat cross-legged on the ground and crushed madder root into powder outside an abandoned stone house on the periphery of her father's orchard. The building was used for storing wool, and colored skeins hung in clumps from the eaves, casting shadows over the doors and windows. Steam oozed from large vats of dye baths boiling outside, releasing sulphates and iron into the air.

Nurdane fed the twiglike roots into the center of two large round stones, churning the mill clockwise with a wooden handle. She hummed songs of a woman who did not wear a headscarf, wondering how Ayse had come to know her, and if Ayse herself went without a headscarf when she left the village, as if the headscarf were a flag or a banner flown only over its native soil, having no use elsewhere.

She paused to feed broken limbs of a windfall into the fires burning beneath the *kezan,* the heavy aluminum pots filled with dyes. She brushed the powdered madder root into a small pan and stood, adding it to the first bath with pinches of copper salts and alum, mordants to increase the dye's color resistance to fading. The particular color of red she wanted depended on the amount and type of mordant. Iron for more muted shades. Alum, potassium aluminum sulfates, for richer, luminous shades of red.

The knowledge of dye recipes had been passed orally from her grandmother to her mother. Her father had learned a special shade of violet from his own mother, teaching Nurdane when she was old enough to understand secrets. He insisted on natural dyes for her rugs, knowing that the colors lasted longest, and despite the availabilty of powders and the cheap chemical dyes peddled throughout the villages, he made his way to the valley each year to pick madder root that grew wild in the cotton fields. There was only one red-producing plant and one blue, madder and indigo, that grew in Turkey, but about twenty different plants that yielded shades of yellow including wild chamomile, wig-shrub, and dyer's-weld among others. Walnut pods yielded brown, and the high tannic acid content of oak bark and acorns, pomegranate skins and mordant, each produced a rich black.

Nurdane stirred the red dye with a flat wooden paddle and added approximately one kilo of wool to the vat, knowing the ratio of wool to root was one to one. One kilo of madder root for one kilo of wool. Attila lay in the doorway of the storage house and watched her, his chin between his paws, unfazed by the grasshoppers trying to provoke him. He pinned back his ears, seeing Ayse riding through the trees toward them. She laid the bike on its side in a pile of stones and carried a small flat package wrapped in cloth.

You never stop, do you?

Nurdane turned to her, laying the wooden paddle on the ground. She smiled, happy to have a visitor.

A bride waits for me.

Don't forget—

Trust me. I haven't. I've been up since dawn. I couldn't sleep. My father and Mehmet played backgammon all night. I found them passed out on the floor before I left, half a game on the board.

Ayse laughed.

I meant don't forget that some of the brides don't mind waiting.

She handed Nurdane the package, encouraging her with her eyes to open it. Nurdane pulled the strings and peeled back the cloth, revealing a record with the photo of a woman on the cover. She had blond, wavy hair and wore bright red lipstick. Her cheeks were round, her smile wide, teeth as white as the shells around her neck. She wore no headscarf.

She's beautiful.

It's Sabite.

The singer?

Ayse nodded, watching the smile grow on Nurdane's face. She turned back, looking over her shoulder as if she held in her hand evidence of a conversation she shouldn't have had, a secret she was not supposed to know.

I want you to have it.

Nurdane looked up at her, shocked.

I want to thank you, Ayse said.

For what?

Letting me talk to you the other day.

You can always talk to me.

I know, Ayse said, staring at her. She pushed the album gently against Nurdane's chest, encouraging the girl to embrace it. She looked around at the mill and the vats, the powder on Nurdane's hands and clothes.

Go home and listen.

Now?

Yes.

But I have to finish the dyes.

What more do you have to do? Everything's already soaking. How much longer will it take?

Four hours. I won't be finished until dinner.

I'll stay.

What?

I'll stay and hang them to dry. Go home and eat something. Listen to Sabite. Your father has a gramophone, right?

Nurdane nodded, dumbfounded by Ayse's offer. Ayse waved her hand in the air.

Take my bike.

Nurdane stood still, staring at her. A wind blew through the trees and lifted the scarf around Ayse's neck. Her skin was purplish, the color of the violet dye.

What happened to you?

I'm happy. I wanted to thank you.

Nurdane pointed.

Your neck. It's all purple. What happened?

Ayse looked down and noticed the dangling scarf. She covered her neck with her hand, then quickly retied the scarf, hiding what appeared to be a bruise.

I slept funny.

Nurdane said nothing, hearing the tension in her voice. Ayse spoke quickly.

I'll take a nap when you're gone. Maybe I'll feel better.

You sure?

Ayse nodded.

I'll be fine.

She sat on the ground before Nurdane could say anything, stoking the fire with a stick.

Go home, Nurdane.

Do you want anything? Food? Some bread.

Just your voice. I want to hear you sing Sabite's songs so we can sing together.

She lifted her eyes, trusting Nurdane to leave her there with the dyes. Nurdane picked up the bike and maneuvered the braces on her legs, ensuring she could pedal without catching her trousers in the chain. She waved good-bye and disappeared through the trees, returning with the soldier in tow. He had seen her ride by the tea-house at dusk and waved her down to inquire about Ayse. He insisted on following Nurdane to the storage house, cursing every time she stopped to catch her breath.

Can't you go any faster?

She was about to tell him to go ahead of her, when she saw embers burning where the fires had been, the steam silver in the moonlight.

Wait here.

Why?

The soldier was perturbed and snapped a twig between his fingers.

I'm not sure where Attila is. I should tie him before you come inside.

She left him standing by a skein of freshly dyed red wool that had blown off the eaves. She laid the bike by the *kezan,* and approached the storage house slowly, pausing at the sound of breathing. She turned quickly, catching the flicker of a candle and the shadow it cast on the wall, a silhouette of two people embracing. A man and woman, the ends of her scarf lifted by the breeze.

Ayse?

She stepped through the door, expecting to find the dog, but instead the flicker of the candle died and the silhouette disappeared, leaving nothing but the play of moonlight on the stones. Still, breathing. She knew Ayse was there.

You find the dog yet?

I can't see.

She turned, finding the soldier making his way toward the door. She pulled it shut and closed the latch.

He must have run off again. Could you help me find him?

Your dog is always running off. Let him go. He needs to learn his lesson.

He's too old for lessons, she said, following the soldier's suspicious eyes that searched the window, trying to see beyond the blackness.

You said she was here.

She probably got hungry. It's been a while.

We were supposed to meet tonight. For dinner at my mother's.

Maybe she's there now, she offered, forcing the hope.

Yeah, maybe.

He eyed a piece of paper blowing about the ground. It had been folded in half, and although Nurdane could not read, she could see words through it. The soldier bent down and grabbed it, crouched on one knee. He opened it and held it up to the moonlight to see the words, reading them aloud.

Were these the hands that used to leap
Out of fables into dreams, were these the hands?
Full of yearning, full of life,
Were these the hands that . . .

He looked up and stared incredulously at Nurdane's lips, which moved in sync with his as he read. *Clutched the pictures and fell asleep,* she mouthed.

Do you know it?

She shrugged, swallowing hard.

I've heard it before.

Do you know it's a crime?

What?

To recite Hikmet's poetry.

It's Daglarca. Not Hikmet.

It's still wrong.

She shook her head, her eyes searching the blackness for some movement from the storage house.

I didn't know words were crimes.

Invisible knives, he said, turning back toward the trees. He drew in a deep breath and crumpled the page, tossing it into the embers, where it caught fire, each word consuming itself until only flakes of poetry blew across the ground and scattered at Nurdane's feet.

Muammer tossed in his sleep and woke to the smell of burning wood. He got up from the pile of wool blankets he used as his bed and crossed to the window. Thin clouds feathered the moon and shrouded the village in a fine blue mist. A stork set forth through the fog, then dropped to the west cliff, where tendrils of smoke curled into the sky, erasing the stars in Orion's belt. The portent spread over Mavisu like a giant sign that only a blind man would fail to see.

He leaned his head against the window and listened to his father snoring in the next room, mail sacks stacked against the wall, letters spilling over the top. They had no doors in the house, and through the archway he could see his younger brothers tucked beside his mother on the sleeping mat. Like cats, he thought. The Koran open beside them on the floor, the thin pages rustling in the cross-breeze. The flicker of an oil lamp cast shadows on their faces and gave their skin a doll-like sheen. They were dead asleep, and he knew they would not wake until the morning prayer.

He crossed back to his blankets and put on his shirt, then walked out the front door, taking his shoes from the rack outside. He took flaps of bread from his mother's oven and tore them into bits, tossing them on the ground to keep the chickens and goats from following him. Then he set down the gravel road and followed the smoke to the west cliff, the stones wet and black in the light.

He could hear them singing first. Then laughing. He followed the tire marks from the bicycles, retracing Nurdane's path, then stopped when he heard the gunshot. The smell of gunpowder drifted quickly toward him, and he jumped into a thicket of mulberry bushes and crouched down to watch. He could see a lamb limping around the campfire, its hind leg shot and dangling. The men stood with their backs toward him, and he could barely make out their faces in the light. But they were familiar now, their half-shaven faces. They were hard to mistake, the strange men he had watched in the mosque. He tried to follow them earlier, but his father had called him to milk the goats.

The men took the lamb and tied up its legs, then slit its throat, bleeding it over the campfire until there were no more flames, only the sizzle of blood on the hot rocks. He could see only their dark forms moving now, the lamb slung over one of their shoulders, its coat silver in the moonlight. They trudged through the olive trees and up the hill toward him. Muammer lay flat on the ground and shoved his forearm into his mouth to silence himself. He felt the ground shake as the men walked past him. They smelled of licorice and wood, smoke and blood. They continued past him, twenty, thirty steps. Muammer waited until he could hear only their voices, then pushed himself off the ground to see where they had gone. When he looked up, he saw them making their way toward the hill, where a candle flame flickered from Nurdane's hut.

They followed the dull thwap of her comb packing the knots tighter on the loom and found her in the dark. They were drunk. The thin mountain air carried their voices, and she stopped weaving when she heard them. They spoke a language she did not recognize, but she understood the grave intention in their tone.

She shifted her eyes from the loom to the window, where three men dragged themselves up the hill toward her hut, hunched over, heaving for air. Clouds of breath in the moonlight. She did not recognize them as the mountain people she knew. They were dark-skinned and unshaven. Two carried guns, the third slung a dead lamb across his back, the head bobbing up and down, mouth gaping as they walked.

They were strangers and yet she knew what they wanted. There had been talk of the pickers. They came to take rugs as they did in other villages across Anatolia and had traveled thousands of miles from Georgia and Armenia for the knots that would make them rich. Her father had warned her but she did not believe him until now. He said there would be intrusions, that she would be hunted for her rugs, but she never felt threatened. The talk seemed the thing of idle time at the teahouse, something that could happen but never did.

The village was too remote for thieves. The altitude at three thousand meters deterred those too weak to ascend by foot. The roads were snow-covered most of the year, and when they weren't, they were mud-pocked and rutted and washed out by summer rains. Even when the roads were clear, Mavisu was impossible to find without a guide. Nurdane did not know how the pickers had found it now.

She cut the last knot and blew out the candle beside her, then lay on the floor, waiting with a knife in her hand. The pickers were getting closer, their steps loud.

They approached her hut cautiously. It sat alone in its superstition, a modest structure of stones built from old tombs that had once housed the bones of fabled men. The spirits were everywhere. Even the pickers felt them and pulled their collars higher over their necks as they followed a narrow goat path strewn with fresh flowers. Orchids and oleanders, iris and poppies, led to the door where candles still burned in rusted cans as if the hut were a shrine.

She had left the door unlocked, but the wind had pushed it open and carried their voices inside. Deep breaths, panting. Nervous laughter. Coarse whispers. Then a splash of something liquid before they kicked the door open wider and stepped inside, ushering the cool air with them. She felt them staring, her back to them, heart pounding against the floor.

They struck a match to see the rug on the loom. A prayer rug, as they had been told. A multiple niche prayer rug, a *saf*. The mihrabs appeared as a series of stepped arches with a pair of birds facing each other on top. The gold contours on the arches gave the impression of a towering series of red and blue steps leading to an imaginary altar.

The rug was only three-quarters finished, but they did not care. They would take it to a rug repairman, who'd finish the job. Then they would make more, copies, as they had done before, and sell the fakes to those who would buy anything they thought was beautiful and rare.

They stepped closer to her, the steel shank of their boots cold against her back. Sleep, sleep, they whispered, careful not to wake her.

Her hair lay in dark clumps around her face. Her skin pale in the moonlight, her lips the color of raisins. They stared at her for a moment in awe and pity. This young woman with the misshapen feet, the girl who had made their prize.

They expected the rug to be finished. They had been told it would be washed, rolled neatly in the corner, where they could take it without waking her and be on their way. But the rug was still on the loom, and they needed something to cut it. The knife in her hand. They mumbled something in Russian. An argument. The man on her left hissed, cursing the man in the middle. One of them spit, and the saliva splattered her wrist.

The man behind her kneeled, his knee in her back. He hovered, the legs from the dead lamb dangling from his back, brushing her shoulder. She could smell the blood and raw flesh mixed with the fetid odor of the man's body, and pressed her tongue against the roof of her mouth to keep from gagging.

He touched her hair, raked the long, black locks between his fingers and held a strand to the moonlight. He touched the wool on the loom, comparing the two, then turned to his friends and whispered in Russian.

It's like silk. She's beautiful.

She's crippled, snapped his friend, eyeing the girl's legs.

Hurry up. You'll wake her, said the tallest man. He took another gulp of liquor from the bota as if he could swallow the courage needed to steal the weaver's rug.

The man behind Nurdane brushed the hair out of her face. She stiffened, clenched her teeth. She felt it coming. His hand toward hers. The nervous heat. The cold metal of his bracelet brushing her arm, wrist. Closer. He wedged his hand between her fingers to pry the knife, but she tightened her grip and he stopped immediately to watch.

She's awake.

Get the knife.

Wait.

He swatted the air to keep the other two men from moving. He leaned closer, studied her face. Her eyes were closed, pinched tightly. Her body suddenly stiff, shoulders up around her ears.

She's scared, he whispered. She knows.

Take the knife!

They raised their voices, abandoned the whispers. Cursed each other. Spit again.

They stopped when they heard the tapping of her knife against the floor. Her hand trembled, shaking the knife so furiously that the man in the middle thought she might cut herself. A single tear slid down the side of her nose.

Don't hurt her.

But before the man behind Nurdane could move, the other man grabbed Nurdane's wrist, wrapped his fingers around her bone like a vice. He gripped her hard, his fingers wedged between her thumb and palm, forcing the knife from her. She flinched, and the blade sliced across the palm of her hand, then slipped and plunged into the man's thigh. He screamed and cursed at her, slapped her across the face. The blood ran like black ink from his

leg and her hand, and he mistook her blood for his own and
slapped her again.

She propped herself up on the floor, staining it with the blood
on her hands. Her eyes wide and wild, glowing iridescent in the
dark, blue-green and metallic, inhuman. She silenced the pickers
with her stare, and they cowered, stepping backward toward the
door, tripping over balls of yarn scattered on the floor.

Eksik olmayiniz.

May you want for nothing, she hissed.

They did not need to speak Turkish to understand her.

The warning was clear in the force of her voice. They moved
quickly, yanked the knife from the wounded picker's thigh, and
ran out the door, leaving a trail of blood in the moonlight.

She did not move for a while, sitting there, staring out the window at the revolving darkness of the sky, the slow shift of stars and
moon. The big dipper fell into the gorge like a dream, and wind
rushed down the mountain, making noises through the trees.

Her face stung where she had been slapped, and her eyes were
wide with terror, looking only straight ahead. Her throat was
tight, and she bit her bottom lip to keep from trembling. She took
a deep breath, and rather than looking down at her hands, slowly
lifted them closer to the sky. They were cold, and she tucked them
away in shame, wondering when Allah would take the gift He had
given her so long ago.

II

John Hennessey negotiated his way among the broken cobbles of Kaleici, the old quarter of Antalya where the Apostle Paul had walked, past the silver shops and tile makers, glassblower and barber, searching for a rug shop open before ten. A thick haze shrouded the limestone mountains rising to the west of the Lycian city, its double-crenellated stone walls defenseless against the heat. It was dusty and quiet. Nothing more than a murmur, the purr of fishing boats in the harbor and the tinkling of tea glasses.

Hennessey turned right at a small corner bakery, crescent rolls behind the steamed windows, the smell of corn bread in the air, taxi drivers in line, smoking. He nodded, watching them steal a glimpse of the Turkish newspaper tucked beneath his arm, their expressions curious, eyes fixed on his face, the blond sideburns, the bangs hanging out of his Panama hat. He had learned to avoid the solicitations of foreign merchants and taxi drivers by carrying the newspaper of whatever country he was visiting. If they thought he could speak Turkish, they would respect his privacy and leave him alone, the way he wished.

Günaydýn, they said.

Günaydýn.

Good morning. His Turkish was not perfect, but they did not detect his accent and continued speaking among themselves, their interest in him waning. He turned in to an alley and followed a string of kilims draped over a brick wall overgrown with purple and pink bougainvillea, the flowers like fluorescent lights against the muted kilim, faded from the eastern sun. It looked like the rug had spent its life on the wall, that its role had been form over function. It belonged in a house, he thought, a mosque, covering the backseat of a taxi. The rug belonged anywhere but where it was, suspended and alone.

John Hennessey did not know much about rugs, but he prided himself on his taste, trusting he would find something good. He considered the request a fair one and did not mind combing the markets and shops as a token of appreciation for the research grant from the women of the Main Line. The wealthy suburb of Philadelphia had been the source of many benefactors after the government had refused his requests for funding. President Eisenhower's defense budget for the military left little for anthropological expeditions among other things, forcing researchers like himself to turn to private donors. Most of the women were widows, wives of late professors, academics themselves who believed in Hennessey's search for the Goddess, intrigued with her revival and survival. They wanted a Turkish rug for their public library. Hennessey wanted to be quick about it, send it by air mail to Philadelphia, get on with the excavation.

He followed a series of wooden horses draped with rugs, staggered in the open courtyard of a dilapidated Ottoman house, its box windows jutting out over the street, shutters crooked and weathered, panes of glass missing from the second floor, steel bars covering the windows below. The doorway was a massive arch of local limestone, still white despite its age. The door, a thick slab of walnut, intricately carved with Arabic letters.

He followed the stone steps into a huge hallway where a Phillips radio played Ella Fitzgerald's "Stairway to the Stars." Beside it lay a half-eaten lamb shank and a dog's bowl, stuck with slobber and dust, bits of wool floating on top. Against the walls were two small wooden chairs and a low, circular table, empty, the tea tray abandoned. He walked over and pressed his fingers against the half-filled tulip glass, the liquid cold, stale, flies fighting for the lone sugar cube left in the nickel-plated saucer.

Hennessey looked around, wondering if the shop had opened yet.

Hello?

Nothing but the clap of shutters against the house. He crossed the stone floor to a crooked stairway, leading to the second floor, the wood stained and bowed, sagging beneath his weight. He stood in the middle, eyeing each of the three rooms, doors clacking against the walls as a hot wind slipped in through the shutters. He could see beyond the middle door a vibrant array of camel bags and flat-weave kilims hanging from the walls, whitewashed and stenciled with mustard and rust-colored flowers. Beneath the nomadic tapestries lay hundreds of rugs, rolled tightly and set in stacks as high as Hennessey's shoulders.

The door was open and he peered inside, finding a man sitting on a pile of rugs, hunched over a backgammon board. Lying at his feet was a large German shepherd that barked in alarm at Hennessey. The merchant turned his head, looking only at Hennessey's shoes, the open-toed sandals. A tourist, he thought, a looker. He rolled the dice in his hand and spoke to the man without looking up, his voice loud, his declaration clear.

No bargains here. My prices are fixed.

May I look?

No lookers. I don't want lookers.

I want to buy. And I don't have much time.

The merchant lifted his eyes to see the man's face, assessing him, the pressed linen suit, tailored, tapered at his waist, the gold watch on his wrist. The pale, freckled skin. Green eyes. The way his blond bangs stuck to his forehead in the heat. The merchant pushed the backgammon aside but did not get up to meet the man.

If you want a deal, go somewhere else.

I don't want a deal. I want a good rug.

I have many.

I want the best you have.

They exchanged a knowing look and the courtship began. Rug dealer to client. He offered tea and sugar. It was hot already but Hennessey did not want to offend the Turk and accepted his hospitality. The man rang a bell and a small dark-eyed boy with a shaven head emerged from the hallway carrying a tray of steaming tea and sugar cubes, lumps of Turkish corn bread wrapped in paper, and a pot of honey.

Hennessey eyed the ceiling, the intricate scrollwork on the beams. Built into the south wall was a huge armoire of solid cherry, its frieze and frame stiles carved into a vine, a relief of diamond points on the door panels.

Beautiful work, he said.

A carpenter lived here with his wives.

Wives?

Four of them. He planted a different fruit tree outside each of their windows. Malte plums here.

He pointed out the window, beckoning Hennessey to see. Hennessey stepped closer to the merchant, aware of the dog, but it lunged at him, baring its teeth. The merchant barked something in Turkish. Hennessey didn't understand, but figured the words were insults since the dog dropped to the floor and whimpered.

Does he bite?

Only if you upset me, the merchant said, nodding from his perch on the rugs, bearded chin cupped in his hand.

You know rugs?

Not really.

Then how will you know if you see the best?

I'd rather ask for it right away. I leave for the mountains tomorrow. The post office closes today.

The post office closes every day.

I have to send it to the States.

Does it matter?

Yes, Hennessey insisted.

You don't have time to find a rug. Have a nice day.

The merchant leaned forward to study the backgammon board again. The dog had fallen asleep and the boy took a pair of scissors and began to repair a rug that sat in a pile at the back of the room.

I can make the time, Hennessey persisted.

Not as long as you keep staring at your watch.

Hennessey shifted uncomfortably, catching the second hand pass the six. It was already ten-thirty.

Go on. Take it off.

What? The watch?

The merchant shifted his eyes, waiting.

I'm not going to steal it, he said.

I didn't say you would.

No. But you thought it.

Hennessey locked eyes with the merchant. He was a small man, round, with a silver beard and glasses. His face ruddy, shiny in the heat. He carried a puckish look in his eyes, intelligent and shrewd, yet honest. Hennessey unclipped the watch and slipped it into his pants pocket.

Feel better? Hennessey asked.

The merchant smiled, crossing his arms.

There are no shortcuts, he said. You can't know rugs by seeing. If you want to know them, you must work at it. You need a *hoca*. Now. What size are you looking for?

Standard.

Large or small?

Large. For a living room. Or a small library.

For your wife?

A widow.

Children?

What?

Does she have children?

Yes.

Grandchildren?

Nine, why?

Look and feel. You'd be surprised.

The merchant got up and disappeared into the hallway, emerging with a coiled rug beneath his arm. He brought it to Hennessey and unfurled it on the floor, tossing it with the ease of a baker flinging dough. Dust and woolen fibers filtered into the morning light.

Beautiful.

Yes. And old. Three hundred years old. She's from a village south of Troy. Ayvacik.

Near Lesbos.

The merchant smiled and nodded.

You've been?

Once.

It's enough, isn't it?

Hennessey smiled and bent down to examine the rug. It was a small piece of something that had once been larger, a threadbare rag of red and blue wool. The merchant paced behind him.

It takes time, he said. To love fragments.

Hennessey looked up.

Yes. I know about fragments.

The merchant cocked his head, anticipating. Hennessey continued.

I study pieces of things. Make them whole again.

You and the weaver. Are you a doctor?

Hennessey shook his head and ran his fingers over the knots.

Anthropologist. Physical anthropologist.

What's the difference?

I study bones. I study the dead.

The merchant searched his eyes.

You're an intelligent man.

I make mistakes.

I didn't say you were infallible. I think I can teach you about rugs. You'll learn quicker than most.

They spent the morning staring at the floor as it changed from one rug to the next. A lesson in composition and balance. The meaning of symbols. The difference between the flat-weave kilims and the knotted-pile rugs. The source of the colors and the native plants that yielded them. The merchant collected only handmade rugs and insisted the dyes were natural. Chemical dyes faded. Factory-made rugs rarely lasted more than a few years. The merchant's criteria for buying his rugs depended on the colors, quality of the wool, and workmanship of the knots. The tighter the better.

I love them like my children, know them as well too, he said, crouching before the sea of rugs on the floor. I can go anywhere in the world and pick them out. I know where they came from, the name of the village. Sometimes the weavers too.

Hennessey kicked off his shoes as the merchant had done and walked across the pile in his bare feet, feeling the quality of the wool. The prayer rug glistened in the light, a simple design, elegant and quiet, a solid wine-colored field, graduating in saturation and hue, situated between two intricate green-and-gold pillars filled with flowers that led to heaven. The merchant ran the back of his hand over the knots.

You'd think it was silk, he said, flipping over a corner of the rug to examine the knots. Look how tight it is. Like a tapestry.

It's gorgeous, Hennessey said.

The merchant sighed, sitting on his knees.

I need her for a while. I can't sell her yet. This rug gives me life. The good ones do.

How do you know?

What?

A feeling. The vitality of the rug.

The merchant stood and took one of the rugs in the stack, holding the coil against his chest, his hands running along the silken pile as he spoke.

I get to know the weaver. The good ones have . . . a certain power. When I see the work of a gifted weaver, something happens to me. I feel her spirit. I know her moods. I know her spells. When she's happy, sad, disappointed, frustrated. Discouragement too. All of her is there, in the knots.

He caressed the antique with the back of his wrist as if he were feeling the forehead of a feverish child.

It must be hard to let them go.

It is. They're like daughters. I wait until somebody falls in love with them, then takes them away.

The merchant sighed, flinging out the rug in his arms, letting it fall on top of the others. It was an old prayer carpet, its wool dyed natural shades of cream, green, brown, and red.

This is a Milas rug.

Milas?

It's from the southwest, along the Aegean coast. Milas carpets are among the most sought after Anatolian carpets for their natural colors and high-quality knotting. Often medium to fine knots. Not as tight as a silk rug, but close enough for wool.

The merchant took out his prayer beads and walked over the rug, inspecting and admiring his piece.

It's from the eighteenth century.

How can you tell?

Look at the colors, he said. Color is its most outstanding feature. The ivory field is most unusual.

Hennessey studied the rug. He had no way of comparing natural dyes to synthetic, but he was struck by the folk-art pattern, the feathery leaf-form trees at the bottom, the stylized flowers at the top. There were two birds in the center, beneath them the heads of two roosters. It reminded him of the quilts he'd seen in Pennsylvania, that of the Amish and Pennsylvania Dutch.

It looks European.

The merchant raised an eyebrow, impressed.

Good eye, he said, tapping the air with his finger.

The motifs are reminiscent of Transylvanian rugs.

How did they get to Milas?

The merchant shrugged.

Nomads. The true Turk is a wanderer.

Hennessey walked over the rug, feeling privileged to be in on the merchant's secrets.

You must have a gift to find ones like this.

I guess I've always had feelings for unique pieces.

Nobody taught you?

I found them on my own. I collected old coins as a boy. Dug them from the silt in the canals by my village. A few kilometers from here. Near Aspendos.

The ancient theater?

The whole plain's been flooded.

I know, said Hennessey. It's a shame. It's impossible to find certain sites now. Most of the excavations have been covered again.

The merchant sighed, flipping back the layers of carpets, finding the tattered rug.

All the beautiful things, *gömmek*. Buried.

What's that?

The beautiful things. They get lost. They go unnoticed for hundreds of years.

Hennessey followed the merchant's eyes roving the abstract symbols in the rug, trying to decipher the archaic code. He could see the merchant was a trained observer much like himself, and he studied the rug with the same intensity as Hennessey would have studied a piece of a pelvis or skull.

Do you ever feel your vision's been . . . compromised?

Hennessey asked the question tentatively. The merchant raised his finger.

I can always find the beauty. I have a nose. Rugs are like that for me. Some people remember a fine meal or wine. The kiss of a lost lover. Some quote poems or sing a song that never leaves them. I remember rugs.

He got on his knees and leaned forward, pressed his forehead against the carpet as if he were praying.

You can smell it.

What?

The flesh of the weaver.

Hennessey stared at him quizzically.

She is with me forever. The weaver never leaves the rug. Her spirit is woven throughout.

He rubbed his hand along the edges, stroked the center, his voice low.

It's sad, he said. You know these great beautiful pieces were probably made in mud-brick houses. Then they leave, enter the world. Great palaces. Universities. The homes of the rich. The weaver never experiences her art. It's like the potter making wine vessels that he will never drink from.

Ironic.

Yes. Very. But it happens. The world wants more rugs. The weaver needs more work. So it goes. But the purpose gets lost. Do you know there's a whole language here, for women?

No.

The merchant continued.

Most of them are illiterate. They can't read or write. What they know is passed through stories and songs. The women of Anatolia have wonderful memories. They commit volumes to their minds. It's extraordinary. The way they listen, too, etching their minds with the words. You see, the rugs have been their only form of communication. The stories recorded in the knots. Most men cannot read the rugs as the women do. I'm lucky I understand. I read music. I play the saz. I'm a musical man. Foreign language has always come easy.

He looked up, eyeing the light that fell through the slatted shutters.

On the days that I doubt Allah, he said, I take out the rugs and smell again, to believe in art, in miracles.

Hennessey smiled, nodding slowly.

The priests used to say art is for the spirit.

The merchant raised his right eyebrow and smiled.

Then you believe in miracles too.

Hennessey flashed a mouthful of teeth. There was a glint in his eye when he smiled, and he looked more like a movie star than a scholar in his linen suit and Panama hat.

On the contrary. I'm a skeptic. I need evidence of everything to prove it existed.

What about love? What evidence is there?

I haven't dug for it yet.

Poor man. Skepticism is your virtue, the merchant said with pity in his voice. Hennessey's eyes narrowed and he jerked his shoulders, a quick shrug.

I believe there's more to everything.

There is. I'll show you.

The merchant began to unfold the kilims and toss them on the ground, piling them up one by one until there were no more to show. Then he unrolled every one of the rugs until the walls of the shop were bare. It was almost dark by the time the merchant decided to open his safes for Hennessey.

No, please. You've shown me so much already. I'm a fool if I can't make a decision.

Which one do you want to buy?

Hennessey shifted on his heels, arms crossed over his chest, fingers massaging the top of his cheekbone.

You don't know. Do you?

Hennessey looked up, helpless.

They should make you feel something. You do know how to feel, don't you?

I can feel. See?

Hennessey closed his eyes, shook his hands out in front of him, breathing heavily. The merchant was amused and bit back the smile creeping over his face. He watched Hennessey's eyes open and his finger point randomly at the rugs.

That one. I feel that one.

The merchant walked over to the pile of rugs and pulled the one Hennessey was pointing at. He sighed, disappointed.

You don't feel *this*, do you?

Hennessey shrugged. The merchant shook his head.

It's a fake. Synthetic. Came from a sorry factory near Istanbul.

You tricked me.

I didn't intend for that. I keep it here to show my clients the difference between the synthetic dyes and natural.

Great, Hennessey said, his shoulders dropping. He was discouraged, if not slightly embarrassed by his haste.

Look. I have an idea to help you make the decision.

If it's not any trouble.

When is beauty ever trouble?

Always, Hennessey said.

Then you have not known the right beauty. Come.

Hennessey followed the merchant across the hall into a narrow corridor, a wooden bridge fenced with latticework so that anyone standing there could see the large entryway of the first floor. The merchant paused, pointing to the latticework.

For the carpenter's wives, he said. So the women could see but not be seen.

He continued across the bridge, bent over, ducking through the low corridor into a small whitewashed den.

This was his harem room, he said, stepping down into a floor covered with rugs. Hennessey had to stay crouched to avoid hitting his head on the ceiling beams, and was relieved to slide down the walls and rest against the handwoven bolsters and cushions. The plaster walls cooled his back.

The merchant pushed against one of the walls and it slowly opened, revealing a long storage room at the back of the house where hundreds of balls of colored wool had spilled from burlap sacks and covered the floor. There were more rugs here than in the other rooms, stacked floor to ceiling, each more vibrant and intriguing than the next.

They're getting to you, the merchant said, I can tell.

He removed a photo of Ataturk from the wall and opened the copper safe behind it. He rooted through a row of rugs, then pulled out one tied with a red ribbon.

This should help you decide, he said. It's my prize. I usually sell them. Even the ones I believe I'll never part with at first. But this one I'm keeping.

He unrolled the rug for Hennessey. It had a light blue prayer niche set into a tree of life motif. The primary symbol in the field resembled two diamonds, one very small set on top of a larger diamond, split by a vertical strip in red. Three circles were woven at each point in the bottom half of the larger diamond, giving the figure an almost human appearance.

What kind is it?

A prayer rug. From the mountains near here.

The Taurus?

Yes. It's not the most beautiful rug I've ever seen, but it's the feeling I get from it. There's a certain . . . *titremek*. A vibration.

Hennessey leaned forward and traced the figure on the rug with his finger. He took out a small notebook from his shirt pocket and drew the figure with the stub of a pencil.

The symbol. It's ancient.

Of course. The symbols are passed from one generation to the next. They've been around for thousands of years.

The rug is old?

No. An infant, really. Only fifteen. I bought it in 'thirty-eight. A young girl made it. She was only eight.

A child?

Hennessey stared at the rug, his eyes wide, incredulous.

Now you know why she's my prize. The knots are perfect. The workmanship is that of a genius. I have seen millions of rugs in my life, but I have never seen such perfection as this. Such passion.

Did you know her?

The merchant crouched on the floor and began to roll the rug, but Hennessey stopped him, holding his hand out to touch it. The wool felt like cashmere, shone like silk in the light. He pressed against the knots, reluctant to let go, but the merchant continued to roll the rug and tie the ribbon around it. His movements were abrupt, suddenly hurried since the question had been asked.

May I be rude?

You're American.

I'm asking permission this time.

Hennessey expected a grin from the merchant. The man had a sense of humor. He had already seen it. But something had suddenly changed. He seemed edgy, even irritated.

How much did you pay for it?

I paid what it was worth, he snapped. This business is not rational. Art never is.

They sat at a secluded restaurant overlooking the yacht harbor and ate grilled trout from the mountains. Local women, hired to make bread, rolled dough by an outdoor oven. The smell of garlic and yeast in the air. Mangy cats roamed beneath the tables, their ribs rubbing along Hennessey's and the merchant's legs. The sun had dropped behind the old clock tower and couples strolled along the pier, embraces reflecting in the seawater. It was hot and sticky, mosquitoes buzzing in the silence between them. The merchant had not spoken since he closed the safe and locked his shop for the night. Hennessey had helped him fold the kilims and roll the rugs. The merchant was grateful, but Hennessey wondered what had changed in the man. He seemed agitated.

Hennessey found it odd they had not yet introduced themselves. He did not know the merchant's name, nor had the merchant cared to ask him his, and he found it even stranger that he seemed to know the merchant better than he did other people he had met along his travels. There was an anonymity about the Turks he admired. A humbling presence he respected, and so he shared the meal and the view as if they were old friends who no longer felt self-conscious in their silences.

A young waiter delivered bowls of cold cucumbers and yogurt speckled with dill and minced garlic. Hennessey smelled it from the tray, his mouth watering through every course right down to the squares of baklava oozing honey and crushed pistachios. It was the first time the merchant had spoken.

Everybody makes this mistake.

What?

They think this is Greek.

It is, isn't it?, said Hennessey, licking the honey from his fingers.

No. We made the first baklava.

It's Turkish?

From Gaziantep. Near the Syrian border.

He pointed east, along the coastline, festooned with cypress and pines.

The stone for the ovens comes from a local mine there. A kind of lava stone that retains the heat. You've probably had the cheap baklava. The tourist kind. But the real thing is divine. A true miracle.

Like a rug, he said, and winked.

Exactly.

The merchant popped the last bite of pastry into his mouth. You know, I have not forgotten your question.

Hennessey swallowed his last bite and pushed his plate away. He was full and flicked his head upward, a gesture to say no, when the waiter approached with a plate of ekmek, a spongy cake dripping with syrup.

What question? About the weaver?

The merchant nodded.

May we have the check please?

The waiter laid a tin plate on the table. Hennessey reached for his wallet, but the merchant snatched the check from him.

You're my guest. When I come to America, you buy me a cheeseburger.

Hennessey laughed, but the merchant remained quiet, his mind pressed by something Hennessey knew not. He could not figure the man out, the graven tone.

You probably wonder why I have not answered you.

You think I'm a fool.

A fool? Why?

For not being able to choose a rug.

Ah. That. I think you're a fool for thinking you could choose one so quickly, like a tie. Or a shoe. It takes days. Weeks sometimes.

I don't have the time. The rug's not for me anyway. It's for friends.

Why don't you have time?

I have to work. I leave Antalya tomorrow.

Americans, he said, and raised his eyebrow. You must make the time if you want to find the right rug. You have to keep visiting them. Eventually, they will speak to you.

I'll leave my tape recorder.

You're a funny man.

Just impatient, he said, taking out a pack of Camels.

The merchant offered his lighter, and Hennessey leaned into it, offering a cigarette in return. The merchant took it between his lips but did not light it.

You want answers.

Yes. That's my job, said Hennessey, and exhaled. He was growing tired, and the merchant seemed far from telling him anything more about the rug.

I've been thinking about *how* to answer you. It's not easy. It's taken me the whole meal to know.

About the girl?

Yes. I'll tell you. But it's a secret.

Then don't bother.

Why not?

Christ! It won't be a secret anymore.

The merchant leaned back into the chair, the rattan bending and squeaking from his weight.

Secrets scare you.

Hennessey blew a small smoke ring, and it drifted slowly toward the merchant, as if it were meant to be an offering. He laughed quietly.

Not really. I've known a lot of secrets in my life.

Yes, but how many have you kept?

Hennessey said nothing, staring down the side-stream smoke.

Why are you telling me?

I trust you.

You don't even know my name.

It doesn't matter. You know something that I don't. You're the only person who can teach *me* about the rug.

The merchant pushed back his chair and stood, pointing to the beach. Follow me, he said.

Hennessey and the merchant disappeared from the city and walked along the beach with their shoes off, the pebbles rough under their feet. Hennessey rolled up his sleeves, let his skin breathe the salty air. They passed an abandoned fishing boat that had broken loose and floated on the water like a dead bird.

Every dealer knows her?

From Antalya to Istanbul. Trabzon to Izmir. Every one has known *of* her. Pickers too.

Pickers?

They search everywhere for rugs. Most steal them. The mosques always get hit first. If you ever see a good rug in a mosque, you must wonder how it survived. I have never seen a good rug in a mosque. They're mostly factory rugs. The wool jumps out when you scratch it. Like a dog shedding. Those rugs won't last a year. The colors fade.

Then how did you get it? Hennessey asked, searching the merchant's eyes. You stole it?

The merchant shook his head slowly, remembering.

I bid at an auction. There was a woman there, Emine. She practically gave it away.

He walked ahead of Hennessey, leading him farther down the beach with his words.

Emine was so dirty, I'll never forget. Her hair was a mess, all knotted, clumped like a nest left out in the rain. Her clothes were torn. She had two children hanging off her arms. Like little monkeys. There was a baby girl strapped to her back. *Allah. Allah.* The wailing. It hurt to listen. The child was so loud, coughing too. I thought she would erupt like, what you say? Poof?

He spread his hands apart, lifting them in the air.

A volcano?

Yes.

His eyes drifted over the water and he hurled a pebble into it, waiting for a tide to roll before he spoke again.

She was alone with the children.

Where was her husband?

Dead. That's why Emine was there. She needed money so she had to sell her dowry. Under Islam, women inherit nothing from their husbands. Some get gold bracelets, if they're fortunate. But Emine's dowry was different. She was a peasant, you know. The rug was her only possession.

Women don't get much, do they?

What is much when they have no rights?

There was anger in his voice and Hennessey turned to him, watching his arms cross his chest.

I wished she would have had bracelets. Gold. Silver, even. Something else to sell. But Emine told me the rug was more precious than gold anyway. She was surprised I didn't know that.

The merchant laughed softly and took out his own cigarettes this time, offering one to Hennessey.

She told me to take extra care of the rug. It was from her village, where the young girl lived. She said the girl had woven prayers into the rug for her. Prayers she believed had given her two sons. Kept her alive through their births.

He chuckled from the next thought, his voice dropping to a whisper even though they were alone on the beach.

Emine said her cow had contracted a lung disease. I don't know what you call it.

TB? Tuberculosis.

I don't know, maybe. She said she took the cow into her house and laid it on the rug in its dying hour and sat praying with it, one hand on the rug, the other on the sick cow's chest, right over its heart. She said the cow was alive and healthy the next morning. Lived a full life.

Hennessey dug his toes into the sand and took the cigarette out of his mouth.

You're a superstitious people.

We trust chance.

Some would call that ignorance.

The merchant tossed his head back, smiling, his eyes aglint in the moonlight bouncing off the water. Hennessey puffed on the cigarette and nodded. From a distance the two men stood as silhouettes against each other, the cherry embers flickering back and forth, communicating the things left unspoken.

Irrationality is not ignorance, the merchant continued. This woman spoke the truth. You could feel it. The look in her eyes when I finally took the rug. She was trying so hard not to cry. I don't think she wanted her children to see. But the baby knew. It kept reaching around and pawing her wet cheeks. She stopped sobbing and got real quiet, but the tears ran and ran. It was horrible. I felt so guilty.

Why?

A woman should never have to cry like that.

You didn't hurt her.

I took her rug.

But she needed money. She came to the auction.

I don't think you understand. When I took the rug . . . it was as if I had taken a life from her. I was tempted to give Emine the money and let her keep the rug.

Why didn't you?

The merchant lowered his head, threw his gaze into the water.

I couldn't. The moment I felt it, I . . . I knew I could never let it go, he said, looking up. And I never will. I knew then I would never see another rug like it.

The merchant walked into the water now, the phosphorescence glittering around his ankles.

You must have looked.

No.

You weren't curious if there were more?

Sure I was. I still am. I wonder about the weaver every day I go to work because nothing compares to her work. Nothing . . . The last thing Emine said to me was *eksik olmayiniz.*

Hennessey nodded.

May you want for nothing, he said.

You know Turkish?

He nodded.

A little. Hikmet is a good teacher.

The merchant smiled.

You like poetry?

I like art.

Then you understand, the merchant said. The woman was right. I had everything I ever needed. My search was over.

It must be hard now to acquire anything else. You've seen perfection.

The merchant sighed and lighted another cigarette.

You know only Allah makes perfect things. Imperfection is human, he said, whispering, which is why I believe the girl is not like us.

The merchant closed the lid over the lighter and they were in darkness again, silhouettes on the beach, silenced by the lapping of the sea and the final call to prayer.

They walked back to Kaleici for a drink at midnight. Most families had returned home, and tourists and men roamed the streets, the cafés full. The grills loaded with lamb kebabs, belching smoke. Talk and raki, flowing freely into the night. A group of old men sat on benches while young boys polished their shoes. Others carried bags of yo-yos and demonstrated under the lamplight with hopes that foreigners would toss them change. Vendors retired their carts of dried fruits, tying them to the horse posts in the streets, and Gypsy girls meandered in and out of restaurants, arms loaded with long-stemmed roses, their dark eyes burdened with desperation.

Hennessey and the merchant watched from the terrace of an outdoor bar overlooking the street. Safiye Ayla played from an old gramophone behind the counter. Her sultry voice spilled into the hot air while the two men drank raki from highball glasses filled with ice, their tongues numbed by the anise, craving honeydew melon and goat cheese, *kavun, beyaz peynir,* the staple meze.

You believe me?

Hennessey reached for a slice of melon.

I told you. Skepticism is a virtue, he said, sliding the fruit into his mouth. He barely chewed, then swallowed, raising his glass into the air. The merchant slid his glass over the bar top but did not meet Hennessey's toast.

You think I'm lying?

No.

Hennessey set his empty glass back down on the counter and signaled to the bartender for more.

You like it.

I think there's more to it.

Tiger's milk, the merchant said, pointing to the glass. He watched Hennessey with a wary eye, unsure if he was already drunk.

Yes. It helps. Your story does too.

The bartender refilled the highball glass and plunked two ice cubes into it, turning the clear liquid gray and cloudy. He slid the glass to Hennessey and winked at the merchant. Hennessey raised it again into the air.

Let's protest.

To what?

Raise your glass. Come on.

The merchant raised his drink.

Higher, Hennessey begged. So the gods can see us.

The bartender laughed and poured himself a small shot of raki and joined the two patrons. Then Hennessey spoke, his voice louder now.

To the cramping social intellectual orthodoxy of the patriarchal and theocratic past!

Hennessey tossed back the drink and swallowed in one gulp. His eyes grew wide, and there was a madness about him. He was a man desperate to make the world understand him. The merchant and the bartender shook their heads. The bartender winked and tossed back the shot, unable to understand a word Hennessey had uttered. But he liked the spirit of the man and welcomed it at his bar. The merchant cocked his head, his eyes drawn to a squint.

What?

There's more to it, Hennessey whispered, and downed the last of his raki.

You're drunk.

I'm Irish. This is a warm-up.

For what?

Hennessey swiveled in his chair and held his finger in the air.

You told me your secret, he said.

I know. Now I'm waiting for yours.

That's the problem, you see. I don't think you can call it a secret. What I know about that rug, many have known before me.

The merchant pushed his glass away and inched closer to Hennessey.

How? It's impossible.

I'm a trained observer. I see a lot. Not everything makes sense to me. Not everything has meaning.

But the rug did. You saw something. I know you did.

Yes.

He raised the glass to his lips and turned it around and around, thinking, reading the merchant's eyes.

Please. Tell me what you saw.

Hennessey dug into his pocket and pulled out the notebook. He flipped through the pages and laid them open on the bar. The pages were covered with a scrawl hardly recognizable as English. Notes everywhere. In the margins, on the sides. The merchant flicked on his lighter to see Hennessey point to the stack of diamonds.

The head and body of a woman.

A woman? Really? You think so?

I know her.

Who?

Cybelle.

The merchant said nothing, did not take his eyes off the figure and studied it intently as Hennessey spoke.

She's a Goddess.

Like Artemis. Aphrodite?

Yes. Except Cybelle's the Mother Goddess. It could be any one of them, really. It's hard to say.

He traced the figure with his finger and continued.

The figure is perhaps a variant of her giving birth.

Your theory?

Mine and others. Based on old clay figures and scratch drawings I've studied. In any case, she's old. Very old. About six thousand to seven thousand years before Christ.

How would the weaver know? Those girls can't read.

I don't know. Stories probably.

There's more to it, said the merchant.

There's always more, right? Hennessey said, and smiled.

A slight grin crossed the merchant's lips too, and he looked up, raising the flame higher to see Hennessey's face. There was a small scar above his right eyebrow that he hadn't noticed, and in his eyes a powerful conviction that even in his drunken state could be trusted.

You're sure, aren't you?

Yes.

How do you know?

I've spent my life following her. That's why I'm here.

The merchant shook his head slowly and turned off the lighter.

Hennessey closed the notebook and stuffed it back into his shirt pocket as the bartender took their glasses and wiped the counter with a rag.

I follow the rugs. You follow the Goddess.

Hennessey smiled and offered his hand, introducing himself for the first time.

My name's Hennessey. John Hennessey.

Hakan. Hakan Topali.

They shook hands and rose from the bar together.

Eksik olmayiniz.

Hennessey smiled. The merchant was still holding on to him with both hands, reluctant to let go too soon. His eyes locked onto Hennessey's.

I hope you find her.

Hennessey lay on the floor of his pension room and wrote in his notebook. A candle flickered over his page as he recorded the merchant's words. The symbol in the rug haunted him, and he turned to it every few minutes as if it held an answer to the questions he wished he could ask the weaver. Did she even know what the symbol meant? Did she have any idea of the history behind it, or was it another abstract shape she had seen in a headscarf, perhaps in another rug from another woman who had never been told the truth.

In every culture of every age, there have been superstitions, he wrote, most of which are spun from fear of the unknown. Rarely do the tales emerge from what is already known, like the story of Cybelle in the girl's rug. Take Medusa. The woman so vilifying and hideous that anyone who looked at her turned to stone. In truth, she was feared for her leadership, for her insurmountable beauty and governing powers. She was a real woman, assassinated by Perseus, who was sent to take her head. When he did, her hair, according to the myth, turned to snakes. Snakes, hundreds of them. The element of darkness and light. Matter and spirit. The revered icon of Goddess cults, now feared and loathed among men.

The message was clear. No matter how hard they tried to eradicate the Goddess, she would manifest in other ways. St. Sophia. The Virgin Mary. And to some, including Hennessey, Jesus himself. Hennessey had always been fascinated with the hypocrisy of religion, a poor Irish immigrant, son of a Catholic widow. His father, a Jew, had been killed in World War One. Religion had been Hennessey's only source of education, a foundation upon which he based the virtues of skepticism. The very god his mother taught him to pray to denied her the support and community she needed to survive the war. She prostituted herself for a boat ride to America, a country that despite the coppery arms welcoming them to Ellis Island swallowed his mother's pride, denying her employment despite her brilliance. He had watched his mother struggle from one job to the next, drunken, married men chasing her around smoky barrooms. His mother was beautiful. She had always reminded him of Medusa with her dark curly hair and light eyes, cursed for her tragic beauty. She was a pious woman determined to condone the hypocrisy of a church whose priest could never look her in the eye knowing her husband had been a Jew. Hennessey believed that if his mother lived during the Middle Ages, she would have been persecuted as a witch. If she had lived during ancient times, he believed she would have died defending a goddess heritage. In either case, the prejudices against Hennessey's mother provoked him to study the rise and fall of matrilineal cultures, and engender the world's respect for them.

That Hennessey would even consider a course on Jesus as the Goddess did not seem heretical. It occurred to him as an obligation to broaden young minds. He had proposed a course on this in the strictest confidentiality to the department head at Penn. He was frowned upon immediately and reminded of his position. He was a professor of anthropology, not religion. Hennessey argued the two were inseparable. Human nature. The nature of spirit. Hennessey argued that the only way to getting at the truth of our spiritual existence was to study our Goddess past, a past that respected and celebrated women. The department head disagreed. It was 1950. Hennessey was only thirty. He had his career ahead of him. He shouldn't risk the reputation he worked so hard to earn.

What reputation?

The one your affiliation with this university is giving you.

End of conversation. Hennessey vowed to find a way to bridge the two despite risking his integrity. He would do it without Penn's help. He would find private donors who would help him attempt what the university deemed impossible, much less futile. Hennessey wanted to reinterpret history. Take the spin out, remove the filters that even he had been guilty of in the past. The historical interpretation of the Hopi, his summers spent on the reservations getting to know the chiefs when the true power of the tribe lay with the women. He had learned it too late, long after his thesis had been written and published in parts in textbooks. He had overlooked the foundation of an entire culture. People believed him, studied his findings, took them as truth. He vowed he would never make the same mistake again.

Despite the skepticism he raised from his colleagues, he knew there were others who believed in him. His circle of artist friends. The painters. The poets. The saxophone player who restored old furniture so he could play in a band at night. He surrounded himself with the believers, with those who made searching for the truth the focus of their lives. They were the ones who accepted him when his colleagues did not.

Hennessey was skeptical of intellectuals, but, ironically, couldn't have been more of an intellectual himself, the best-looking man on campus, who was more interested in the book in his face than the flock of women at his feet. His colleagues were intrigued by him, by his charm, his ease in social situations, but his alternative views challenged them most.

Hennessey thrived on anything and everyone who opposed mainstream reality. He hated that word. Reality. An acidic sound on his tongue. A laziness about it, the rolling "l" as if the letters forced themselves together to form the word. He eschewed his Catholic upbringing for more Eastern philosophies. He liked the possibility of multiple truths. The philosophy suited his lifestyle as an anthropologist, the trained observer in a world he believed had gone blind.

He wanted to share his vision but did not broadcast his views. They slipped through conversations. Asides, really. The comments between coffee breaks, strictly entertainment. *What's John Hennessey brewing these days?* It's not that they didn't appreciate him, they didn't take him seriously. His views posed no threat to them, only, perhaps, to his colleague Rodney Young.

When word leaked of Hennessey's proposed Goddess course, Young immediately eliminated him from the list of candidates to accompany his dig at Gordion, the legendary Phrygian capital where King Midas ruled and was buried. Young wanted only those who demonstrated sound judgment. There would be interviews. Radio. Film. Print. *Time. Life. National Geographic.*

Hennessey wanted to go. He had planned on it, dreamed about it as a student, the camel caravans, the desert, entire civilizations buried beneath the silt of ancient rivers. The thought was a pleasant one, gave him hope that his skills as a physical anthropologist would be used for something more than the identification of the war dead in Europe.

The expedition at Gordion would go on without him. History would be recorded without John Hennessey's observations. Young made sure of that. He had ranked Hennessey as the top candidate but was too afraid of risking his funding to subscribe to the maverick's point of view. Young's affiliation with Hennessey would not only jeopardize his expedition and career, but also the history of the world as it had been interpreted until then. He left Hennessey in Philadelphia, boarding a plane for Turkey, unaware that Hennessey would be there before he arrived, sleeping on a thin mattress stuffed with wool in a corner of Asia Minor that smelled of lemon and wild rose. Prophecy and fate. His duffel bag stuffed, notebooks spilling out of the top with the hope they'd be filled with evidence, not of King Midas but of the Goddess.

Hennessey reviewed the maps again, copies he had made of the initial ground surveys taken in the late nineteenth century. They were nothing more than swirls of ink on the page. Hardly a topographical guide, more like a giant thumbprint. Nobody had excavated Mavisu. Attempts had been made. None succeeded. Hennessey would be the first. He closed the book and lay on his back, staring at the wall.

He was anxious, restless. His stomach ached and his forehead was beaded with sweat. He had suffered cramps since he had returned from dinner. He figured it was jet lag. His window was open for the heat, the door propped with a rubber shoe to generate a cross-breeze. But the air was still and hot, moving nothing but the sound of horses clopping through the cobblestone streets. Then he heard it, the faint titter of a flute. The music grew louder and drums began to beat.

He crossed to the floor in his bare feet and looked out the window, trying to see beyond the lemon trees. The music drifted toward him through the alley, growing louder, the rhythm faster. The stutter of a flutist lured him outside. He put on his shoes and walked into the street, feeling the music in his chest, pulsating, making his breaths slow and deep in the warm night air.

It was three in the morning. Hours it seemed since the last call to prayer, yet Hennessey was wide awake, restless. He had not adjusted to the time change. It was only eight in the evening in Philadelphia, and he was grateful for the diversion. He turned down a side street, climbed up a flight of stone stairs, and stopped. He felt a sharp pain across his abdomen and stood doubled over, trying to catch his breath. He felt nauseated and for a moment couldn't see. He got down on his knees, crawled to the closest tree trunk, then sat with his back against it, trying to focus. Out of the corner of his eye, crossing the park, was a wedding procession. He could make out a white horse and a woman covered with a red veil. It was the last thing he remembered before he collapsed.

He dreamed of the site. The bones he'd find. The radiating pattern of boar jawbones laid around the skull. The chambers full of earthenware vessels and bull horns. The grain bins, the relief figures on the walls. Splashes of ochre and real blood. Leopards ran around him in circles, chanting names. *Inanna, Artemis, Athena, Demeter, Rhiannan, White Buffalo, Pele, Ixchel, Cybelle.*

As far as Hennessey could see in the dream, he was hovering over an open grave, where the skeleton of a neonate lay inside a coiled basket. Strings of beads covered the figure. Beside it, the skeleton of an adult man lying on his back with flexed legs. He had been decapitated, and there were slash marks across the vertebrae. A plank and pellets had been placed over him, ochre stains on his wrist bones where owls emerged and flew up around him, wings flapping dust. He could see nothing through the circle of leopards moving closer, backing him into the edge of the grave until he fell into the dark pit, crushing the skeletons to powder.

He woke instantly and tossed in his bed, the sheets damp and twisted around his hips. The window was open for the heat, but he was shivering. He did not remember the window, and when he opened his eyes, there was nothing familiar about the room.

This was not his pension in Old Town. Several beds were lined up against the wall, military style, tidy and empty. Mint-green tiles covered the walls, and he could smell the bleach in the basin beside him. A large blue glass evil eye the size of a dinner plate hung

from the door, and he wondered what he had done to need such
protection. He had seen the Turkish tokens of good luck everywhere, hanging from the rearview mirrors of taxis and buses, dangling over butcher blocks in shops and kitchens.

A gardener stood outside the window trimming grass with a
push mower, humming prayers above the shuffle of patients in the
courtyard. A ball bounced on a distant sidewalk, and children
laughed. Mosquitoes buzzed around his head.

His arm was sore, and when he pushed himself off the mattress
to sit up, he felt the IV tugging. He was connected to a bag of glyc-
erin, dripping slowly from its perch above the bed. The floor was
white where the drops had splattered and dried.

He felt weak and groggy. His stomach was sore where the intestines had cramped, were cramping still. He rubbed his hands
over his lower abdomen, his thighs, and then it dawned on him.
His pants were missing. His passport gone.

Shit.

It had happened to him before. He had lost his passport twice.
The first time in France during the war. He lived at the American
embassy for a week before they could issue another one. Nobody
would come near him because he smelled so bad, reeking of death.
But they were kind to him and gave him food and shelter because
he was identifying their sons and husbands and brothers who had
been killed in battle. Their forensic hero. He was not so lucky on
a dig in Greece, where the passport was stolen and he was no hero.

*There are regions in the world where conflict is endemic no
matter how good your intentions,* he remembered telling his students. Thirty-eight degrees latitude. Thirty degrees longitude. *Tem-
per your searches with patience there. Step lightly. Gather your
data and leave no traces. Be a ghost to the culture. Remain objec-
tive but trust your instincts and follow them wherever they may
lead.*

Now, lying there on the sagging mattress, he wondered how he
could trust so easily, even the merchant. He had no idea how much
an American passport would sell for in Turkey. A lot. That's all he

knew. He was too weak to care, his stomach was empty, his body heavy, feverish. Scenes from John Ford's wagon master flickered in his head. *Chuckawalla Swing. Chuckawalla.* He wondered what time it was. What day.

You look nothing like your photo.

Hennessey turned his head to see a relatively tall man, a few years older than himself, maybe forty, standing in the doorway with a clipboard. He wore a white medical coat, and his dark hair was stiff, parted to the side, and combed with oil. His posture was stiff too, as if he had not yet accepted the formality of his uniform. He stood in the doorway for some time, conflicted, eyeing the patient before him with uncertainty. He appeared blurry to Hennessey, an apparition, it seemed, the shiny floor tiles reflecting light through the tails of his lab coat. He locked eyes onto Hennessey's face with a look of resigned recognition, as if by crossing the threshold into that room his role would take on more than the dictates of his profession. He shifted his weight and leaned against the door frame, carefully considering his first words.

You look much better in person, even if you're sick.

The doctor was a Turk but spoke with a slightly British accent. He waved the passport in the air, then stuck it in his breast pocket and washed his hands in another basin of bleach outside the door. Then he entered the room, walking extremely erect, and crossed to the bed. He laid the passport and a *Time* magazine beside Hennessey's fingers.

Thank God, he groaned.

The nurses are wondering about you.

Already?

The doctor grinned.

You kept touching yourself. Checking your pants.

I do that.

You intrigued them.

Circumcised men don't touch themselves?

It's not our habit.

Never?

Not in public.

The doctor stood with his hands crossed over his pelvis, heels together, military style, with an almost majestic air. He pursed his lips until he could no longer contain the laughter. Then he howled.

I told them you were American.

And single. Did you tell them that?

Don't break any hearts in my country, please. I have enough patients already.

The doctor laughed again as Hennessey rubbed his fingers over his temples.

Tiger's milk got me?

The doctor shook his head.

Raki had nothing to do with it.

Why do I feel like hell?

Dysentery.

Shit.

This is true. We gave you a shot to stop that. The IV will rehydrate you. You can imagine, you lost a lot of fluids.

Hennessey tossed his head back into the pillow, jostling the warped steel frame of the bed. He stared at the ceiling. The brown paint had peeled like chocolate in the heat, and the loose chips drifted slowly over his head.

How long have I been here?

Since early this morning. You were found passed out in the park. Do you remember a bride?

Hennessey rubbed his forehead, thinking.

Not really. I saw a horse. That's all I remember.

She saw you against the palm tree and took it upon herself and her husband to bring you here. She sacrificed her wedding night to help you. Said it was an omen. A chance to do good, to make Allah happy.

Come on, Hennessey said. He did not believe the story.

It's true. She wants to visit you tomorrow.

Hennessey glanced up at the wall clock. The second hand was not moving.

What time is it?

Lunch is coming. You need to eat.

Hennessey threw back the sheets.

I'm supposed to leave Antalya at four.

The doctor chuckled, shook his head.

You can't.

I have to work.

So do I. You're contagious. And as long as you're under my care, you're not going anywhere.

But I hired a driver. Everything's been arranged.

The doctor smiled, glanced down at the clipboard.

Mr. . . . . Hennessey. I'd lose my job if I let you go out and infect others. Especially during tourist season. My hospital is already understaffed.

Hennessey took a deep breath.

Can I send a telegram?

Yes. Of course. Anything to help you.

Today. I have to send it today.

We have phones here.

Not in Mavisu. It's a small village in the mountains.

The doctor dropped the clipboard to his side and studied his patient intently.

Mavisu? By the river Nurdane?

You've been there?

The doctor paused.

Many times. I do rounds.

He spoke emphatically now, a little tighter-lipped than Hennessey expected. The doctor took off his glasses, trilling them between his fingers, inquiring.

What takes you there?

The Ministry of Culture. For an excavation.

You're an archaeologist?

Anthropologist.

The doctor nodded slowly, arched an eyebrow, skeptical. Most Turks who learned of Hennessey's profession gave him the same look. Hennessey was used to it. It was his challenge to make them trust him because his search was different. The Turks were leery of diggers since the British had begun to haul off pieces of the past, ancient statues, columns and tombs of the great civilizations that flourished here. All for the price of admission to their royal museums. Hennessey clarified his role.

I'm a physical anthropologist. I study bones.

That makes both of us.

The doctor smiled, running his finger along the pen tucked behind his ear.

Who funded the excavation? It is an excavation.

A surface scraping first. A preliminary dig. Most of the money came from my country. Mostly private donors.

What about the villagers? They know you're coming?

They've arranged to pick me up.

The doctor cocked his head, surprised.

The postman. He comes to Antalya once a month. For mail, I assume.

I'm surprised he offered to drive you.

You know him?

The doctor shifted on his heels. He had about him an odd tick that preceded any comment more important than simple banter. He rolled his shoulders back and spoke.

I know everybody in the village. They're mountain people. They don't trust strangers.

I don't expect them to. But they have nothing to worry about.

The doctor and Hennessey held each other's gaze. The doctor turned, stepping aside for a nurse and her tray full of glass tubes. He pulled the sheet over Hennessey, who had turned his head toward the window and held out his arm for the nurse to draw blood. A group of schoolgirls in blue uniforms were skipping down the sidewalk, plucking mulberries from the trees. He was thankful for the distraction. His arms were sore from the needles, and the blood loss made him dizzy.

Suddenly, he found the doctor, not the nurse, prying open his fist. The two of them alone.

It's over. You can relax.

He uncurled his fingers and shook them over the edge of the bed. He turned to the doctor, his mind spilling.

Did you find a notebook last night?

Only the passport.

I had a notebook. A small one.

The doctor shook his head.

I'm sorry. That's all we found, he said, unscrewing a bottle of Coke, setting it on the bed stand.

I'll let the postman know you won't be coming with him. I'll make other plans for you.

The doctor turned and walked toward the door.

Doctor?

He pivoted on his heel, turning. His light brown eyes, wide and healing, almost russet in the light.

Thanks for helping me.

When I help you, I help myself, he said, then left.

Hennessey slept and woke, tossing restlessly during the muezzin's prayer calls that broadcast from the bullhorn five times a day outside his window. The nurses took him off the IV by the next morning and brought him a plate of hard-boiled eggs and cheese, chunks of thick white bread, and light tea so his stomach would not be upset.

He picked through the pages of *Time* left by the doctor, an issue from May 25, 1953, the full-page color advertisements making the hospital seem like a prison. Pictures of men seated around a palm-studded swimming pool, drinking tumblers filled with gin and quinine water. It looked good to him. Joan Crawford's legs, too, in their fishnets and strappy black heels propped on a barstool, promoting *Torch Song*. He didn't want to hear more devastating news about the war in Korea and instead read about heroes, mountain climbers who scaled Mount Everest as a special coronation present for the twenty-seven-year-old Queen Elizabeth II. More ads for toasters, tires, cameras, and cars. He was tired of reading and pushed back the sheets, then stepped down to the floor.

He could see his face in the cracked mirror hanging from the wall across the room. He walked slowly toward it, feeling the blood drain from his head, then stood in front of the broken glass to study his face. His beard had grown thick, his face thinner. For a moment, he did not know where he was, where he had been. A bride. He remembered a bride. Nurses. He looked down at his arm, bruised where they had poked him with needles. It was not enough for him to move. He was happy to see the fresh blood on his skin, relieved to know he was alive.

His stomach growled. He grabbed his robe and walked into the hall, where a string of evil eyes hung from the walls. There were no doors on the rooms, and he could see the other patients in their beds, five of them stuffed into each room. They each stared at the ceiling, women separated from the men, feeding prayer beads through their fingers to pass the time. He was lucky to be contagious, he thought, to have a room of his own.

He passed a small cat licking its paws on the cool tiles, cleaner than the streets from where it had strayed. He turned left at the end of the hall and found the doctor in his office.

A small boy sat on a chair with his hands beneath his legs. His lips were swollen and a rash had spread over his neck. The doctor was giving him a shot, then turned to Hennessey.

Too many seeds, he explained.

What?

The doctor spoke in Turkish.

He ate too many sunflower seeds. Salted.

The boy looked up at Hennessey, guilt-ridden.

But the movie was good, he said impetuously.

Movie?

He came from the drive-in, the doctor explained. He should have been in school.

The drive-in?

Over by the old temple.

Gilda, the boy said, flashing a toothless grin. Do you like Rita Hayworth?

Hennessey winced.

They use ancient ruins for a movie theater?

The doctor nodded as if this were nothing new, then looked back at the boy.

No tomatoes or citrus. Promise?

The boy nodded slowly, pursed his lips.

Take these after your dinner.

The doctor pressed two white tablets into the boy's hands.

You're not going to tell my mother, are you?

Only if I see you here again. Go easy on the seeds.

The boy nodded once, smiled, then left.

Hennessey eyed the office. Black-and-white photos of villagers, mostly children, hung from the walls. A group of young girls washing clothes by a well. Boys hanging upside down from the limb of a tree. Babies clutching onto their mothers' backs, eyeing the cameraman with amused suspicion. A drummer. A tea bearer. An adolescent with webbed hands and a permanent wink on his face, arms extended, offering a bag of lemons. Hennessey stopped at one particular photo, a small girl with huge light eyes, almost silver. The girl was sitting at a loom, her back toward the photographer, her head turned slightly over her left shoulder so that her eyes caught the light. She wore an expression of fear and slight disgust, regret, it seemed, as if she were defending herself against whatever existed beyond the frame of the photograph. She was the only person not smiling.

A warm breeze came through the window and the photos flapped against the wall. The photo with the girl had been there for

some time, edges frayed and yellowing, positioned in the center of
the others. Hennessey leaned toward it to get a better look.

Your patients? he asked.

Yes.

She's young, he said, focusing again on the girl. And beautiful.
Look at her eyes.

The doctor nodded.

Yes. They're unique.

She looks Balkan. A bit Laz too.

The doctor cleared his throat.

Very good. She comes from nomads. You a detective?

Trained observer.

Hennessey leaned closer to the photo.

She's a weaver.

Yes.

You treat her?

She can't walk.

Hennessey turned back to the doctor, looking for an explanation. The doctor opened a file folder and stuffed papers into it,
avoiding eye contact with Hennessey.

She had polio. She walks with braces now.

You saved her life.

The doctor said nothing, standing from his desk when an older,
rotund woman squeezed her way through the doorway. Her face
was wrapped in multiple headscarves, each more colorful than the
next. The doctor greeted her by kissing her hand, then touching it
to his forehead as was the custom. The woman smiled, her mouth
full of gold. She handed him a box.

She'll look beautiful.

Thank you, the doctor said, taking the box rather quickly, then
dropping it on his desk.

Don't you want to see what it looks like, Adam?

I like surprises, Mother.

He spoke forcefully and the woman scowled, her eyes sunken,
her face beaten by the eastern sun, shriveled and ashen, elephantlike.

Fine, have it your way.

She nodded, then stormed out of the door, mumbling a prayer of salvation for her son. The doctor turned to Hennessey and shrugged. He suddenly looked like a teenager, so vulnerable and embarrassed. His face was flushed and he wiped his forehead with the back of his sleeve. He paced the room, staring at the box.

Would you like me to leave?

The doctor paused and turned to Hennessey.

No. I want you to get dressed.

Hennessey cocked his head.

Now?

As soon as you can.

I'd like to eat first.

You will. On the road.

The road?

I thought I could take you to Mavisu with me . . . since you lost your ride.

The doctor cleared his throat before Hennessey could respond, then removed the stethoscope from his neck and set it on the desk.

They drove east along the lush Mediterranean littoral into cotton fields where nomads lived in tents by the road and worked the land. The mountains loomed large to the north and west and castles dotted the foothills, completing the fairy tale of ancient Pamphilia. They passed banana plantations and grape farms, groves of olives and figs. Irrigation ditches criss-crossed the fields, and everywhere greenhouses breathed steam into the air. The road rolled flat before them into the openness, already green with summer. The air was heavy and warm, sweetened with tomato.

Hennessey pressed his head against the window of the truck, wondering how many had come and gone through this great thoroughfare, either taking Alexander's route to Syria or Bahce's to Mesopotamia. The land was part of a great chain of mountains that once girded the ancient world and dropped one by one to the sea. The route was treacherous. Hennessey knew if he found what he wanted, he would be more fortunate than other men who had come before him. The risks had not bothered him until then, but as they got closer to the village, he could feel his heart beating faster, his palms wet.

Are you always this quiet? the doctor asked.

Hennessey turned to him, watched him drive with his right hand on the wheel, prayer beads in his left, rotating as they always did in the hands of those who worried. But it was Hennessey who could have used the beads.

What is it that they don't trust?

Who?

The villagers in Mavisu.

The doctor chuckled, flashed Hennessey a smile, and slapped his thigh.

They don't trust a lot of things. Politicians. Christians. City folk. Foreigners. Intellectuals.

Great. I've struck out on four of five.

They're mostly suspect of intentions.

They know why I'm coming.

The doctor turned to Hennessey.

What are you looking for?

Bones.

Only bones?

Human bones.

You're digging up graves?

The necropolis there.

The doctor chuckled.

There's a necropolis in every village.

Nobody's located the one in Mavisu.

What makes you think you're going to find it?

Hennessey turned to him.

It's in my gut.

Be careful, the doctor warned. Your gut has made you quite ill.

Why did you let me out?

What?

I thought I was contagious.

You were. Still are. Your enthusiasm for Mavisu is infectious, Adam said, slowing down for a wedding party to pass. He pulled over on the shoulder to watch the nomadic tribe cross the flood plain. A team of horses carried hand-painted wooden chests, bright tapestries, a rifle, and a mirror that caught the late-day sun. The bride sat on the lead horse, accompanied on either side by two men on foot. From the distance they appeared to be twins. A father and his brother perhaps. They wore caps on their heads, one black, one white, as if the bride sat between them to settle an age-old dispute.

Gold bracelets covered the bride's arms, and on her hands were white chiffon gloves, her white dress billowing about her like giant wings. A red scarf covered her face, and the men led her slowly across the road. She looked back over her shoulder every now and then and waved to the weary children, her cousins perhaps, who lay behind her collapsed over the backs of donkeys.

The doctor watched the bride until she was a silhouette in the orange light of the plain. He knew she would be losing her family. Her home. A small price to pay for becoming a woman, the arrangements of tradition.

I wonder if she loves him.

Hennessey turned to him, confused.

Thought that wasn't an issue here.

For Islam, no. There is only love for Allah. In Turkey, it's different. There is love for a woman. There is love for a man. And that is love for Allah.

The doctor ran his hands along the steering wheel, his two

index fingers splitting at the top, each tracing the rims as if he were drawing a heart. Then he shifted gears and gunned the truck down the road until nothing but a veil of dust separated him from the bride.

They climbed the foothills by nightfall and stopped by the lip of the canyon to fix the front headlight. A large stone lay wedged between the shattered glass of the bulb. The doctor kicked the bumper.

The other one still works, Hennessey said.

It's not enough light for us to continue. The road only gets worse.

Hennessey shined a flashlight up the road, where toads hopped across in packs, splashing through the puddles made muddy by melting snow. The air was cooler up here, and Hennessey shined the flashlight through the trees to see where they would camp. Nothing flat. Only scrub and stones and pieces of sarcophagi scattered along the slopes.

The doctor looked around, cocked his head, cupped his ear. A tambourine jingled in the distance.

There's a tavern around here. About two kilometers. I know the owner. We can stay the night.

Hennessey looked back up the road, but the doctor shook his head.

Don't even think about it.

How much farther to Mavisu?

Far enough. Trust me.

I can hold the flashlight, he offered.

Forget it. I'm not taking any chances. If you want to walk, I'll pick you up on the way.

Hennessey thought about it for a moment.

Where's your sense of adventure, doctor?

This way, he said, and waved his hand through the air, pointing in the direction of the music.

Trust me.

I'm beginning to trust you less each time you tell me to trust you, Hennessey said.

Really. You'll like it. There's always a dancer here.

A belly dancer? Hennessey asked, his teeth aglint in the moonlight.

No. A dervish. We're going to spin until we lose our minds.

They climbed down an old goat path and entered the mudbrick building through the back door, a smoky haze their guide to the teahouse.

They sat at a table whose top had been carved into a backgammon board. Boar's bone inlay. Miniature dice. Hennessey took the seat facing the window. He could see a group of women sitting on cushions in a small house across the road, the flicker of a candle illuminating their faces, long and rueful in the dying light. Even then, in the privacy of their own homes and the company of their own sex, they did not take the headscarves off. Hennessey wondered if the Prophet had ever allowed his wives to do so in his presence. It was hot even in the mountains, and he felt sorry for them.

He looked around the teahouse, at the men sitting on the floor, their hands dirty, fingers gnarled and wrapped around cigarette stubs that had long since been smoked. They spoke with their hands, waving the extinguished ends around as if by doing so they would give them life once more. Tobacco was cheap but hard to come by in these remote areas, so Hennessey got up and offered them his pack of Camels. They stared at him with wide eyes, incredulous. He spoke Turkish.

Share one with your wives.

They laughed.

I mean it. Take one for yourselves and take the rest to the women in the house over there.

They don't smoke.

Have they ever tried?

The men shook their heads. They were confused by the strange man before them. His sandy hair. Eyes the color of cut granite. They wondered if he was German.

If you want the cigarettes, go.

He pointed to the window.

Now, he said, his voice forceful. He was twice the size of them, at least. They stood quickly, then dashed out the door. Hennessey smiled when he heard the women howling from the house. He returned to his table to find Adam with two teacups and a bowl of sugar.

You can't play games with them.

Why not?

They'll kill you.

But their wives will be happy.

The doctor raised an eyebrow and offered a tea glass. Hennessey took it, each man holding the other's gaze until they finished the last drop of tea, setting the cups down together on the table. By then the men had returned to the teahouse and lifted Hennessey in his chair and carried him to the center of the room. They cleared the tables and chairs around him and for a minute he thought they would shoot him right there for breaking Islamic law.

Instead, they began to play a tambourine and drums. A flutist sat with his legs dangling over the tea counter, playing a sultry, hypnotic tune. A fat man began to dance, dervish style, hands waving over his head. Gold bracelets jiggled on his wrists as he spun in circles around the room until the song ended. He was bent over his knees, heaving for breath. The extra flesh of his chin seemed to pull his whole face forward. He coughed, choking on the smoky air.

Not a man in the teahouse was without a cigarette by then, and if they were, they were rolling more by hand. Hennessey clapped for the fat man, winked at Adam, who was pointing now to a belly dancer who had walked through a beaded curtain from the back room.

Thunderous applause. Hennessey could feel the stomping of the men through the seat of his chair. The belly dancer was approaching him, her dark skin visible through the pink chiffon costume. She eyed Hennessey as the music started, soft drums, the wispy strokes of a tambourine.

The dancer touched her fingers to her lips and eyed every man before her as if to consummate her dance with strangers. The men fell silent, their feet rubbing each other nervously beneath their chairs.

She moved only her arms at first, long and smooth, back and forth like wings over her head. The rhythm grew faster. The shake of the tambourine louder, almost violent now. The music pulsated through her body, and she waved her hands, flexed her wrists, delicate yet strong. The tips of her fingers had been dyed red with henna. The thumb and middle fingers slipped between the elastic holds of tiny brass cymbals. She clapped them together and let the chimes resonate through the smoky air before she clapped them again. Her hips followed the sound, thrusting up and down. Then double time, up, up, down, down until her entire body quivered. She was young, no more than seventeen, and yet she moved like a sultan's courtesan, aware of every curve in her body, every dip and hollow. Powerfully innocent. She rolled her stomach to the beating of the drums. The muscles rippled, breasts to navel.

Hennessey sat watching her, mouth gaping, completely unaware of himself. He was fixated on the girl, smitten not by her dance as much as by the mystery of the woman this girl would become. Would she be like the others in the house next door? Bound and gagged by the veil, body swimming in clothes that hid her graceful figure. Would she dance for others, outside the village, beyond the canyon walls? Would the world share her gift or would the confines of her submission make her forget the movement that made her eyes glow, gave her such joy. She moved closer to him, as if she were dancing for him alone, her movements unrestrained, uncommitted to anybody but her own soul as if she knew he understood her. She whirled around him and he closed his eyes, overwhelmed by the passion in her dance. She touched the nape of his neck with the tip of her finger and he shivered. When he opened his eyes, she was gone, and the teahouse was empty and dark.

H ennessey and the doctor found a lightbulb in the morning and fixed the truck. The air smelled of burning wood. The men from the teahouse met them with loaves of fresh bread to thank them and say good-bye. They were freshly shaven and dressed in clean clothes. They smelled of soap and cologne and they wore funny grins.

A good idea, they said, lining up to shake Hennessey's hand. The men elbowed each other and winked. A lanky fellow with silver sideburns stepped forward and whispered into Hennessey's ear.

It's the best night we've had in a long time, friend.

Hennessey smiled and climbed into the truck, where the doctor sat waiting for him. He opened the window to let the men pass him the bread.

Try massaging their toes next time.

The men straightened, their eyes wide. Hennessey flashed them a smile as the doctor turned on the truck and pulled into the road, the sound of gravel crushing beneath the tires. They drove north along the western bank of the river to Aspendos and its ancient theater that rose unexpectedly from the valley. The parking lot was empty, save a gaunt mule that stood sleeping under a fig tree.

I want to show you something, the doctor said.

They climbed down from the truck and walked toward the

gate. Two young guards stood outside, stiff-chinned and bored in the heat.

We're closed.

The doctor stopped in front of the soldiers, eyeing them. They were of medium height, thick, square builds. Dark eyes. The doctor turned to Hennessey.

They won't let us in.

Hennessey dug into his breast pocket and tossed a pack of Camels to the guards. They said nothing more and unlocked the gates. Hennessey followed the doctor through a dark corridor toward the stage, where a young peasant girl stood singing, her head bound in a white scarf. Knowing perhaps the beauty of her profile against the stone pillars, she turned from the men, out of tradition, and faced the backstage wall, her voice floating up to them as they passed.

Hennessey took a deep breath. The mountains rose around him in every direction, and he could see the lush plain roll out to the sea as if he were looking down on it from the air. Low clouds pulled themselves over the valley and cast shadows on the land.

Hennessey had been to many ancient theaters but nothing as large and well preserved as this. The theater was massive, seating roughly twenty thousand. The semicircular construction consisted of two sections, twenty tiers of seating with ten staircases in the lower half and nineteen tiers with twenty staircases in the upper. Barrel-vaulted colonnades crowned the top, and slender double columns divided the two-story stage. Ionic capitals with their bull-horn scrolls on the first floor, and Corinthian capitals on the second. Medusa's head, now broken, united both the stage walls, effecting blessings and warnings to the audience. Vaulted passages at either end of the stage led to the orchestra, which had once been covered by a wooden roof.

The theater was the most perfect he had ever seen. Its rough-hewn stones, immaculate still, thousands of years since its construction. The stones, white as bone in the light. He walked toward the steps, speechless, overwhelmed by his insignificance against the grandeur. According to the legendary Mopsos, Aspendos was founded by the Greeks in 1000 B.C., enjoying its glory days under the Roman Empire. Here, actors from every age had entertained noble men like Alexander the Great and other statesmen who had come to settle disputes between locals and the citizens of Perge.

There was something sacred about the theater, a place, proud and limited, where men could lay down their weapons to understand and celebrate the human condition. Hennessey wished that somehow he could put to rest the dispute between himself and Rodney Young, share the moment with him, show him the importance of his excavation at Mavisu, why unearthing a Goddess site, the oldest one in Asia Minor, he believed, had more political and historical implications than opening King Midas's tomb. Hennessey had become as respected as he was feared, a loner among his colleagues, an enemy of the Vatican, promulgating the notion that God was a woman. He had battled so much ridicule that most of his recent life had left him numb. The petty trials. The tireless research. The draining hunt for funds. He had placated too many for the merriment of few. Doubt and fear, his beasts, trundled defeat and a despondency he usually experienced, temporarily, after he began a dig, not before he started one. His mission to Turkey was not just to prove himself right, to save face in his department, but to prove the world was wrong. The Goddess was not dead.

Hennessey rubbed his hands along the armrest of a seat carved from local limestone. The ruin was alive. He believed there was life in inorganic material, and he knew that if he listened long enough to rocks and bones, they would always take him to where he needed to be. He had spent many evenings alone in the basement study of his apartment, holding the pieces of human skeletons from ancient times, the buzz of a single lightbulb the only sound before the pieces vibrated, resonating meanings that only he could understand. Listening had become Hennessey's ritual, his way of respecting the sanctity of the sites, and although he had not come to dig beneath the theater, he could feel the presence in the stones surrounding him. He could hear the clapping of millions, too, through the breeze, yelling and cheering as he climbed higher, two steps at a time, stopping to catch his breath at the top. The doctor lagged behind.

Were the men like us . . . who built these things?

No, said Hennessey.

You think they were greater? Smarter?

Hennessey nodded emphatically.

They were women.

The doctor watched Hennessey stare out at the river, framed by a large window cut into the south wall of the theater. The turquoise waters shimmered in the light.

Are they always so blue?

Only this one. It's a very special river. Alexander the Great stopped to drink here in his quest for eternal youth.

Hennessey turned to him, curious. He did not know this story.

A stripling instructed him to arrive on a virgin mare, Adam told him, because it was believed their eyes were made of light.

They stood staring at the river for a while, the waters carving their myth through the distant canyon. The bank was bordered by the bright pink blossoms of oleanders in bloom, like a garland laid down by the gods.

What do they call the river?

Nurdane.

Noordanna?

It's Arabic. *Nur*. Light. *Dane*. Piece. Piece of light.

The doctor closed his eyes, breathing deeply, his chest expanding through the thin white shirt on his back. He took the prayer beads from his pocket and kissed them. Then he opened his eyes and turned to Hennessey.

Will you pray with me?

Depends on what Allah you pray to.

The one that listens.

Hennessey offered a half-smile.

I can do that. What are we praying for?

Nurdane's strength.

Hennessey nodded, waiting for Adam to close his eyes. He closed his too, turning slowly on his heel to face the cerulean water and pray for Nurdane, the prayer that would make things whole again.

They followed the road north along the river, climbing into a forest of stone pines and wind-shorn cypress, the bearded trees like hoary men, bent and bony, whistling in the wind. Beyond the stars, the distant peaks glittered with snow, offering enough light to set up camp.

Adam collected pinecones and roasted the seeds over a small fire Hennessey built near the water. They wrapped themselves in wool blankets and sat facing the east with their shoes off, sharing a can of sardines and feta they bought from a shepherd in the valley. There were no stores now, nothing but the occasional villa and yala that appeared as they gained elevation. Here solitude floated up from the valley, and they were free to let their thoughts roam in the solitary wilds, far from the threatened hurry of the city. They said little as they ate, the silence punctuated only by the random pop of burning wood. The rush of the river carried the voices of men.

They stopped eating when they saw them come into the firelight. They were heading south, following the current. The white waters tugged at their clothes and pulled them under. They coughed and choked on the water, cursing in a language and dialect neither the doctor nor Hennessey could recognize at first.

The current pulled their shirts tight against their backs, tugging at their pants and the dead lamb that they dragged through the water with ropes. They slapped the snowmelt, cursing it, struggling to cross to the bank where Hennessey and the doctor sat eating. There were three of them. Two men dragging the third, his arms draped around their shoulders. He was limping, shouting every time they jerked him the wrong way.

Iceriye yagmur giriyor! Yagmur giriyor!

Evet. Taman.

Korkarim ki!

They spoke a kind of Turkish learned from the streets, their accents stilted and abrupt. If the doctor and Hennessey wanted anything, they wanted a good night's sleep, and so they decided it was in their interest to help these strangers on their way. They stood and met them by the river, lifting the injured man's legs. They carried him closer to the fire and laid him on a blanket. He howled, grabbing his right thigh where blood oozed through a slash mark in his pants. The doctor crouched beside him, removing his boots and socks. His skin had grown white, numbed by the water. His ankles were wrapped with a piece of red yarn, and the doctor pulled it off slowly, examining the wool. He smelled it once, then dropped it in his pocket as if he were collecting a souvenir.

Can you move your toes?

I don't understand.

Adam turned to Hennessey.

Do you speak Russian?

No.

He's speaking Russian. I need him to move his toes.

Hennessey crouched down beside the doctor and massaged the man's foot. The skin was cold, not from lack of circulation but from the chilled water. The injured man lay stiff, his face frozen, only his toes moving, mimicking the bend of the doctor's finger.

Can I use your knife?

Hennessey took the knife from his pants and gave it to the doctor. The injured man's eyes grew wide, like a spooked horse's, the whites glowing in the firelight. He inched back from the knife, kept pointing at the blade.

No!

Hold him still. I need to cut his pants.

Hennessey moved behind the man, supporting him with his knees, then held his thin arms back as Adam sliced through the pants. He took the two flaps in his arms, pulled and ripped the cloth open to expose the wound. It was still tender, raw. Blood had dripped down the man's leg and covered most of it, concealing the source of the wound. The doctor took a handkerchief from his pocket and dabbed at the blood, uncovering a short, thick slit in the man's thigh, right over the saphenous nerve where the femoral artery had been punctured and was still spurting blood and pus. An infection was setting in.

The man flailed on the blanket, hysterical. He hadn't stopped talking since they laid him on the ground, and now that he had seen the wound for the first time, he threw his arms and knocked Adam in the jaw.

Iceriye yagmur giriyor!

Relax!

Iceriye yagmur giriyor!

Hennessey moved in to help Adam restrain the man, pulling his arms back.

He's saying the rain's coming in.

Firtina cikacak.

He was whispering now, his arms limp, as if he had surrendered. His lips trembled and he drummed his fingers over them like a child, repeating himself.

Firtina cikacak.

He's afraid.

Adam locked eyes with him.

What are you afraid of? What happened? *Ne oldu?*

The man said nothing, his eyes fixed on the fire. His expression was a mix of fear and lassitude, as if answering were a waste of energy, that any answer would be wrong. His partners stepped back, hissing. They kicked the ground and spat into the fire.

Ne oldu? Adam asked again.

He looked up at the men, expecting an answer, but they said

nothing and retreated, their shoulders drooping, burdened with what appeared to be guilt.

Did one of you do this?

They shook their heads.

He's our brother.

Were you in a fight?

Not this time.

Tell me what happened.

The two men turned to each other, searching the other's face for an answer.

Adam turned to the injured man and locked eyes with him in the firelight. There was something evil about the man, something the doctor had felt many times before, but he had taken an oath to help the sick, and took the man's head in his lap. He spoke to him softly, in Turkish, an unconditional kindness in his voice to get the answers he wanted.

If you want help, you must tell me what happened.

The man bit his lip, turned his face away from the fire to hide in the dark. His oldest brother spoke first.

He fell on rocks.

The river's full of them, his brother said.

What were you doing?

Hunting.

Hunting?

Boar. Wild boar.

I see, he said.

The doctor gently pushed the man's head forward, then got up, gesturing for Hennessey to follow him to the truck, where he took a black medical bag from the backseat.

They lie. There are no more boar here.

Why?

They were contaminated from the water years ago. Wiped out by polio.

From the river?

The virus is carried in fecal matter. Runoff.

Adam took a small lantern wedged between the seats and shut the door.

He was stabbed. The mark is obvious.

Think one of the brothers did it?

I don't know.

Will he need a hospital?

No. Rest. And a doctor's care. We'll have to take them to Mavisu.

Hennessey studied Adam's face in the campfire's dim light.

Is it even worth it?

Adam struck a match and lighted the lantern. He held the light up to Hennessey's face.

A doctor's oath has no options.

You're a good man, Adam.

Only out of circumstance, he said, quickly closing the medical bag. Feed him while I clean the wound.

Hennessey nodded and followed him back to the injured man, the light of the lantern casting shadows on the ground. He covered the stab mark with strips of cloth soaked in calamine.

Will I be okay?

Eventually. You going far?

Yes.

The injured man turned his head, craning his neck to see his brothers, who hovered over him, inspecting the doctor's work.

I'm taking you with me.

Where?

Mavisu. It's a little ways from here. Another day of travel by car.

Mavisu?

Yes. The village on the mountain. We'll give you a bed and food. You're welcome to stay while your brother heals.

We can't.

What?

We must keep going.

Not now. He's in no condition. He runs the risk of infection. It's my duty to get him well. You'll like the village. Travelers usually do. At least those lucky enough to find it.

The brothers shifted uncomfortably, mumbling again in Russian, their voices low, guarded. They walked toward the river and stood, smoking.

They won't go, he said.

Don't they want you to heal?

Yes.

Of course they do.

The injured man looked up, locking his eyes on the doctor's face, his words defensive, as if he were trying to convince himself.

It was an accident, you know.

The doctor wrapped the last strip of calamine and looked down.

There are no accidents, he whispered. Who stabbed you?

The injured man's face grew tight, jaw clenched, holding back the words.

The doctor pressed on the wound.

Tell me.

The injured man winced.

Who?

A girl.

What?

A villager.

The doctor lifted his fingers from the man's leg.

Where?

Mavisu, he whispered, his eyes darting back and forth from the fire to the river's edge, where his brothers were pacing, arguing again.

Mavisu?

The injured man nodded, remembering.

She was scared.

Why?

I touched her hand.

Adam said nothing more and walked back to the truck to be

alone. When he opened the door, he found the oldest of the brothers sitting on the driver's side, slumped over the wheel.

You can sleep in the back, the doctor offered, his voice pinched
with disdain.

I'm not sleeping tonight.

I'm trying to help you.

We don't want your help.

Excuse me?

The man pushed himself off the steering wheel, the leather seat
buckling beneath him. He stepped down from the truck and stood
in front of Adam, waving a fishing knife in his hand. He backed
the doctor against the door and pressed the blade of the knife
against his throat, nicking the skin. He slid the knife to the doctor's ear, turning his head in the direction of the injured man and
his brother. They had turned on Hennessey too, holding his arms
behind him and a knife to his heart.

Bastards! Hennessey shouted.

Tell your friend to shut up.

Hennessey! Adam pleaded.

But we're trying to help them.

Help yourselves, the man said, pressing the knife harder against
the doctor's right ear, suddenly slicing off the tip of the lobe.

The doctor gasped, hearing the piece of flesh hit the ground like
the body of a small snail, sticking on impact. He felt the warm
blood against his neck, soaking into the collar of his shirt. The
man pressed his face against the doctor's cheek.

Learn to listen next time.

He shoved him against the door, shouting to his brother, who
immediately picked up the injured man and hauled him into the
woods. He dug his hands into the doctor's pocket, pulling out his
wallet, then took a wad of lire and hurled the rest at the doctor's
feet.

Esik olymandiz, he sneered, running after his brothers.

Some thanks! Hennessey shouted.

Shhhh.

The doctor grabbed a cloth from the truck and pressed it against his ear to stop the bleeding. He waited, listening to the footfalls of the men through the woods, twigs snapping beneath their boots, until he could hear only his heartbeat. He threw his eyes on the contents of his wallet, business cards and photos scattered on the ground, Nurdane's photo staring up at him, splattered with his own blood.

III

Nurdane stood beyond the reach of light in the doorway of her father's house, hesitant to go inside. The door was open for Attila, and she could see the shadow of her father's prayer positions move along the wall, the chant of suras through his labored breath. She wiped her hair out of her face, the smell of blood still on her hands. She had tried to stop the bleeding by wrapping her headscarf around the wound, but it had bled through the cloth and felt heavy now, as if she had carried a small weight in the palm of her hand.

Attila met her first, his face still swollen. He sniffed her, tracing the blood to her hand, then stepped back, smelling the men. He bared his teeth and whimpered. She waved her finger in the air, begging for his silence, but he began to bark. The chanting stopped, and she heard the crack of her father's knees as he rose to meet them.

Attila?

Ali stepped into the light of an oil lamp that hung in the hallway and took the dog by the collar.

What is it?

Attila growled. A warm cross-breeze blew the door back, the hinges creaking.

Who's there?

Nurdane stepped into the hall, hand clutched over her chest. Her blouse black where the blood had stained it. She said nothing and stood still. Her father moved slowly toward her, his eyes following the trail of blood.

What happened? he whispered. His voice was hoarse from prayer. Nurdane searched for the words as he stepped closer.

My knife slipped.

What?

It was an accident, Nurdane explained, shifting her eyes to meet her father's. Ali nodded slowly, trying to understand. It made no sense. She had never dropped a knife. In the seventeen years she had been weaving, there had been no accidents. He took the oil lamp off the wall to get a better look, eyeing the blood seeping through her headscarf.

Come, he said, leading her through the darkened hallway to the parlor.

She sat on the prayer rug. Attila dropped to the floor beside her, watching Ali unlatch the braces on her legs. His hands slid over the metal, nervous. He didn't have to unfasten the hinges. Her legs had shrunk so much that he could slip the braces over her feet and be done with it. Her calf muscle hung from the bones like two unripened tomatoes, he thought, unsnapping the braces one by one, honoring her simple dignities. When he was finished, he wiped the braces clean with a small rag and set them alone by the door. Then he paced the room, thinking, watching her eyes rove the camel bags on the wall. She seemed distant.

Were you alone? he asked.

Yes. With Attila. Why?

There are no accidents.

He ripped a clean rag in half. The tearing of the cloth startled Nurdane, and she shifted nervously on the floor. She sat crosslegged and pressed her hands against her thighs to keep them from shaking. Her father was wrong. There were accidents. She did not intend to stab the picker. It happened, unexpected, an accident.

Ali took the pot of water from the samovar and set it on the floor with a bar of soap. He took her right hand and began to unwrap the bloody headscarf. She turned her head and shifted her eyes toward the ceiling as he exposed the wound. *Allah. Allah.* He held her hand palm-up toward the light and stared incredulously. Clots of blood had formed along the arc of a slash mark cut deep into her flesh from the left pad to the base of her index finger. He could flip back the skin with his thumbnail. He drew in a deep breath. Only the ticking of a small wall clock broke the silence. Nurdane covered the wound with her fingers.

We must clean it, Ali said, prying her fingers back.

I'll do it.

She held her hand in a tight fist, her eyes squeezed shut, fighting the tears. Ali noticed her fingers were touching the open wound, pressing it hard, yet she seemed unaffected by the pressure.

Nurdane?

What?

Don't you feel it?

She pressed harder. Her fingers turning white.

Give me your hand. Please.

He fought her, wedging his own fingers beneath hers as the pickers had done, trying to get her knife. He took her hand and laid it flat on his leg, then squeezed the soapy cloth over the wound. He expected her to scream, for the soap to sting. But she sat still, and her stillness unnerved him. He tried again, this time dunking her hand into the hot water. She looked at him and answered before he spoke.

I don't feel anything.

He looked down at her hand and traced the slash mark with his finger again.

Nothing?

She shook her head.

I must have cut a nerve.

Ali searched her eyes, following the sudden drop in her voice, detecting the confession as if she had planned her injury long ago.

If you needed a break, you could have asked me.

She turned to him, confused.

A break?

If you needed more time, I mean. To finish the rug. I realize the pressure once the bidding begins. It seems heavier this year. More intense for you.

You too.

She looked up into her father's eyes.

Do you think . . .

· Her voice trailed off as she considered the consequences of the picker's touch. *As long as you keep your hands pure, Allah will continue to make the rugs through you.* Her father's words rang in her head as he stood silently in front of her, trying to read her face.

What?

It was a mistake, she said.

He nodded slowly and watched as she lifted her eyes to meet his. She felt her heart racing. She wanted to tell him everything but asked him only one question.

Does Allah understand mistakes?

Ali wrung the bloody cloth over the pot. He laughed softly, then grew silent and turned to her as if she had reminded him of something he had forgotten.

He creates them, Nurdane.

Why?

They teach us to be good, he said, then threw his gaze into the pot, watching the blood cloud the water slowly, moving and curling like a lie.

A warm, tropical rain fell on the village that night. Poplars bent backward in the wind, and the cypress tossed their long branches like arms casting spells. Ali lay on a mat stuffed with wool and listened to the wind blowing from the mountain. The breath of angry spirits, he thought. Every now and then streaks of lightning came through the window, and he could see the entire village, the clay roof tiles fiery red with nothing but blackness behind them.

He could not sleep and threw back the thin sheet of cotton. The wind changed direction and blew rain through the window, causing a cool mist on his arms. He rose quickly and crossed the floor in his bare feet to shut it, then pulled his trousers on in the dark and walked quietly back across the room to the hallway.

He entered the parlor where Nurdane lay on her side, sleeping. Her legs were tucked into the flap of her skirt and her hands crossed each other, the left clutching the right. Ali approached her quietly, picking up a piece of bread from the table. He crouched beside her and rubbed the bread over her wounded hand. She tossed in her sleep, her teeth chattering. A mohair blanket lay at her feet, and he took it and covered her until her breaths were heavy and he was certain she had returned to her dreams.

He stuffed the bread into his vest pocket and crossed the room to the camel bag on the wall. He reached into the recess and took the box with the dress pattern, set the ledger in its place, and slung the bag over his shoulder. He walked quietly to the door and picked up a fountain pen from the desk before he let himself outside.

Rain had flooded the garden and washed out the road. Streams of water ran white, like a million beards through the village. Mud clung to his heels as he trudged to the cemetery and waded through a field of wild wheat that lay matted on the southern slope. Ancient tombs dwarfed the headstones of the modern dead, and he stumbled over those overgrown with weeds.

A small patch of poppies surrounded his wife's grave. He crouched before it and pushed back the flowers to run his hand along the prayers etched in the stone. She was believed to have gone to heaven for dying in childbirth. They called her the *logusa,* postpartum woman. She had sacrificed her life for another, and her sins, if any, were forever pardoned.

Her tomb had lain open for forty days after her death. It had been twenty-two years, but he could smell her still, in the rain. The storm aroused her spirit. Rosewater. The ablution haunted him since her passing. She was eighteen. A Laz girl with nomadic roots from the Black Sea. The only legacy that survived her were Nurdane's blue eyes. The fact that her daughter could not walk separated her from the nomadic history they would have shared.

There was no place for his wife in the mosque, and so he came here, where he could feel her still in the quiet mist, to be with her and seek guidance. He set the camel bag on the ground and sat cross-legged in the wet grass, facing the grave. First he took the bread from his vest pocket and tossed it into the graveyard. Then he pulled the dress pattern and pen from the bag and waited for lightning to begin the prayer he had come to write for Nurdane. He dragged his pen across the page, hoping his wife would help him find the words to tell Nurdane the truth about her hands. He could see it in her eyes, begging him to tell her what she was too scared to know. He pretended he didn't understand her. That what she wanted to know had nothing to do with what she was asking him. He could not tell her the origin of the virgin's knots yet, but wondered how long he could keep the myth before her questions drained its power.

He listened for answers between the thunder and the rain. The sky crackled with electricity and carried with it the fragrance of storm, ozone-rich and furtive, culling memories he would have liked to forget. The polio had struck Nurdane in a storm like this. She was five and had followed a group of women to pick wild herbs on the mountain. Sage and thyme. Bitter tastes to him now. She had wandered too far and had gotten lost, her cries muffled by the thunder. His search lasted hours. He had found her lying on the ground motionless, face planted in a patch of poppies like a stone that had tumbled from the hill in the storm. She lay barely breathing, hands clinging to a clump of petals, now crushed between her fingers. He told her to get up, but she only moved her eyes, straining them toward the crags of the mountains. He shook her shoulders, yanked her legs from the ground. Told her to get up and walk. She staggered forward, tripped on the ends of her dress, tearing them, then slumped onto the wet earth. She lifted her head slowly and gave him an apologetic stare. She could move only her upper body and walked her fingers through the flowers into her father's hands. Her tiny fingers were stiff like bits of broken clay, and he squeezed her gently and promised her she would walk again. Then he built her a loom and taught her how to weave, to give her a life beyond the stillness. Her hands would take her where her legs could not. As long as she kept them pure, he believed, Allah would make the knots through her forever. He wanted to soften the blow of her harsh misfortune, wanted to insure she had a way to provide for herself long after she survived him.

In ancient times, his people had built small temples at crossroads, first for Apollo, then later for weary travelers who had lost their way. If they did not know which way to go, they could step inside and rest awhile, meditate, and listen to which direction called to them in the silence. He preferred the cemetery. The way of the dead. He bowed his head and waited for hours until the words escaped him and prayer flooded the page.

When he finished, he took the dress pattern with him toward a wind-shorn cypress on the crest of the cemetery. The trunk was twisted, the roots gnarled. The tree was reputed to be more than one thousand years old, and the villagers believed it had special powers. Their *tuba,* tree of paradise. Pieces of frayed cloth dangled from the branches and contained the prayers answered there.

Ali stood under the damp branches and read over his own prayer, the rain light and steady. He held the paper up toward the sky until the ink bled down the page, and cupping it, held it to his mouth and drank the stream of words until the prayer was inside him.

She wore her braces and walked the perimeter of the west cliff. She wanted to know if Muammer was right about the pickers. The ground was still damp and pocked from the rain, the weeds collapsed. She glanced down at the gully where the pickers had been camping and spotted a dark circle where the tall grasses had been charred from the campfire. The trap was still there, coated with what appeared to be resin. Nurdane pressed her finger against it, then tasted it. Honey. It was obvious now. The pickers had set the trap for Attila, and she wasn't convinced that they had not intended to kill him. They had succeeded in keeping him away from the hut the night they had come to take the rug. The bandage wrapped around her hand was a painful reminder. It was hot and her skin perspired beneath it, softening the scabs that had formed in the night. She could feel only pressure on her fingertips, other feelings lost.

With her eye she followed a band of light over the wooded area and wondered if the pickers would be back. She thought about moving the loom to the house, where the rug would be safe. But there would be questions and stories. Rumors ran rampant through the village, and no person was safe from the accusations that coupled a change in tradition, even if it was slight. The villagers considered her hut more sacrosanct than she did herself. They would rather have abandoned it than change anything for fear it would diminish the power of the rugs. She considered telling Mehmet but was too scared he would tell his father, and his father would tell hers. So she decided to carry the secret as long as she could. She would have to leave the rug alone and trust Allah with its safekeeping.

She turned back and followed the road, stopping for a flock of merinos and their young shepherd. The sheep pranced across the road, their bodies freshly shorn. They looked funny to her, half their size, misshapen without the wool, their skin pink and shriveled, nicked with razor marks. They passed her, then stopped, bleating, as if they wished to exchange words for the sacrifice they had made for her rugs. It took the wool of a hundred sheep to make ten thousand knots, and she thought they were reminding her now not to take them for granted. She waved to the shepherd.

Go on. They want to see you, he said.

She negotiated her way among the flock until she stood in the center, and only when she thanked them did they let her pass. The shepherd blew into a small flute hanging from his neck, and the sheep trotted down the road, their bleating carried by the wind.

What happened to your hand?

Nurdane turned to find Muammer riding up to her on his bicycle. He was with his younger brother, who sat on the handlebars, lips stained with berry juice.

Nothing. It was an accident.

It was the razor blade.

No, Muammer. It wasn't.

She tried to move past him, but he rode beside her.

They hurt you.

She picked up her pace.

Don't you have music lessons?

Yes. Tuesday.

She said nothing. The boy persisted, riding on her heels.

You told me to go to the mosque and pray for you. So I did.

Thank you, Muammer. I could use every prayer.

He stopped and pushed his younger brother off the bike when he heard a familiar bell ringing in the distance.

Go home, Adel. I'll come later.

His brother jumped off the bike and ran through the grass toward his house. Nurdane kept walking along the road, hoping Muammer would tire and leave her alone. He coasted beside her, keeping with her slow, steady pace.

I saw them, he said.

Who?

The men. Somebody was passing them money in the mosque. They weren't from here. They didn't even know how to pray right. They touched their foreheads to their knees.

Nurdane adjusted her headscarf. The tassels had slipped forward, over her eyes. The boy knew too much, and as much as she did not want to hear his story, she could not help but ask him for more.

Who were they passing money to? she asked.

Mustafa.

The owner of the general store?

Yes. I think that's his name.

Nurdane shielded her eyes from the sun with the back of her hand. She did not want the boy to see her face, to learn more than he already knew. Mustafa's daughter was one of the brides to be married within the month. She was eligible to receive the rug, and she wondered if Mustafa had placed a bid, and if he had, why he was paying the men to steal it.

How many? she asked.

What?

Men. How many men did you see with Mustafa?

Three.

He stopped and looked up at her. She shifted on her braces, her face still covered by her bandaged hand.

Their eyes were puffy and red, he said. And they were dirty.

With big, thick beards. I know they were the men at the campfire.
I matched their boot prints. I know they trapped Attila.

Nurdane paused and turned to him. Muammer put his bare feet
on the road and skidded to a stop. He blinked earnestly, his eyes
glazed, teary. She knew he was telling the truth, and it broke her
heart to see him so frustrated, trying so hard to help her. He
blinked and a tear fell down his cheek.

They didn't do this, Muammer. You must believe that.

He reached out to her injured hand and touched the bandage
with his trembling fingers. His voice low.

What if they come back?

They won't, she said.

Who will help you?

Nurdane turned and looked out among the pediments that had
tumbled down the steps of the ancient theater. The faces were
cracked or turned every which way, mouths open, laughing.

I'll be okay.

Muammer shook his head.

I could have stopped them. I saw them walking toward the hut
last night, and I could see you from my window. You're always
there so late.

I was weaving.

The boy nodded, turning the events in his mind. The dead
lamb. The path through the snow. It was so easy for him to follow
them. He turned back only when he saw their gun.

I'm sorry they hurt you.

They didn't. I told you, Muammer. It was an accident.

The boy sighed and ran his hands idly over the handlebars.
They won't get away with what they've done. Allah will punish
them, he said.

He made a wide arc around her, then disappeared over the hill,
only the clank of his chain in the distance. She stood there for a
moment and turned her face to the sun. You're wrong, she
thought. Allah will punish me. *When Allah takes something from
you, he gives you something in return.* The words came again, this

time not in her father's voice but her own. She reversed the refrain, wondering for the first time what happened when you took something from Allah, what it was you gave Him in return.

Nurdane entered Mustafa's store at noon. The muezzin's cry echoed throughout the village, and she paused in the doorway and bowed her head, praying the boy was wrong. She pulled the door shut behind her and negotiated her way among stacks of unopened boxes and crates of bananas brought up from the valley. The store was a cluttered addition to Mustafa's house. Nothing more than whitewashed cement with a small window blocked by racks of fruit juice. Shafts of light moved through the bottles and cast orange shadows on the walls.

She stood behind a shelf crammed with jars of olive oil and soap and pushed them aside to see Mustafa, kneeling on a faded prayer rug. He faced a picture of Ataturk on a calendar nailed to the wall, his postulation appearing more for the great leader than the prophet to whom he prayed. He looked small to her, hunched on the floor. He was thin and she could see the bones poke through his shirt, his spine snaking along his back. A gold watch dangled from his wrist and slid down his arm when he stood, lifting his hands over his head. He turned right, then left, greeting the protecting angels, but froze when he saw her. She watched the lump in his throat rise, then fall. He slowly lowered his arms to his sides and instead of facing her, turned his back.

I'm praying. Can you come back later?

No.

Her eyes roved the shelves, the cheap headscarves from the city folded in tiny triangles among yellowing tablet paper, rusted canteens and dusty bottles of Coke that had not been touched since the war.

I don't see any knives here.

She felt him turn to her, but she kept her eyes fixed on the shelves. He caught a glimpse of her bandaged hand before she moved it behind the headscarves.

You do sell knives here?

She shifted her eyes toward him and he nodded, his eyes slipping from her, lower, below her hip, where her hand was resting.

They're in the house.

He pointed behind him, but his finger aimed toward the window. She turned and saw the tip of the minaret in the frame, shimmering in the sunlight. She turned back.

There?

Where?

The mosque?

No.

You do your business in the mosque?

He dug his hands into his pants pockets and shifted on the thin rug. A quiver crept in his voice.

I sell many knives. What do you need?

She stared at him.

A small one.

For what?

To cut knots. I lost mine last night.

He gave her a strange look, one eye twitching. He batted the air, pretending it was dust.

I think I have what you need. It's in the house.

He left the prayer rug on the floor and walked past her. He paused briefly to glance at her hand, but it was she who spoke first.

It slipped.

What?

She looked up at him, surprised he did not understand.

The knife. It slipped.

He nodded quickly and moved toward the door. He fumbled with the latch as she spoke.

Did you place a bid, Mustafa?

He stopped and turned. She repeated herself, her words fused with anger.

My father didn't mention you wanted the rug.

He glanced up at the evil eye hanging above the door and said nothing. Only the beating of a rug could be heard from the yard.

Will it happen again? she asked, her heart pounding.

He said nothing and opened the door, grateful for the breeze. He found his daughters outside, ears pressed against the wall. Their faces were wrought with confusion.

What does she want?

Too many answers, he said, and walked past them.

They scrunched their noses, perplexed, and watched their mother enter the store. Mustafa's wife was a heavyset woman, pregnant with fleshy jowls that hung over the edges of her head-scarf. She stood in the door frame and spoke to Nurdane.

You're in time for lunch.

Nurdane forced a smile.

Perfect timing.

Please join us.

Before Nurdane could answer, the woman pointed at her hand.

An injury always loves a meal.

The woman lumbered across the store like a bear, leading Nurdane outside, past a very disgruntled Mustafa and his flock of daughters. The age gap was so great between them that the eldest could have passed as a mother to the youngest. There were twelve girls, one of the biggest families of Mavisu. Nurdane wondered if Mustafa and his wife had spent their lives trying for a son, draining them of honor and resources. They were a poor family and wore threadbare clothes. The youngest bodies swam in hand-me-down dresses, torn at the hemlines from tripping so much. Nurdane recognized none as her students. They couldn't afford the lessons of the loom, and for this she pitied them and thought it a cruel injustice that Allah had not made all women weavers.

They brought her into the house and tossed bolsters on the floor to make her comfortable. Mustafa disappeared down the hallway and left her alone with his daughters. His wife dashed into the garden and returned with a tray of olives and peppers and pearls of fresh garlic.

Nurdane ate little, still nauseated from the accident. Everything tasted metallic, smelled of blood. She rolled an olive pit around the palm of her left hand and studied the dowry collection of Mustafa's daughter Cennet piled in the corner, stacks of blankets and towels, hand-woven socks, headscarves bordered with coins. The gifts had been folded neatly on a pine chest hand-painted with flower designs and abstract figures reminiscent of those found in her rugs. A few factory-made rugs lay rolled up beside the trunk, the chemical dyes discordant and unpleasing to the eye. But the rugs were necessary to complete the girl's trousseau no matter how they were crafted. Nurdane considered the dowry complete and wondered what difference it would make, if any at this point, should Mustafa's daughter receive her rug.

She moved her eyes among the tower of gifts. They were so beautiful to her and rare. She often caught herself daydreaming at the loom, imagining what her own trousseau might look like. The only dowries she would know were the ones she made for other girls. And that was her fate and that was her luck and she believed it was not her place to question it.

It must be hard to give them up.

Nurdane turned to Cennet, confused.

Your rugs. How do you let them go?

Ah, Nurdane said. You get used to it.

You shouldn't.

Nurdane felt her body stiffen. Cennet was brazen and seemed not to care either way if what she said offended the weaver.

The rugs aren't for me.

They should be.

They're for happy marriages. For Allah.

Nurdane looked down at her hand. Cennet huffed and reclined against the wall.

Have you ever seen Allah sitting on a rug?

Nurdane shook her head. Cennet continued, waving her finger in the air as if she were conducting her own private symphony.

Have you ever seen Allah sit?

Again, Nurdane shook her head. The girl continued, whispering this time.

Have you ever seen Allah?

She tucked her finger back into her hand and looked over at Nurdane.

If you can't see him, how can he see your rugs? How can he know how beautiful they are if he's never had the chance to walk barefoot across the silken pile. It doesn't seem fair. You give up your rugs before you ever get to use them.

Nurdane nodded, considering, and tossed the olive pit into a shallow tin on the floor. She did not think about these things and found her mind trying to untangle the ideas. It made her head hurt. Cennet turned to her with a strangely resolute look on her face.

I'll promise you something.

Nurdane locked eyes with her, waiting.

If I ever won the rug, I'd give it back to you.

You'd be a fool.

Nurdane and Cennet turned to find Mustafa standing in the doorway. His face was drawn with worry, his eyes blazing, furious. The boom of his voice silenced the room. The girl sat up and spit a look of defiance toward him.

Then you should keep it. I never said I wanted the rug. My marriage does not depend on it.

Cennet pushed herself off the floor and slipped into the hallway to be alone. Her mother entered with a tray of tea and shelled pistachios. Mustafa held up his hand.

It's time for Nurdane to leave.

But there's tea.

We've given her enough!

Cennet stared at him, and his wife shrunk back and threw her eyes upon the tray with shame. We still have cake, she said, disappointed.

Another day. My father's been expecting me.

Nurdane pushed herself off the floor and stood. Her braces had slid down her legs, but she did not stop to adjust them, following Mustafa outside, her steps awkward as she limped past the girls. She stopped on the steps. Mustafa pulled a knife from his pocket and passed it to her, his hands trembling.

Leave my girls alone.

He spoke through his teeth, lips pressed together as if he were withholding a curse, his face filled with bitterness. She took the knife from him and ran her finger slowly along the blade, testing it.

It's sharp.

I took it to the whetstone.

Strange too.

Strange?

She looked up at him. A horsefly had landed on his cheek and he slapped it, splattering himself with blood. Nurdane turned the knife, catching the sun on its blade.

It's so small but it can cut so deeply, she said, as they exchanged a knowing look, then turned and walked down the path.

Attila followed her, trotting closely behind, whimpering when her legs buckled, as if to warn her she'd gone far enough. She refused to stop and dragged her body up the rocky slope until she reached the hut. She stood outside the window and held on to the lower branches of a cherry tree to catch her breath and take in the view. The twilight sky held the moon like a giant persimmon. The air was still and cool, sweetened with pine. She followed the rim of the aqueduct with her eyes, striding for miles to the gorge where the river ran black.

She could make out two figures in the water. Her body stiffened and she felt the hair rise on her neck. A rush of white water erased them, and for a moment she thought her eyes were playing tricks on her. But the figures resurfaced as one this time. She gripped the knife tighter, then pulled the dog into the hut and locked the door. She moved quickly through the dark, feeling her way with her feet, over the balls of wool, the wooden beaters, her spindle. Her hands crawled along the loom until she felt the hurricane lamp and a box of matches.

She lit the lamp and set it on the floor. The soft glow cast odd shapes across her face, the weft and warp crossing her like a net. She spotted the tip of the knife under the bench and pulled it out. Streaks of blood had dried and caked on the blade, the surface dull with dust. She did not want to look at the knife any longer, and wrapped it quickly in a cloth she pulled from her belt. She looked over her shoulder at the door, making sure she was alone, then pulled the new knife from the scabbard and laid it on the bench as if it had always been there. Then she took the old knife outside.

Attila lay in the doorway, his head between his paws, watching her move along the hill. She walked a few yards from the hut and got down on her knees and laid the knife beside her. Then, using her left hand, she dug into the earth. The soil was moist and stuffed with worms, and they wrapped themselves around her fingers as she worked. When the hole was deep enough, she laid the knife inside and, shaking the worms from her fingers, packed the soil around it with the heel of her hand. She worked delicately, carefully, but was overcome with anger, and began to pound the ground with her fist, striking it as hard as she could, pushing the knife farther into the earth.

Eksik olmayiniz!

Her scream echoed across the ravine. She cried again and again until her voice grew hoarse and her throat hurt and her lungs could no longer support her will to be heard. But her strength of hand surprised her, and she hammered harder, releasing the hatred she had for the pickers and the resentment she harbored for herself. It was an accident. She knew this, but it was her hand that touched him. It was her knife that cut into his leg.

As long as you keep your hands pure, Allah will make the rugs through you. Her father's words rattled her mind like old seeds in a dried gourd.

Her hands were no longer pure and there was nothing she could do to change this. Now what? She could feel nothing in her right hand. The slight pressure in her fingertips. What good was that? Allah teasing her, she thought, reminding her of what she had lost. Her hand for the loom, for the rug still upon it that begged her to finish it. She turned toward the hut and saw the rug through the window, sitting there in the darkness.

Her cheeks were wet, and she moved her hand down them, mixing the dirt and tears. She struck the earth again with her fist. Her body grew warm, wisps of hair stuck to her neck. She pounded harder until the soil gave way and sank a few inches, leaving a shallow depression for her tears to collect.

She looked around and grabbed the closest rock, a small chunk of limestone. She did not wish to use the rock like a headstone to mark the site, but, rather, to cover the knife with the hope that one day she would forget it was ever there.

She lifted her face to the sky and closed her eyes, feeling the hot wind from the mountain. She sensed something strange about the days, the shift of the earth perhaps. The approach of the solstice. She felt a change beyond the light, something in her heart, a new space opening up to her for forgiveness or shame. She did not know which.

She leaned forward and pressed her cheek on the ground, and felt something move. The sound of a heavy object being dragged. Then footsteps. Attila barked and stood in the doorway, ears pinned, tail thwapping against the frame. Nurdane sat up and looked over her shoulder. An old man approached her from the opposite side of the hill, his silver hair blue in the light. He was hunched over, his chest nearly touching his knees. He carried three logs on his back and had somehow tied them to his bony frame with a network of rope that ran across his chest, over his shoulders, ending in a slipknot around his waist. He wore a ragged wool sweater and baggy plaid trousers rolled up around his thin ankles. His feet were bare, and he walked so slowly, his movements were almost imperceptible from a distance. He stopped short of Nurdane, as if to keep a formal distance between them, then lifted the small cap from his head. His voice, high-pitched and puckish.

Do you have tea?

Tea?

I'm rather thirsty. The air up here. It's dry.

She did not recognize the man, but Attila stood at the door, wagging his tail as if he had expected the guest, and wouldn't he please come inside?

Are you from here?

He pointed behind him.

I live in the yalas by the river.

She sat kneeling with her hands on her thighs, studying his shriveled face in the light. It reminded her of a dried fig, shrunken and scorched by the sun. He was a nomad, a wanderer, lost perhaps among the ruins tonight. She had never invited anyone into the hut before, but the man stood shivering, the veins on his neck bulging from the weight of his load. He wanted tea. He would be on his way.

I have to heat the water. It will be a few minutes.

The old man nodded, pleased.

Thank you.

Nurdane wiped her face with the flap of her skirt, trying quickly to clean the dirt. She did the same with her left hand but her fingernails remained black. She adjusted the braces and pushed herself off the ground and gestured for the man to follow her inside.

She put a kettle over a small samovar and set matches to the charcoal. The old man stood at the threshold and scratched Attila between the ears. The dog was content in the old man's presence and nudged his hand with his nose.

He likes you.

I was a shepherd as a youth. I had a dozen dogs. Kangals, of course. They're the most loyal dog in the world.

She smiled and nodded, happy to see Attila himself again.

He was stung the other day.

What?

That's why his lips are so swollen.

The old man moved a shaking hand around the dog's mouth.

Yes. Yes.

Nurdane studied the man. He did not seem interested in the rug. His eyes focused only on the dog. She was relieved. He had probably seen hundreds of rugs in his long life and had no interest in them. She looked around the hut for food to offer.

Would you like cherries?

If it is no trouble. Do not go far to please me.

She gave him a curious look and pointed to the tree outside the window.

I can practically pick them from here.

She moved across the hut, her braces creaking. The old man cocked his head and held his arm out as if to stop her.

Take your time, he said. I'm in no hurry.

She turned to look at him and stiffened. His eyes were colorless and watery. He seemed to be looking straight through her, and she turned to look over her shoulder, wondering if somebody else was there. He immediately threw his gaze downward and stroked the dog again.

I'll be right back.

Nurdane stepped outside and walked around the hut to the cherry tree outside the window. She could see the old man, down on one knee, trying to play with the dog. There was something odd about the way he moved, so calculated. He reminded her of herself, trying to maneuver with the leg braces, but there was some-

thing beyond his age that made her curious. She picked the cherries with her left hand and dropped them into her vest pockets,
then walked back into the hut.

Please, sit down.

The man shook his head. He was still standing in the doorway.
The dog had not moved and seemed to stay beside him, as if to
guard or guide him. It was an odd arrangement, and Nurdane
wondered how he could stand for so long with the logs on his
back.

I thought you wanted to rest.

I am, he said. I'm not walking.

The teapot whistled and Nurdane crossed the hut and carried it
and two tulip glasses back to the man. But before she even filled
the cup, he extended his hand, palm-up. She set it down carefully.

It's very hot.

That's fine. Thank you.

He took the cup to his lips and drank. His eyes still. Like a dead
man, she thought.

Where are you traveling?

To see my wife.

You don't live together?

It's been a long time, he said, finishing the tea.

Nurdane did not take the glass but stood beside it and watched
him wave it in the air, searching for her hand. She watched him for
a few moments longer than she should have, and realized from his
struggle that he was blind. When she finally took the cup and freed
his hands, the old man patted the air until he found Attila's head,
then moved slowly toward the door.

Esik olymandiz, she said, blessing him.

He nodded and smiled.

You too. Finish the rug.

Excuse me?

He shifted his head in the direction of her voice, but his eyes
faced the moon.

No matter what happens, you must finish.

On Saturday she went to the lodge. She was early but the door was already open and she could hear the soft music of fingers plucking the weft and warp of a loom. She paused under the shade of a pomegranate tree to listen. The thwap of fingers usually soothed her, but today the sounds were unnerving.

She stopped in the doorway. The looms had been pushed against the wall, except for one, where a young girl sat weaving, a bota of *ayran,* yogurt and water, tied around her waist. The cap had rolled off and a trail of thick milky liquid had spilled on the girl's dress and onto the floor. She did not seem to notice the spill, nor did she pause to look up at Nurdane. There was a focus about her, something serious, a fierce determination she did not recognize in any of the young weavers she taught. Her brows knitted in concentration. She moved her lips quickly, counting the spaces in the pattern.

Shadows fell across the loom and blocked her face. Nurdane stepped closer, and the girl pivoted slightly, keeping her face hidden. Her body seemed strangely contorted, her trunk twisted to accommodate her still legs. Her head was wrapped in an elaborate arrangement of silk scarves hand-painted with flowers. A chain of red and white poppies crowned her forehead.

Nurdane approached the girl slowly. The floor was slippery with dust and stamped with footprints. Divots marred the wood as if it had been scratched by nails. Nurdane stepped around the odd markings and the floor creaked. The girl sat still and faced the loom, her back to Nurdane. The closer Nurdane got, the faster the girl wove. The thwack of the beater louder and harder, punctuating Nurdane's every step. She could see only the girl's left side, her angular profile against the window. Her young skin was smooth and flawless, almost waxy in the light. Beads of sweat clung to the hollow of her cheekbones, her slender neck looked warm and pink. She did not seem bothered by the hair that hung in her eyes and continued to weave, using her left hand to maneuver a strand of red wool between the weft and warp, tying the final knot in a motif that filled the entire field. The *elibelinde,* "arms akimbo," they called it. The Goddess figure, her arms outstretched, legs spread wide across the field. Beneath her was an inverted image, forming a cross.

Nurdane recognized the figure. Something passed on to her from her grandmother. She had never taught the design to any of her students. They were not ready. It was too complicated and yet the young girl had mastered it. Her craftsmanship was perfect. The design flawless.

Nurdane stepped closer now, standing behind the girl's left shoulder. She looked down and noticed the girl was using only her left hand and, when she searched her lap for her right, she found only the stub of her wrist among a mass of wool balls. Her right hand was missing and in its place was the knife Nurdane had bought from Mustafa, slicing through the knots with a certain ease that made it look like the arrangement was typical, natural even.

Nurdane stiffened. The girl continued to work harder now, conscious of Nurdane's stare. Nurdane lowered herself to the girl's level and the girl suddenly stopped. She laid the knife down on her lap and turned her head slowly, her blue eyes as wide as the woman staring at her. She moved her hand to the crown of poppies on her head.

It's good luck.

Poppies?

When a white blooms with a red.

It's impossible. They never bloom together.

They do when death is impossible.

Nurdane clasped her mouth with her hand and drew in a breath. The young girl's voice was identical to her own, and when she looked directly into her eyes, she realized she was staring at herself. The girl opened her mouth to speak, when Nurdane heard the sweep of a broom. She turned her head and saw the village gardener cleaning the floor while the muhtar supervised him, checking off a list from a small notebook.

The lodge is closed, Nurdane.

What?

Your classes were canceled yesterday.

She stared at them, confused, slightly dizzy.

Didn't anybody tell you?

She shook her head.

No.

I'm sorry you made the trip. Seems like it's the hottest day of the month. We should be in the river, swimming, but we promised your father we'd work today.

She wiped the hair from her face. Nothing was making sense.

Work? For what?

The muhtar put his arm out to stop the gardener from sweeping.

Didn't he tell you?

I . . . I haven't been home since yesterday. I slept in the hut last night.

The muhtar turned to the gardener. An eyebrow arched slightly. An odd grin on his face.

We're having a dance, he said. In your honor.

The gardener began to sweep again, this time humming a folk tune as he worked. Nurdane watched him move in front of her and realized the young girl and the loom had vanished, leaving nothing but the knife on the dusty floor.

She sat alone on the floor of the lodge and waited for them, listening. The windows were open for the heat, and she could hear the strains of a ney flute and the flutter of capes in the wind. They permitted no light and had her sit in the dark, back to the window, so the moon could not meet her eyes. A dark veil covered her face and draped her shoulders, hiding her hair. She was not to look at the dancers.

The musicians entered first, each carrying an instrument to summon the spirits. The seventy-two-string zither, the tambur, the kenece, a small three-string violin, the cymbals, a double drum, and the ney flute. The musicians were men except for one woman, the village soothsayer with the silver braids that fell out of her scarf. She wore white trousers and a white vest. An elaborate white scarf bordered with gold coins was wrapped around her head like a belly dancer's. She took her place on the floor beneath the men and faced Nurdane. She nodded once to acknowledge her, then whispered.

Do not be afraid.

Nurdane nodded back, surprised to hear the old woman's voice and equally grateful she was with her now, to guide her through this dark and lonely place where she was told she would heal.

A drum solicited the dancers. They entered slowly, one by one, and surrounded her in a circle. The floor sagged beneath them. She could see their bare feet beneath the ends of their black cloaks and skirts. She counted twenty of them. Maybe more. Large steel nails were wedged between their big toes and glimmered in the moonlight.

They started with soft, gentle turns. Heads slightly tilted. The tops of their conical hats barely skimming the ceiling. They moved in a counterclockwise direction, left to right. Left, because that was where the heart was. They used the nails to keep them in place so they would not touch one another.

The music grew richer, more vibrant as the dance continued. The deeply hypnotic rhythms induced each dancer into a trance, whirling faster, moving the cool air with them. They extended their arms, right hand heavenward, the left facing down to the earth. The gesture symbolized their faith in the world, in matter and in spirit, their longing for providence. They believed one place would deliver them from their earthly wounds. Their order, one of faith in suffering. They trusted pain for the lessons it concealed and believed there was no true beauty without it. And yet Nurdane's pain was of a different kind, neither solicited for some great evolution of spirit nor understood, and so they danced longer and faster, asking the spirits to reveal it and endow them with the capacity to heal her.

They were sweating and she could smell them through their clothes. Olive oil. Garlic. Thyme. Sage. The spices seeped through their pores, wafting through the room when their cloaks flapped in the air. Occasionally the edge of a cloak would fly up and caress her veil as if the cloth itself were reaching out to touch her, to bring her into the dance.

She sat erect, shoulders square, shifting only her hips when her legs grew sore. She closed her eyes and breathed deeply, concentrating on the music, bringing the voice into her. An older shepherd. She had heard him many times before. His voice was rich and melodic and made her body tremble. Deep vibrations. She felt a warm tingling and wondered if this is what it meant to feel Allah.

The dervishes did not perform the dance for anyone. It was not a scheduled event like the call to prayer. The lodge had been banned since all Sufi orders were outlawed by Ataturk in 1925 and had since been turned into a school of music. Despite its ruling, the lodge continued to function as it had for centuries, bringing the villagers closer than the mosques could ever take them to Allah.

The dancers stepped closer to her now, still whirling without one touching the other. They clapped deliberately, four times to welcome the spirits. One for each direction. East, west, north, south. The way of the spirits, good and evil. They stomped once and tossed the black capes over their shoulders, revealing starched white tunics.

The room had grown hotter and the heat pulled Nurdane out of her trance. She looked up, forgetting her pact, and saw the dancers' faces glistening in the moonlight. Her father was among them and stepped forward from the circle and crouched beside her.

Give me your hand.

She did as she was told, seeing only part of him through the veil.

Palm this way.

Ali unwrapped the bandage, each turn accompanied by the whirl of the dervish behind him. He pulled a small atomizer from his robe and sprayed her hand with rosewater.

Prepare for *sama*.

He chanted softly, eyes fixed on her hands. *Makan zaman ikhwan*. The place, the time, the brethren. He needed to recite the words only once, but he repeated them over and over in his mind, as if to convince himself he could still bring light to Nurdane's eternal darkness. He believed there was still time. He believed his actions had not yet drained the myth of the virgin's knots.

They carried her home in the dark and upon her request, laid her on a mat on the veranda. She fell asleep watching the slow shift of stars and woke to a cold brilliance surrounding the village, as if everything could begin again in the morning. But she remembered the blood in a dream and still tasted the bitter iron in her mouth. Smelled the wet leather. She could hear them too, the bray of drunken laughter like a petulant ass.

She had not slept well. Her eyes were puffy. Her legs sore. Her hair was wet with dew and lay twisted like a long rope draped over her shoulder. She was too tired to move it and lay there on her side, gazing up at the mulberry tree in the yard. Her headscarf blew off in the night and billowed now from the top branches, where a raven sat watching her. The bird had not moved all morning, and she wondered if Allah had sent it. Not an angel or a guard, she thought, but a gargoyle, sharp and black as a conscience to remind her of her mistake.

Her hands. Now more than ever they felt like strangers, odd appendages that she would be better off without. They were both a responsibility to Allah and a liability to herself. The rugs had given her a livelihood beyond the bids they summoned. Weaving proffered her a direction and identity that few women of Anatolia had known or would ever know in their limited lives. She had respect. She had money, a little. She had an odd independence because of her craft. She could wander where she wanted. She could swim in the river alone, sit in the mosque, play cards in the teahouse, but the smoke stung her eyes, hurt her lungs. She preferred the hut. She hated the villagers who were always looking up in awe, not realizing she was trying to find the best way to climb down and join them. She wanted to leap from that high place and land in the road and dance with the stones between her toes. Just once. She wanted to be like them.

She wished her honor could come through her womb and not her hands, but she knew she would never give birth. She came from a people who believed women were vessels who gave their husbands children, and she knew she could never be that woman, any woman. She would never bear children. Her legs, she had been told, would not allow her to care for a child, to wander as her ancestors did among the mountains. Only the loom would give her children, the rugs. Her marriage had already been arranged to Allah.

She possessed many things other women did not. Talent,

beauty, grace. A life of honor, of purpose and privilege, because of that. But these things never threatened the women she knew or solicited envy. What they had she would never know. A husband, children, families. And some of them, she knew, had love. The kind of love nobody talked about, tender and kind and shared only between a man and woman. The kind she knew Allah dispensed at will like a secret only the privileged few could be trusted to hear. She put a certain kind of love into the rugs, but it was not the kind she longed to know. She could hug the crossbars and bury her head into the wood, but it would never touch her in the way she wanted, nor comfort her in the way she needed.

She had sat alone many times in the hut and spilled her tears into the knots. Whatever she had inside her fell away to the rugs. Love, compassion, laughter, life. Allah through her. She let it go through her fingers, letting her hands become a vessel for Allah's work. She had spent a lifetime of giving and believed in its honor.

IV

They entered Mavisu by way of the cemetery, passing ancient sarcophagi, Lycian tombs, and a series of stone pediments carved with faces whose mouths had been stuffed with grass. Child's play, Hennessey thought, watching the shadows of tombs slice the earth like spears.

It was a country of patchy farmland and pasture, a series of chalk ridges and narrow canyons flanked by pine and beech, cedar and oak. Where the forest stopped, the slopes were rocky and barren and dovetailed like hands. They looked red in the light and reminded him of the outcrops over Jerusalem. There was nothing hospitable about the fallow slopes, parched and cracked like the skin of its people. He could see it already in the contrasts, the determination to thrive here despite the elements. Green against brown. Wild roses pushing their way through the rocks. Clumps of poppies poked out of snowfields, and everywhere the dusty leaves of olive trees glittered like sequins across the land.

In the course of his travels, Hennessey had come to believe that those who inhabited desolate places possessed a certain vitality not found in lusher climates. Mountain people had always been the most spiritual in every culture. Pisidia was not an easy place to inhabit. Life was both given and taken here. Earthquakes, fires, famine, and drought plagued the region and reminded its habitants that nothing was ever safe, nothing permanent. It was precisely why its people defended their traditions so fiercely. Not even a natural disaster could alter their will, and it was this steadfastness of character that Hennessey admired most about the Turks.

He could see the Goddess everywhere now, in the curve of the mountains, the slope of the hills. There was a site ahead of him now, looming in the foreground. He could make out the fallen columns and imagined them tumbling down the hill during earthquakes. He heard the thunderous boom of greatness crumbling, the shouts of villagers running for their lives, and the cries of those who perished.

Hennessey could see a narrow switchback running up the mountain toward a small stone structure, a hut of sorts. Goats grazing in the grasses. He did not recognize the structure as Hellenistic or Roman. Something more modern yet primitive in its simplicity. Two windows and a door, the glint of sunlight on the corrugated tin roof that lay crinkled like the folds of an accordion.

They drove through the village gate, a stone archway connecting an old aqueduct to a fountain, where a group of barefoot girls worked in pairs filling wooden buckets with water. Their dresses bright, darkened with spills. Giggles in the air. The girls waved to the truck and Adam honked playfully, luring a group of boys on bicycles closer to the bumper for a tow through the village.

It was a kaleidoscope of color. Muted pastels on wind-scrubbed stucco. The minaret and mosque, stark white in the light. The houses were modest yet neat, each with a garden of poppy and wild rose seen only through the courtyard gates. Women in headscarves stood behind them, gripping the bars as they stole a quick glimpse of the truck. Most of the villagers had already clamored out of their houses and sat crouched on their heels in the shadows of doorways, on rooftops. A group of men, sitting with crossed legs, crossed arms, hugging their elbows, had gathered on a pine log running the length of the teahouse. They moved only their fingers around prayer beads. Their eyes like black stones. Even in the shadow against the slow movement of the truck, Hennessey could see the history in their faces. The cross of cultures. The sloping foreheads, lined with stories. The round, dark eyes of the Orient, the storm-colored eyes of the north and west. He could feel them watching, shifting their eyes to the right as the truck passed.

They turned down a gravel path and drove beyond Ali's orchard, where a flock of ravens scattered from the trees. They stopped on the side of the road to wash their faces from a stone pipe jutting from the earth. The water was cool and ran muddy from their hands, and they took turns until it was clear and they were clean again. Adam walked to the edge of the road and stood combing his hair with a small metal pick he had taken from his back pocket. He pointed below him to the eastern slope of the village, where a farmhouse filled a shallow depression of wheat.

That's where you'll stay.

That's the postmaster's house?

Adam nodded.

You'll have to walk from here. The truck will never make it back up the hill.

You going to be okay?

Hennessey looked at the doctor's ear.

I'll be fine.

Nice job, he said, staring at the stitches that stuck out like whiskers from the doctor's earlobe, the wound red and raw.

They got you good, didn't they?

I can still hear. That's all that matters.

Hennessey nodded. The doctor had spoken little since the men had left. He seemed intensely focused, exhausted from lack of sleep.

Take care of yourself.

You too, the doctor said.

Hennessey grabbed his duffel bag and a small typewriter from the truck, then closed the door. Adam caught him reaching for his wallet and held up his hand.

Don't. You must understand. Good Turks try to do one good thing for another person each day. It makes us happy.

Hennessey offered his hand and a cigarette.

Will I see you again?

Adam nodded.

It's a small village, he said, climbing into the truck. The door closed with a sudden boom. The finality of their parting disturbed him, and he felt obliged to offer something, even words, to the doctor to show how much he appreciated his hospitality. The window was open.

I hope your patient heals quickly.

Adam nodded.

With Allah's will, he said. With Allah's will.

He started the engine again and rolled forward, disappearing, only the glow of his taillights in the thick blue mist blowing down from the mountain.

Adam stood in the courtyard of the old Ottoman house and watched Nurdane through the window. She lay on her side and stroked the old sheepdog that lay on the floor in front of her, the flicker of a candle on her face. Her profile had changed in recent years. Her face was longer, more angular. She was no longer the *yar kizi*, a village girl. She possessed the grace of a woman and a vulnerability that made her beautiful.

He felt more comfortable examining her from a distance and wished it had always been this way. It was easier to diagnose her progress in the dark without making her feel awkward. Darkness allowed his face to reveal the losses. The musculoskeletal problems, her swollen elbows, signs of bursitis, tendinitis, the curve of her spine, her foot and toe deformities, the carpal tunnel burrowing into her wrists, the premature degenerative osteoarthritis from the chronic strain on her joints for overcompensating with her upper extremities. Her complaints of morning headaches and confusion, shallow breathing, restless sleep, nightmares. Hers were the textbook symptoms of postpolio syndrome.

She had been sick the last time with a wet cough, and he was relieved to hear her singing along to the soft strain of Hamiyet Yuceses playing on the radio. My black-eyed love, she sang, asking her lover to save her. The song had always chilled him. It was the story of a woman who cries to be helped by her lover, but he never comes because he can't hear her. *My black-eyed love pays my cries no heed.*

Nurdane's voice was softer, more subtle than the famed nightclub singer. There was a transparency about it, as if light itself could vibrate the cords in her throat. An angel, he thought. It was her nature to inspire this kind of wonder, the beauty tied up inside, reserved only for her rugs.

He had come to love the knots not for aesthetic reasons. Sure, he could appreciate them. He knew her craftsmanship was unparalleled and not a single girl from the northwest coast to the southern villages had ever come close to creating the kind of rugs Nurdane produced. But it wasn't the beauty or even the feeling he got when he looked at them or walked barefoot over the lush merino pile. He loved the rugs for the way they made Nurdane feel. The quiet pride he glimpsed on her face whenever she finished one. The strength and will and sense of purpose they imbued within her. He loved the rugs mostly for their healing capacity. The weaving helped Nurdane in ways he could never do as her doctor. He could remember every rug and how it had changed her, making her wiser, stronger, braver, but he could not remember the moment when he first loved her.

She was his first patient, his first case during medical school. He was twenty, living in London. His mother had sent him the nearly illiterate letter from Ali, pleading for help for a disease he had never known. It had been seventeen years and yet the words still haunted him, night after night. Her father's terror that his daughter would be crippled and alone. Could he save her life?

He rocked back and forth on his heels, watching her. She was not wearing her headscarf and her dark hair fell thick and glossy over her shoulders like raven's wings. She had pushed the sleeves up her arms, where little hills of muscles were bronzed by the sun. From what he could see from the distance, her upper-body strength had not changed. Her shoulders were broad for a woman, from years carrying the rugs across her back, from dragging her own body weight across the ground like she was doing now, trying to get to a glass of water sitting on a small table in the middle of the room.

Attila got up, stretched, then crossed to the window and sat facing Adam. But he was not prepared to go in yet, to see Nurdane's hands and the damage that had been done. She would probably never tell him about the pickers. Why would she? They had never been friends. Her trust in him was nothing more than professional. He had learned to control his love. Keep things platonic. She was only his patient. She owed him nothing.

Adam heard the crush of gravel and looked up to see the cherry ember of a cigarette glowing in the dark. Ali stood in the half-light of a small lantern hanging from the porch. He tossed a pot of potato skins into the garden. Then he whistled and Attila trotted through the door. The potato skins of no interest. He turned, sniffing the air, then stepped lightly over the broken loom until he came upon the walnut tree and barked. Adam leaped out at once and waved to Ali, startling him so much, the old man dropped his pot on the ground.

Iyi aksamlar, Ali.

Ali cupped his fingers and held them over his eyes, trying to ward off the glare from the lantern. Adam stepped closer, facing him, Ali frozen, repeating to himself over and over, *Allah, tamam. Tamam . . .* He stood at attention with his hands on his hips, chin up, shoulders back.

Adam smiled and Ali nodded slowly as the doctor approached

him. He stepped into the light, standing still, long enough for the old man to get a good look. Adam lowered his hand for the dog to sniff. The two men stood staring, each afraid to look away, as if there had been too much time since their last meeting. Ali's forehead glistened with sweat, and Adam wiped it for him with the back of his wrist. Then, as if he had been silently negotiating, Ali lunged forward and took Adam's face in his own, tilting it toward the light, searching his eyes the way a father would his son's.

Thank Allah! he whispered. His voice cracked and he ran his finger over his bottom lip to rub out the tremble. Adam smiled.

Sorry I'm late. I would have been here last week.

Ali smiled, then kissed Adam's forehead, pulling him into his arms. Adam could feel him shaking, and he moved his arms around the bony shoulders and squeezed hard. He could feel the man's tears soaking through his collar. His voice muffled by the cloth.

I was so worried.

Why?

I thought you changed your mind.

Adam gently pushed him away and looked into his eyes.

I promised you, Ali. I would come back for her.

Hennessey fell into the arms of darkness and woke to the ritual of hospitable rites, the destiny of every traveler in Turkey. He lay on a low bed built of walnut and watched the postman's oldest son, Muammer, polish his boots. The boy was no more than seven years old and yet he worked with the fervor of a businessman, eyebrows furrowed in concentration as he spit and shined the leather.

You're a hard worker, Hennessey said in Turkish.

The boy giggled, scratching the buzz of black hair on his head, trying to understand the man's strange accent.

My father taught me.

He's a smart man. Think he'll let me hire you to dig?

The boy stopped shining the shoes and looked up. His soft brown eyes were filled with concern.

Who died? he asked.

Hennessey laughed.

Nobody.

The boy drummed his thumb under his chin, thinking.

We dig only graves here, he said.

Hennessey sat up and swung his legs over the edge of the bed.

Nobody has died.

The boy swatted the boots with the cloth.

They will. They always do, he said, then set the boots beside the bed and stood.

You'll need a guide.

A guide?

To show you the ruins.

Oh, yes. Of course. I'd like that very much.

Then hire me for that.

How much do you charge?

Gum?

What?

Bubble gum.

I'll see what I can do, said Hennessey.

The boy walked over to the bed and looked straight into Hennessey's eyes.

It's a deal, mister.

Muammer shook the man's hand and offered a one-toothed grin, looking over his shoulder to the moth-eaten lace hanging from the door.

He's awake, he announced with a singsong voice.

Within seconds, a short, squat woman with thick ankles delivered a tray of tomatoes and cucumbers, two hard-boiled eggs, and flaps of bread that reminded Hennessey of wet parchment. Her skirt was covered with flour handprints and several generations of patches, each a different material sewn neatly over the last, her poverty worn with pride. She scurried quickly out of the room, returning with a jar of olive oil, pressed fresh that morning.

Avison, she said, and set the olive oil on the tray.

Thank you, Hennessey said to the woman, but before he could see her, she had already exited, leaving him alone with her son.

Please. Eat with me.

Hennessey sat down and crossed his legs. The boy shook his head.

After you're done.

It was the Turkish way to serve the guest before oneself. Hennessey was too hungry to argue, and so he tore a piece of bread and wrapped the egg in it like a sandwich. He bit down so hard, the hard-boiled yolk shot across the dusty floor. The boy scooped it up and let it roll around the palm of his hand.

See? Somebody *will* die, he said. You lost the yolk. The life.

Hennessey chewed slowly, pouring olive oil onto the tray, dipping the ends of the bread into it.

Know any jokes, kid?

The boy looked out the window, watched a stork fly over the fields.

Ataturk dancing as a dervish.

Hennessey stopped chewing.

That's the best you can do? No donkey tales? No great *hoca* jokes?

The boy seemed preoccupied, anxious even.

My father says you're a teacher.

Hennessey nodded.

I was. Before I came here.

Then you should know better jokes than me.

True, Hennessey said, biting into a tomato. The juice trickled down his chin, and he caught it on his tongue. The boy watched him impatiently, thrust his hands in his pockets.

You eat too slow for a hungry man.

I'm enjoying my meal.

There's other things to do here than eat.

Do you mind?

The boy lowered his head and slid down the wall until he was seated cross-legged on the floor. He stared pleadingly at the strange man with the golden hair and ran his fingers over his type-writer.

Did you write to my father on this?

Yes. See the coffee stains? The keys are sticky.

The boy punched them with his two index fingers.

I want to be a writer.

A poet?

The boy shrugged.

Or a movie star.

You've been to the movies?

Once with my dad. Can you hurry? I want to show you the hill.

Hennessey sighed, took one last bite of cucumber, then wiped his face with his sleeve. The boy was not going to leave him alone.

Where's your father?

Delivering the mail. He's the postman. Remember?

The boy cocked his head.

You're not very clever for a teacher.

Professor, Hennessey corrected him. The boy's eyes grew large. Hennessey cracked a grin. Then he pushed himself off the floor and lifted the tray.

Leave it, the boy said. It's my mother's work.

Wouldn't it be nice to help her?

Why?

The boy looked utterly confused and scratched his thin stomach with his hands. His ribs were sticking out through his shirt.

My mother never asks for help.

I know, Hennessey muttered in English. The boy stood in the funnel of light coming through the window.

What did you say?

Nothing. I'm thinking.

Hennessey debated taking the tray to the postman's wife and carried it as far as the door, then decided not to offend her and set it in the doorway, sliding it forward with his foot. He wanted to help, to show his appreciation, but he also knew it was the role of a Muslim wife to serve the man out of duty and obligation. Had the Prophet ever cleared a plate in his life? He couldn't remember. He wondered if anyone had ever served the postman's wife other than the village midwife who had helped to birth her four sons. Hennessey looked through the lace at the back of the hunched figure, punching a wad of flour dough with her fists. If only she knew her history, how different her life was from that of the women who had come before her.

This way. Out the back door.

The boy tugged at Hennessey's hand.

I'm coming. I'm coming, he said, then moved quickly to the bed and grabbed his shoes, pulled a white T-shirt over his head, and picked up his shirt from a small wooden stool that looked too small to sit on.

What's your hurry?

It's a surprise.

I don't like surprises.

You'll like this one.

Hennessey followed Muammer through a path of wild wheat, trampled, it seemed, from the play of goats. The path steepened, forking to the left, and followed a narrow switchback over the hill to a grove of olive trees near the hut. The ground was covered in fallen columns, mediotopes, and pediments, some whole, some split. Hennessey stepped around the fragments, in awe, piecing together the puzzle of the once-great city that had occupied the hill. He could see the contours in the stones, the carvings of horses and soldiers, women carrying baskets, and the heads of mythic figures, those with wings and snakes for hair.

The library was over there, said the boy, pointing to the stump of a pillar overgrown with weeds and dry grasses, like a stone thumb jutting out of the earth.

They shopped here, in the agora, he continued, climbing over a pile of rocks, standing with his feet spread, arms outstretched, catching the cool air blowing down from the mountain, owning the view.

Think Allah can see as much as me?

Hennessey flashed a smile.

Never know. You're pretty high up here.

On a clear day we can see the sea, the boy said, pointing south, tracing the crevice of the canyon with his finger in the air.

Have you seen the sea?

In a book once.

Muammer caught a lizard with his eye and scrambled down the rocks, chasing it until it darted into a small crack in a tomb. He poked at the hole a few times, then gave up.

They're odd, he said.

Who?

The lizards. They like to hide with the dead. They feel safer there.

Hennessey walked over to the ancient tomb and crouched down until the hole was eye level. He leaned forward, trying to see inside, past a spiderweb, beyond the darkness. He ran his fingers along the gritty marble, traced the Arabic letters carved along the sides.

There's nothing left, the boy said, kicking the tomb.

Hennessey jumped back.

You sure?

Why? You think there's treasures?

The boy laughed.

We've taken everything into our homes.

Hennessey looked up, shielding his eyes from the hot morning sun.

Bones too?

The boy shook his head.

What would we do with bones?

He giggled and ran farther up the hill, then peered into the window of the weaver's hut. He glanced quickly over his shoulder and beckoned Hennessey to come see.

Hurry, teacher.

Hennessey pushed himself away from the tomb and followed what remained of the goat path. He stood on the crest of the hill, looking up at the hut, more than the makeshift dwelling he imagined. It was a rough-hewn stone building whose frame had been carefully constructed of raw timber, pine, and beech. The door itself was patched in squares of tin, some rusted, some new. An evil eye hung over the door with a braid of camel hair. Muammer crept up to the door slowly, then reached around his belt to a leather sheath and pulled out a small knife.

What are you doing?

Being your guide.

I didn't hire a thief, Hennessey said.

We're not stealing anything. Only a quick look.

The boy jimmied the lock with the knife. The door popped open, swinging forward, creaking on its rusty hinges. Light slipped through the opening and fell across the loom, where the dust glittered, drifting slowly toward the rug.

Hennessey gently pushed the boy aside and stepped inside. It was damp and smelled of wool and straw. Balls of yarn covered the floor, and from the raw pine beams of the ceiling hung a series of pages, each with a blue handprint imprinted over Arabic text. There had to be at least a dozen pages, the edges jagged, as if they had been torn from a book.

Hennessey slowly traced the hand, a right hand, then spread his fingers over it, careful not to wrinkle the paper. The hand was much smaller than his own, more narrow, with long, thin fingers. A woman's hand.

He felt a chill and stepped back. The pages rippled in the breeze. He turned his head to the boy, now silent at the loom, mesmerized by the rug. He ran his fingers back and forth over the knots, mumbling a prayer of thanksgiving and praise. He turned to Hennessey.

Have you ever seen anything as beautiful?

Hennessey shook his head, remembering the rugs from Antalya. He wondered what value the merchant would have given it. He stepped closer to the rug, taking in the thousands of knots tied on the loom. The bright scarlet field. The blue arches. The Z-shaped border. Symbols for water. He approached the rug like the invisible altar it alluded to and offered his hand. Then he touched the knots. The wool was soft under his fingers and shone like silk in the light. Hennessey closed his eyes again and drew in a breath. When he opened them, he was overcome by an overwhelming feeling of longing and sorrow, dread, too, as if the rug, hanging there, suspended between the ground and the heavens, had burdened him with its secret. He was reminded of the rug tied with the red ribbon in Kaleici, and he knew now what the merchant had meant when he said that a weaver leaves a part of herself in every knot.

Is she sad?

Who?

Hennessey looked down at the postman's son. The boy was craning his neck, searching the tall man's eyes.

The weaver.

The boy thought about this and nodded.

Her mother died when she was little.

When?

At birth. She never knew her, the boy said, biting his lip, his mind wandering. Wouldn't it be hard to live without knowing your mother?

Hennessey shook his head, the world's greatest misfortune, he thought.

Do you know her?

She's dead, mister.

The weaver. Do you know the weaver?

The boy nodded.

Nurdane's my cousin.

Hennessey eyed him curiously.

Nurdane?

Yes.

Nurdane's a weaver?

Yes, mister. Are you listening?

The boy looked over his shoulder, scowling at Hennessey.

Yes, he said, roving over the handprints. I thought . . .

What?

Nurdane is the river.

They named her after it. Piece of light, you know. That's what Nurdane means.

Yes.

You know?

The doctor had mentioned it. We stopped by the river on the way up. *Noordanna,* Hennessey repeated to himself, rolling the double *o* and *r* with his tongue.

Arabic, he said.

Yes. We were nomads.

Hennessey stepped closer to the loom, ran his hands along the crossbeams, plucked the warp strings with the ring finger of his right hand as if he were a child again, unskilled at the violin.

If she's your cousin, why did you have to break in to see her rug? Couldn't you ask?

Nobody sees the rug before it's finished.

Why?

The boy rolled his eyes and sighed.

It's bad luck, he said.

For who?

The bride.

Why?

It hurts her chance of having a happy life. Having a baby. A boy.

What if she has a girl?

The boy scratched his head and shrugged. The thought fazed him, as if he had never thought about it before.

A girl?

Hennessey nodded, biting back the kind of chuckle that made his stomach churn.

The bride could have a girl.

It happens, the boy said, considering. But it's not what's supposed to happen.

He lowered himself immediately to his right knee and faced the rug. Hennessey looked around the hut and stopped on a curious bundle of cloth on the floor. Beaded tassels were sewn on the edges. He recognized it as a headscarf. He waited until he was sure the boy turned his full attention to the rug, then walked over to the bundle and pulled back the cloth to reveal a copy of the Koran. The pages were watermarked and the spine was covered in layers of tape. Indigo stains of fingerprints everywhere. He ran his fingers over the holy book, then covered it quickly with the cloth.

We should go now, he said to the boy, but Muammer was too rapt in the rug to listen.

I want to stay.

Now, said Hennessey. It's not right.

He yanked the boy up from the loom and pulled him through the door.

You forgot to lock it.

Shhh.

He squeezed the boy's hand, silencing him, keeping him close to his side until they reached the olive trees that grew in the middle of the hill. Hennessey paused, seeing a shadow move across the grass. He lifted his eyes, following the shadow to its source, a young woman bearing her weight on crutches. She stared, motionless, as if she were a part of the tree's shadow but not her own, the elongated shape of the crutches in the grass inverted, like two minarets flipped upside down, balancing her. A pale yellow scarf covered her dark hair, the loose strands blowing across her neck. Hennessey straightened when she moved into the light. Her blue eyes shone like bits of broken seaglass, so still, fixed on his face.

You didn't need to lock it, she said. I'm going in.

Hennessey looked over at Muammer.

I'm sorry, he mumbled, burying his face with his hands.

Too late, she said. You know better, Muammer.

Nurdane moved awkwardly out of the trees, through the grass. Hennessey noticed her bare feet, snared by ugliness, sharp as talons, scraping the earth in their struggle to keep her balanced. She drew in a breath, stopping short of Muammer.

Go home.

Muammer backstepped, cowering like a dog.

I saw it for only a moment.

Long enough, wasn't it?

Don't tell. You won't tell, will you?

She lifted her eyes to meet his.

Who's to tell? Allah already knows, she said, moving past him.

Nurdane got as far as Hennessey's feet, when a breeze lifted her headscarf. The yellow cloth floated through the air and landed on Hennessey's boot. Nurdane knelt down to pick it up like Hennessey did, his shoulder brushing the braces beneath her skirt. She drew in a breath and held herself there, smelling him. His oils sweet. His shirt clinging to his arms and back. She felt his eyes on her and quickly threw her gaze at the ground to keep them from meeting. She did not need to look at his face to remember it. The stubble across his chin. His square jaw and hook nose, geometric shapes she would weave into her dreams. She took the scarf and stood. Hennessey stayed on the ground and looked up.

I didn't mean to scare you. I was trying to help.

Thank you, she said.

I'm a bit clumsy.

She smiled but quickly covered her mouth with the scarf. Her hair, glossy black waves in the wind, until she quickly retied the scarf and tucked her hair into the folds.

You didn't scare me, she said, turning slowly on her crutches to make her way up the hill.

Hennessey took the boy's hand and ushered him quickly down the path. They stopped only when they had crossed the boundary of the postman's farm. The boy was panting, trying to catch his breath, and fell exhausted onto a tree stump.

You're lucky you didn't touch her, mister.

Why?

You're a stranger. She doesn't know you.

Hennessey searched the boy's eyes, confused.

If you touch her, you'll break her spell.

Hennessey leaned back in the grass and stared up at the hut, catching the weaver watch him through the window as if she had been listening.

She turned her back slowly and sat in front of the loom. The late morning sun came in through the window and left shadows over her face. She extended her left hand to the last row of knots and dragged it slowly through the mihrab, mumbling prayers. They flooded her but meant nothing. She used words only to sever the silence, her heart racing as she pressed into the pile. When she reached the bottom of the loom, she started over with her right hand, holding her fingers an inch above the knots, and traced the field again.

She sat on the bench when she finished, and using the tips of her crutches, dragged the bundle of cloth toward her, then took the Koran in her lap. She opened the book and laid her right hand on the page, then bowed her head and prayed to Allah to help her finish the rug.

A gentle wind pushed through the hut. The pages fluttered and brought her out of her concentration. When she looked up to focus, she saw Hennessey's face in the rug as if she were remembering a dream. Then she leaned forward, pressing her nose against the wool, and smelled him in the knots as if he had always been there.

Hennessey spread the maps on the floor, studying them by candlelight, trying to figure a way around the hut. The maps were old, the edges torn, the paper thin and flaking like dry skin. He traced the grid, the roads leading to the agora and library, the path to the gymnasium. A dotted line curved behind the citadel and switched back to the hill where the weaver's hut had been built. Small triangles marked the remaining sarcophagi. X's over those believed to be the tombs of statesmen, religious leaders, citizens of status. Here and there, a small X over a surviving tree.

The princess of Pontus, Loadice III, the seventieth great-granddaughter to the Persian king of Anshan, spent her youth here in the third century, when Hellenistic kings ruled the land. Scholars had debated for centuries if she had been returned to Pisidia upon her death. Hennessey doubted it, challenged more by the deaths of the Goddess and her culture. If he were to find evidence

of her anywhere, it would be there, on the hill, somewhere beneath
the weaver's hut. It would take years to excavate the hill, pending
the success of the initial surface scraping. He had only suspicions,
strong intuitions about where the burial chambers were and what
they contained.

He looked over the maps one more time, turned them around,
stared at them from different angles, snapped a half-dozen pen-
cils, thinking. The problem was not taking down Nurdane's hut.
The stones had been cut neatly. He could disassemble the structure and rebuild it in its entirety, but he did not want to touch the
loom. He had been on many digs throughout the world and had
helped to tear down buildings and trees that obstructed an excavation. It was part of the process. It was part of reclaiming the
past, his prerogative as a physical anthropologist. He was even
entitled to it, by law, by the Turkish Ministry of Culture. Yet despite his professional privilege, Hennessey believed he was putting
the weaver at great risk by moving the one place that seemed to
keep her safe.

He folded the maps and sat up to smoke a cigarette. He
hadn't eaten since breakfast and his head throbbed. He got up
and wandered into the parlor, where the postman and his wife
sat on the stone floor, drinking tea. The woman stood immediately seeing Hennessey, then disappeared into another room, returning only to give him a clean glass and sugar cubes before
leaving again. Hennessey stared after her, helpless, but the postman had already filled the glass with tea and beckoned Hennessey to join him.

Sit, he said.

But your wife . . .

Can wait. Sit down.

Hennessey nodded and sat on the floor. The postman eyed him
curiously.

You're a funny man. So nervous.

I have a lot on my mind.

But you're in Turkey. Your home is far from here. What can be

so heavy to make you pace like a chicken? Is your bed too hard?
Are you not sleeping?

I'm sleeping. The bed's very comfortable.

Muammer said you talk in your sleep.

Hennessey took the tea and dropped the sugar cube into the liquid, watching the crystals dissolve.

Your son's a very curious boy. He asks a lot of questions.

Very good, said the postman. Skepticism is a virtue. He's a quick learner. I've taught him everything he knows.

He seems to know a lot about my work.

I tried to explain what you're doing as best as I could. We've never met a professor. Never met an anthropologist either. It's very new to us. Your love of . . . antiquities. We're used to them. They are not so unique to us. My wife took one of the fallen columns and turned it into a planter. For garlic.

Hennessey's eyes went wide.

Garlic?

Sure. Tomatoes too. The stones stay warm after the sun goes down. We've found uses for that old stuff. The muhtar has one of the original theater chairs, stone, of course, in his house. He reads the Koran from it. Says it inspires him with the Prophet's word.

The postman threw his eyes at the ceiling, where layers of blue paint were peeling. He sighed, weary.

I wonder what Rita would say about this.

Rita?

Hayworth.

Rita Hayworth?

I named my truck after her. Gilda. You know she's one of *us* now, he said proudly. Married Ali Kahn.

They're divorced.

The man sat up, stunned.

They got divorced in January, Hennessey said.

No.

It's true. I read it in *Time* magazine. Adam showed me in the hospital.

The postman crossed his arms, brushing off his elbows as if the words soiled his sleeves.

Is nothing sacred to you Americans?

Hennessey shrugged.

Yes. Some things. Baseball.

The postman clicked his tongue in disapproval.

At least *I* still see Rita once a month.

You?

Rita is my ritual. I see her in the outdoor theater in Antalya. Makes the trip to the post office a little more exciting.

He lowered his voice to a whisper as his wife entered.

Keeps my mind full on the way home, he said, winking.

His wife delivered a tray of dried chickpeas and fresh cherries. She set the food on the floor and left her husband and his guest alone to eat in the silence, the only sound the ting of cherry pits hitting a tin plate. When they finished, the postman reclined onto his elbows, stretched out his legs, and closed his eyes to listen to the cicadas coming through the window.

They are the fourth best sound, he said.

Oh, yeah?

Hennessey rolled the stem of a cherry around his tongue. What about the other three?

The postman opened his eyes.

The sound of money.

Yes. Of course.

The sound of water.

And the fourth?

The postman closed his eyes again and smiled.

The sound of a woman's voice.

Hennessey let out a chuckle. The postman looked over at him, agitated.

What's so funny?

When do you ever listen to a woman's voice?

All the time, he protested.

I've been here two days and I haven't heard your wife speak once.

The postman nodded and leaned closer, lowering his voice.

Between the sheets, my friend. Between the sheets.

Hennessey smiled faintly; he did not want to get into it with the postman, but this was exactly what he had come to challenge. The postman's feelings no different from the other men in the village or from those he had met over the years in the cities. From what Hennessey discerned in the conversations he had between the postman and his son, women were feared as much as they were revered. They were ostracized as much as idolized, embraced as much as shunned. Their culture was one of the great contradictions, an irony, really, he thought. *Anatolia.* Full of women. Islam, the submission of them to Allah. The veil, in fact, was not for the woman's sake, but for the man's, to keep him from seeing her. The face of a woman could lure men from their true intentions, their devotion to Allah.

From what Hennessey had observed, even in Mavisu, the men did everything in their power to prevent themselves from being enamored with the opposite sex. Women walked behind the men in the streets or kept hidden behind the walls of their homes. They whispered prayers behind a curtain in the mosque because their voices distracted the men. A friend had whispered this to him in the Blue Mosque in Istanbul. *Women can control themselves. Men cannot.* The postman's belief that a woman's voice was the most beautiful sound in the world gave Hennessey hope. He sat up and lit a cigarette, then handed it to the postman.

Tell me about the weaver's spell.

The postman rolled over on his side and took the cigarette between his lips. He filled his lungs with the sweet tobacco, exhaling tiny rings of smoke.

The polio was more of a curse.

How old was she?

Five. She was paralyzed.

He followed the trail of smoke with his eyes and offered Hennessey another cigarette. But Hennessey refused, too engrossed in the girl's story.

It's a miracle she can walk with the braces.

Thanks to the doctor, the postman said.

Adam saved her life?

Yes. Saved Ali's too. I don't know who was more devastated when they learned about the disease. Nurdane was too young to understand what had happened. What she had lost. Ali spent six months writing letters. I took them to Antalya and waited eagerly for a response. We waited and prayed. But there was nothing. No letters for almost a year.

She couldn't move for a year?

The postman nodded.

That's when Ali made her the loom. To give her something to do in the stillness. We're nomads, you know. At least we were. It's our nature to move.

Hennessey met his eyes.

Ali taught her to weave?

His mother was one of the best. His wife too.

Where is she?

Dead. Died when Nurdane was born.

The postman cracked open a walnut and let the shells fall to the floor.

Ali was a broken man then. Still is in many ways. Everything he lost, is losing still.

What?

Things. You know. The way things *should* be.

No. How?

Stable. The way he expected. The way we all do. He's never understood why it happened. None of us do. But that's life. These things happen. We would be lost without losing. Makes us face things. You know?

Hennessey nodded.

Yes, he said, and narrowed his eyes. Tell me about her other spell. The rugs.

Ah, the postman said, tracing the remaining smoke ring with his finger.

Nurdane's gift, this weaving of hers. This art. It's very special. Very rare. A gift from Allah, really. But it is conditional. As is everything. Our lives. We all owe somebody something.

Hennessey cocked his head, trying to understand.

Debts you mean?

Obligations. Duties. We take vows to prove our faith.

Like a priest, Hennessey suggested.

Yes. Or a prophet.

It's funny.

What?

Proving faith.

The postman chuckled sadly, agreeing, then dragged his thumbnail across the floorboard.

I guess her vow is like a priest's, Hennessey said.

Who? Nurdane?

The postman drew in a breath, as if his words were the result of a great feat, belief or blind faith, Hennessey thought.

As long as she keeps her hands pure, Allah will make the rugs through her.

She can't touch a stranger?

She must stay a virgin, the postman said.

Hennessey studied the man's face in the light. He wanted honest answers.

Do you believe it?

For her sake, the postman said, lifting his eyes. We all want to believe in the virgin's knots.

She moved awkwardly toward the doctor, pausing every now and then to loosen the new braces he had given her. They were cold and tight around her legs, heavier than the others. Her movements more sluggish and sloppy now, but she was determined to keep her balance, to prove she had not lost any strength since Adam had seen her last.

He stood a few feet in front of her and continued to step backward the closer she got, like a parent teaching its infant to walk, to keep reaching, stretching farther and farther. He searched her face, waiting for her eyes to meet his, but they were far from him, lost somewhere between the slats in the floor and the abstractions in the prayer rug.

She was warm, her dark hair matted and wet beneath her headscarf. She had been walking for Adam since dinner, once in the garden, and later inside to see how she handled the stairs. They were not as difficult as they appeared. She preferred climbing to walking because it masked her handicap and she could compensate for the swoop of her legs by pausing at each rise in the stairwell. But now, walking on a flat surface, in a straight line, frustrated her.

How do the braces feel?

Wrong, Nurdane said.

They take time to get used to.

I liked the old ones.

You liked the crutches, he reminded her. You must learn to walk without them.

He's right, Ali said. Those braces are better.

They're too tight.

They'll adjust in a few weeks, Adam said, rubbing his ear where the stitches had been.

Does hurt adjust? she asked, moving past him.

It can.

He wanted to help her, to reach out his hand and ease her frustration, but he knew she needed to figure it out for herself. It would take patience to adjust to the changes. All he could do was provide tools to manipulate the hurt, bend it, tuck it in, fasten it to something other than her own nerves, the impulses that sharpened her tongue with comments that seemed uncharacteristic.

She took a few more steps and stopped in front of Ali. He was kneeling on the ground, hammering finishing nails into a wooden bar on the wall.

Try to learn from the pain, Ali said. It is meant to help you.

Is that what Allah says?

It's suggested, he said, and straightened. He tapped the hammer one last time against the bar, pulling down on it to test its strength. The doctor had prescribed the bar for Nurdane's therapy. Here she would practice walking without the crutches until she could maneuver with the braces only.

It's ready, Ali said.

Nurdane sighed.

I'm tired.

Give it a try. Go on, Adam persisted.

I've been walking for an hour.

Move, Nurdane, Ali said. You've been still long enough.

She shrunk back from her father. His words lifted the hair on her arms.

You told me I would never walk again.

That is what we all thought, Ali said.

Adam interrupted.

Things change, Nurdane.

Why? Because you say? Or Allah?

She was looking at Adam when she spoke.

Adam's been studying.

What? she asked. What does he know that Allah doesn't?

Silence, save the ticking of the wall clock. Nurdane looked down at her hand, then lifted her eyes to meet Ali's. He turned to the doctor for encouragement. Adam cleared his throat.

Your disease *can* be cured.

Since when?

To a degree. There've been studies.

Studies?

Yes. In America. Research facilities. Centers for care and rehabilitation. There's even been talk of a vaccine.

Isn't it a little late? For a cure?

He nodded.

But not to get you walking without the braces. There are many survivors all over the world.

Nurdane shifted her eyes to him as if he had breached the pact between them, his words unsettling.

I don't understand.

She took a few more steps until she could reach the bar, extending her hand to touch it. Then she turned and looked over her shoulder, her hair spilling out of her headscarf.

You tell me I won't walk, then you tell me I will. I don't see Adam for months, I figure he's forgotten about me, given up. You tell me nothing about the doctor, and when I ask about him, you don't give me answers. Then he suddenly shows up and expects a miracle.

Nurdane!

He does. You both do. You want me to walk. But look at these legs? How can they ever walk?

They already do.

Nurdane kneeled, clutching the braces with her hands.

This is not walking. This? This is struggling each day. You give me new braces year after year, then this bar, hoping to see me walk. But what do you expect? You want the braces to fall away. So do I. But they won't. They can't.

You haven't tried.

I try every day, she said, her voice graven, resolute. I've tried every day since I was five. Every night before I go to sleep, I promise myself that in the morning, I will rise without the crutches. And every morning when I wake up, I try. I push myself up from the mattress and look at my legs and I tell them what I want them to do, but it's like the shepherd's son, Cyrus. My legs are deaf. They don't hear me.

How do you know?

I know my limits, *baba*.

Ali dropped the hammer on the floor.

Only Allah knows your limits.

He turned abruptly on his heel, then marched out of the room, leaving Nurdane with the doctor. Adam drummed his fingers nervously over his lips.

He only wants you to heal.

He wants too much. He wants a miracle.

Will you try?

What?

To walk without crutches or braces. For him?

She nodded.

I'll try, she said. To believe in miracles.

She turned from him and faced the wall, then, using the bar, moved hand over hand until she could slip outside to the veranda to be alone. She fell asleep watching the stars shift, wondering how many miracles it took to make them shine so brightly and if there were any left to spare.

Ali entered the mosque to pray. A few stray cats lay inside the doorway, sleeping. It was late. Oil lamps burned from the ceiling and cast shadow fingers along the walls. He could hear the murmur of a woman's voice behind the curtain at the back of the mosque. She stopped praying when Ali passed as if to honor his presence, then started again when he took his place up front and sang, kneeling.

Allahu akbar . . . praise be to Allah, Lord of the Creation, the Compassionate, the Merciful, King of Judgment Day! You alone we worship, and to you alone we pray for help. Guide us to the straight path. The path of those whom you have favored, not of those who have incurred your wrath, nor of those who have gone astray.

He repeated the chorus until his voice grew hoarse and his throat was sore. He sat still, eyes heavenward, lost in his thoughts. He wanted to tell Nurdane the truth. Tonight more than ever he wanted her to know everything about her hands. He could not bear to look at her like that, struggling. The pain on her face. She was trying so hard, trying as she had always done to get better, to walk, to return to that day when she could run, but she was too old. Her muscles had gone too long without use.

Seventeen years the virgin's knots had held tight, and the myth was now stronger than ever, so strong, he believed it himself. *When Allah takes something from you, he gives you something in return.* Half-truths. He hoped Nurdane would forgive him someday, accept the lie and understand. Ali did not consider himself a deceitful man, and like any man ensnarled in the web of his own affairs, he truly believed he had done right. He was simply doing what the Koran had instructed, what he believed was his right, to honor his daughter and defend her life. He wondered many times what the Prophet would have done had his wife died and left him with a crippled child, a girl. He read the Koran over and over, searching for advice, and finding no hadith to comfort him, he made up his own.

When Allah takes something from you, he gives you something in return.

He had worn the rugs thin at the mosque, his corner, on the left, still reserved for him even years after he had mourned his losses and his daughter's. Nurdane had no idea that because she would never walk, she would remain a virgin forever. Who would marry her? Who would trust her body to bring life into the world? Ali could find no man to marry his daughter. Half a woman, they would say, and move on.

He looked up at the dome, eyes squinting, trying to hide his wet eyes from Allah, but there was so much anger inside him. The constant vibration, the thumping in his head. The headaches. The sleepless nights. The worry that carved his face with lines and made his neck stiff, the kind of worry that could twist his tendons and nerves into rope. He promised himself it would be over by the end of the month, after the solstice.

He felt a sudden chill. The door opened and ushered in a blast of cold air. Holding an oil lamp, Adam walked over to Ali and sat down beside him. He reached out and put his hand on Ali's shoulder.

She'll be all right.

Ali turned to him. His lips trembled.

What if it's too late?

Adam shook his head.

It's not.

I want to tell her, Adam. I should have told her years ago.

How would you know?

I knew you loved her then. You've always loved her.

Adam locked eyes on the man's face.

What?

I was too stubborn to believe it was true.

Adam felt his stomach churn, and he pulled his hand slowly from the man's shoulder.

What more could I have done to show you?

Nothing.

Ali turned to him.

I'm sorry, Adam.

Adam rubbed his eyes, scratched his beard.

I told you I would come back as often as I could. Year after year. I promised.

Ali nodded.

I know this. My wife came to me in a dream and told me that you would come. That was before the polio. Nurdane was three. I didn't believe it because she was healthy. You know. Running. Jumping. Doing everything a child could do. I guess I forgot about it until the other night. I saw her again.

Your wife?

Yes.

But she's dead.

Not in my dreams.

Adam looked at him, surprised. Ali continued, lowering his voice. She told me I didn't need to worry. That Allah had a plan for Nurdane. But I didn't trust her. It was a dream, you know. It's hard to trust a dream.

You did what you had to do.

I always do. I lie.

Adam stiffened and lowered his gaze to meet Ali's, but Ali turned his head, watching the flicker of a candle flame along the walls.

I tried to play Allah.

Ali's voice broke and a tear slid down his dirty cheek. He looked so desperate. So frail, his sharp eyes suddenly gone soft, like an old man dying. He could barely make out the words.

What a fool. To think I was helping her.

He pounded the prayer rug with his fist.

Adam took his arm and squeezed him gently.

You were scared. Any father would have done the same.

Ali looked up.

Do you think she'll forgive me? he asked.

Of course.

Adam held on to Ali's elbow. He could feel the bones through his sweater.

I'd feel better if I could tell her.

What good would it do after all this time?

Ali sighed, I'd feel better. I can't sleep. I'm never hungry.

You can't tell her now. You can't afford it. There's no time.

Ali threw his eyes on the hole in the rug beneath him.

It's cruel, he said, the cost of truth.

Nurdane spent the morning pulling weeds from the garden. She remembered stories of her mother doing the same, burying her hands in the earth, unloading her thoughts. Her hand still hurt, but it was not why she hesitated. She was reluctant to work for the very reason that she could still weave despite her mistake. It was already hot, the flies buzzing by nine o'clock. The air was heavy and wet. She rested her chin on her rake and looked up, sensing a storm in the thick band of clouds gathering over the mountain. She had not slept well and felt anxious, tossing and turning with thoughts of the rug.

It had been nearly two weeks since she had touched the picker, but the knots still came as they always did, tight and packed against the warp. The injury had slowed her, yes, but it had done nothing to her workmanship. Touching the picker had been, it seemed, an inconsequential act. But as much as she wanted to be-

lieve that thought, she found herself suspended and waiting, bid-
ing her time like the lone crag watching lightning draw closer. She
expected a strike at any moment, the hand of Allah crashing down
on her for breaking her promise, but still, her act yielded nothing,
demanded nothing, and rather than thrill her with possibilities, she
felt terrified, trapped by her new freedom. She was afraid of what
may follow if she finished the rug without suffering for her mistake. And that truth was too unbearable now, too heavy in the
heat before noon.

A sputter and clacking brought her out of her concentration.
She looked up to find Mehmet driving toward the house in a Jeep.
The inner tubes of old tractor tires were strapped onto the roof
and skimmed the branches of a fig tree where he parked. He
hopped out of the car, grinning, his feet bare.

You ready?

For what?

Mehmet smiled.

Get a towel. We're going to the river.

Now?

You promised we'd swim.

She held up her hand, the bandage covered with dirt.

You can still put your toes in, right?

There was no arguing with him, and she knew nothing but a
natural disaster could cancel his plans.

It'll do you good. Everybody's making such a huge fuss about
your hand. These people really need to find something better to
do. They'll kill you, worrying. I mean it's only a cut. It will heal.
Everything heals.

She smiled, raised an eyebrow, and dropped her rake. He
helped her into the Jeep and drove in reverse, hammering his way
down the gravel until they reached the road to the village.

They wound through stone-walled streets where groups of boys
played marbles and scattered at the moan of Mehmet's horn. He
drove like a madman past the teahouse, the Jeep rattling as he cut
a corner to avoid hitting a flock of chickens. He stopped only to

let a procession of older men pass, their bony frames burdened by prayer rugs as they made their way to the mosque.

Mehmet pressed on the gas and drove through the village gate, past the cemetery where the road opened into a firebreak and distant snowfields. They passed a shepherd and his black-eared lambs, and on the mountain, groups of women had gathered to cut wild sage. Nurdane had not been this far out of the village in years, her heart light as they bounced along the road.

Mehmet looked at her from the corner of his eyes, the grin. It was nice to see her relaxed, happy. But there was something wrong, the headscarf so tight around her face, cutting off the slope of her cheeks. He loathed the scarves and had written countless poems on their futility. It was in his presence alone that his own mother removed hers, and then for only a few minutes. He could understand. She was old and slow to adapt to the new ways, a married woman when Ataturk had lifted the mandatory veils in 1926. But Nurdane was too young and too beautiful to cover herself. He turned to her and, without asking, pulled the scarf from her head, as he would have for Ayse.

That's better, he said, pressing on the gas, speeding until her black hair fluttered in the wind.

She said nothing, only eyed him as he stuffed the scarf between the seats.

It gets in the way.

She turned to him, watched his lips fold into a crooked smile.

Of what?

Seeing all of you.

Of me?

Women. Beautiful things should not be covered.

He focused on the road, driving around the splayed fringe of cypress that had fallen.

You find them useless, don't you?

He nodded. She continued to stare at him, curious.

Ayse finds them useless too, she said. She's found other ways to wear a headscarf.

Nurdane pulled out the scarf from the seat and tied it once around her neck, as she had seen Ayse do that night in the storehouse, letting the tassels blow in the air. She was enjoying herself, her eyes wide, beaming, testing him with his secret. He could tell she was trying hard to hold back the smile.

Ayse's good at that, she said.

What?

Finding ways around the way things seem to be.

He nodded once but did not look at her. It had been Mehmet with Ayse in the abandoned house. The poem was enough. She had no need to ask him about the incident. And he felt it now, the trust in her. He studied her profile, her face lifted, dignified by her silence, as if she were passing their secret to the sun.

No wonder he has your picture everywhere.

What?

They bounced over a network of roots and stumps, and he raised his voice so she could hear him over the racket of the engine.

The doctor has your picture in his office.

Adam?

He nodded.

I see him every now and then in the city. We have tea. Play backgammon. He's the one who taught me, but don't ever tell your father. He'd never forgive him.

I'm sure he would. He treats Adam like a son.

Mehmet laughed again.

I know. He's always asking about you, but I have to laugh because he probably sees you and Ali more than I do now that I'm studying.

She pulled back her shoulders and narrowed her eyes, curious.

He paints?

No. It's a photo.

A photo?

Right beside his calendar, in the middle of the wall.

She squinted, shielded her eyes with the back of her hand. Mehmet continued. He spoke proudly.

The one at the loom. Your back is toward him. Your face is slightly tilted, enough to see your eyes.

I don't remember.

It's striking. The way the light comes through the warp. Your fingers reaching into it. Adam's got a bit of an artist in him. Surprised me, you know, for a doctor.

Nurdane nodded. She could not remember when the photo was taken. In fact, she could not remember the doctor with a camera.

You sure it's me? He sees a lot of weavers.

Mehmet nodded.

Your braces were leaning against the loom.

Of course.

Her voice fell and Mehmet turned to her.

It's beautiful, Nurdane. He's very proud of it.

She lifted her eyes slowly to meet his, parting her lips, but did not smile. She had absolutely no recollection of the photo. Nobody watched her work.

I'm sure, she said.

What?

That he's proud of his work.

She shifted uncomfortably in the seat, eyes fixed on the passing hills, wondering about the pride in the poppies that ignited them.

They looked like coffins from the distance. The raw wood trunks filled the flatbed and slid toward the back of the truck as it heaved uphill past Muammer. He rode his bike behind it, weaving in and out of the fumes. His shirt was tied around his waist and his bony back glistened in the harsh afternoon light. The air was thick and oily with heat, blackened now with exhaust. But the truck thrilled the boy, and he followed it through the village to the lodge where it stopped. Ali and Adam jumped out and shoved logs beneath the tires to keep it from rolling down the hill. They motioned to the boy.

Give a hand.

Muammer dismounted and leaned his bike against the great walnut tree growing beside the lodge. A spindle lay cracked at the base of the tree, and wisps of wool covered the ground where the women had been carding. Muammer picked up the spindle and walked over to Ali.

Can you fix this?

Not now. We need to get these trunks into the lodge and painted. You good with a brush?

The boy shrugged and wiped his forehead with the back of his hand.

I shine shoes.

Can you paint?

I thought they were coffins.

Adam laughed. They're wedding chests.

Trousseau?

Adam nodded.

Whose?

Adam turned to Ali, reading the concern in his eyes.

A bride's.

All of them?

Muammer squinted, counting the trunks. There had to be about a dozen crammed into the flatbed, and he could see the intricate carvings in the wood. They reminded him of his cousin's wedding chest, his mother's too.

Ali cleared his throat, tried to change the subject.

They're a bit plain, don't you think?

Muammer pushed his bottom lip out, assessing.

Yeah. I guess.

They could use a little color.

Muammer looked at Ali like he was crazy.

Of course. No bride wants a coffin.

Ali looked over at Adam.

We have the paint. Between you, Adam, and myself, they could be done in a few hours.

Muammer shifted his eyes from one man to the other, reading the proposition.

How many?

Twelve. We'll be done before dinner.

How much you going to pay me?

Ali turned to Adam and smiled, amused by the boy's business acumen.

Did your father send you?

No, the boy snapped, offended. I followed you here.

Ali pursed his lips, crossed his arms.

You always business?

Are you?

He stared at the man, challenging him. He had watched him for years, collecting the bids for Nurdane's rugs, haggling with villagers over the price of cherries, bartering with the furniture makers over windfalls in his orchard. Ali was as much about business as was his father and the other men he knew in the village. He had learned good business was not about how much he gained but how little he had to compromise to get what he wanted. He refused to surrender.

I'm a good painter, he said.

I bet you are.

I have a lot of experience.

Ali turned to Adam.

Do fences count?

Adam smiled, glanced down at the boy. He got the joke and stood stiff, rubbing his hands over his shaven head.

So how much am I worth to you?

Adam cleared his throat and tossed Muammer the keys. The boy stared at him, then looked up at Ali. Ali eyed Adam suspiciously.

You know how to drive?

Muammer shook his head.

Yes. Of course.

What have you driven? Adam asked the boy.

A few tractors.

Any trucks?

My father's. Once.

Muammer straightened his back, giving himself another inch through the lie. Shoulders back, square. Eyes sharp.

If you help us, you can drive the truck, Adam offered.

Muammer nodded. Fair deal. He dropped the keys into his pocket and climbed into the flatbed. Then, pulling a small knife from the scabbard hidden by his shirt, he began to slash through the hemp tied around the trunks.

Adam turned to Ali and winked.

Acts as if he's untying the Gordion knot.

Ali nodded and took a cigarette from his pocket.

In a way he is.

Nurdane and Mehmet descended roller-coaster style into a thicket of juniper and pine and bounced along the stone blocks of an ancient road. It was hot and dry and smelled of burning brakes. Nurdane held tight to the bar as the Jeep rolled onto an old bridge that spanned the river where mercenaries and marauders had crossed before them. The waters ran swift and white, each current chasing the other past artesian springs where trout moved in the shadows.

It's strange.

Of course. Adam prefers Shakespeare over Rumi.

Mehmet turned to her, waiting for her to smile, but her brows were knitted, jaw clenched. She twisted the tassels of her headscarf around her left hand, not from boredom, but a certain tension he sensed since he had told her about the photos.

Nobody goes into the hut, Mehmet. They know better.

Mehmet considered and shifted into a higher gear as they picked up speed. He focused on the road, trying to remember exactly what he had seen above Adam's desk.

Maybe it wasn't the hut. It could have been any loom.

Nurdane turned to him, incredulous, sarcastic.

Where? The lodge?

Maybe. Now that I think of it.

But I never weave there.

Nurdane spread her fingers to catch the wind, remembering the young girl's face at the loom. Mehmet turned to her.

Maybe you forgot. I mean, how many rugs have you made in your life? Hundreds, right? It has to be hard to keep them separated. To *remember* them all.

Nurdane narrowed her eyes and locked onto his face.

I remember every one as if it were a child. I can tell you the bride who received it and when. How many knots it had. The pattern. The story I was telling in the rug. The rugs are like your poems, Mehmet. They stay fixed in the mind forever. You never forget.

He felt her eyes bore into him, begging for answers. He saw the photo. Remembered the window, the way the light bled through the weft on the loom. He knew the photo had been taken from her hut. There was no mistaking it.

How old was I in the photo?

Mehmet looked at her face. It had grown more angular over the years. The dip below her cheekbones deeper, more severe. Her eyes somewhat tired and sad. Like the photo.

It was recent.

I don't remember.

You have a lot on your mind.

Shapes. Symbols.

What?

I have rugs on my mind. I remember patterns. The shape of certain light. Why would I forget this photo?

She watched him throw his gaze at the road. The lump in his throat. He gripped the wheel when she asked again.

Why would he take it without telling me?

To remember you. He likes you, Nurdane.

Likes me?

He's proud of you.

She turned to him.

He's proud of himself for helping me.

But he has.

He only helps to remind me of what I've lost.

She could feel his eyes on her. She turned and lifted her gaze to the granite outcrops crowned with fuchsia oleanders.

He doesn't truly understand the disease. He thinks the braces and the exercises help. Thinks that's my biggest problem. But there's so much more. It's like a ghost, you know. The polio. It comes back. Haunts me. Sometimes I feel burning on my skin, but when I look, there's nothing there. I feel it in the dead of winter too, on the coldest days. I feel the burning as if somebody put a hot skillet on my skin.

How long does it last?

A few minutes.

Have you told Adam?

There's nothing he can really do about it. The feeling leaves eventually.

He probably knows something.

No. It will make him anxious. He'd visit more than he does already. And I don't want that. I don't need that sympathy.

Mehmet had never heard Nurdane speak like this, the frustration in her voice. He respected her silence and said nothing, then turned onto a goat trail that spiraled down to the river. He parked under a pomegranate tree and turned off the engine. The stillness eerie.

He's only trying his best.

She nodded.

I know.

He wants to see you walk again.

Like you, my father, and everybody else.

Things could be worse.

I don't think so, Mehmet.

She smiled sadly.

You've run with me. You remember who I was before the polio. I'm not broken in your memory. You don't try to fix me. You see me as I am. As I always was. But to Adam, he sees only the pieces. Nothing whole.

She fixed her eyes on the river and watched the waters toss themselves like the manes of wild horses. She lifted her skirt and showed him the new braces.

Last night he gave me another pair.

I thought you got new ones last fall.

I did. And the summer before that.

It must cost a fortune.

She nodded.

I've never asked my father. He won't talk about the money, said I'll always be cared for. But I wonder how he's paying. How much debt he owes. I wonder how much it's really worth to Adam too. What he really wants for this work.

Her voice trailed off. She threw her eyes on the cigarette papers littering the floor of the Jeep. Then she looked up. Her voice choked with frustration.

I wish I could read that look in his eyes and know what it is . . . I'd give him whatever he wanted if it meant he'd leave me alone.

It was dark inside the store and smelled of cigarettes and dust. Suzan Yakar Rutkay's "Chain of Love" played from an old transistor radio in the back, where Mustafa sat hunched over a desk, dealing himself cards. He sang, oblivious to Adam's presence.

Good afternoon.

Mustafa was startled and dropped the cards on the ground. He squinted through the late-day sun that squeezed through the window, and seeing who had entered the store, stood immediately and wiped his hands on an old rag that hung from the wall.

Adam! Old friend.

Adam smiled and offered his hand. Mustafa took it and kissed it.

So good to see you. How long have you been here?

A few days.

You staying long?

As long as Nurdane needs me.

Mustafa studied him. His neatly trimmed mustache. His manicured fingers.

Ali paying you well?

We work things out.

Adam searched the metal shelves mounted on the wall.

You have any paint?

Mustafa chuckled.

He's got you painting too?

Adam turned to him. I offered to help.

For how much?

Adam jerked his head quickly upward, as was the custom when men shared ill-spoken words.

We need every color you have.

Now?

Adam nodded, then dug into his pockets and jingled the coins there. Mustafa quickly moved out from behind the counter and opened a few boxes on the floor. He tore open the flaps of cardboard and spoke quickly.

How is her hand?

Better. It's healing more slowly than I'd like.

Mustafa looked up, alarmed.

Is there an infection?

The cut was deep. One of the worst I've seen. Tore right through her nerves. She's lucky she can still move her fingers.

She's still working? Mustafa asked, searching Adam's face for a positive response.

She doesn't like to discuss the rug.

She's close, right?

Close?

To finishing. We're all waiting.

Adam locked eyes with Mustafa. His brows scrunched with worry.

Why does it matter to you?

It matters to everyone, doesn't it?

Mustafa set a few cans of paint on the floor. He pried open the lid with a screwdriver.

You want blue?

Every color you have. I need the rainbow.

Mustafa looked up, curious.

You painting Ali's house?

We have a project.

Mustafa stood.

My wife has others in the house. Used. If you don't mind. Wait here.

Mustafa disappeared through the back door and returned with various sizes of paint cans. He set them on the counter, running his fingertips along the tops of the cans.

Your rainbow. Nurdane deserves that.

Adam stiffened, his face drawn in the dusty light.

I don't think you understand.

Mustafa put his finger over his lips.

Shhh, he said, closing the door behind him. He turned up the music as he spoke.

We want her to finish the rug.

Adam nodded, confused by the man's insight, and yet he did not want to confirm or provoke his suspicions.

She will. As soon as her hand heals.

Tell me, Mustafa whispered, pushing the cans of paint across the counter. Who got the bid?

Adam sighed, dropped his shoulders.

I told you I have the money for the paint.

I don't want your money, doctor. I want to know who's getting the rug.

Adam slid the paint back to Mustafa, but Mustafa pushed it back.

My gift to you.

Adam chuckled.

I don't need your gifts.

He pushed the paint cans back, but Mustafa stepped away from the counter and stumbled over a can of olive oil.

Take them, please. Just tell me who it is.

Adam sighed, defeated. He did not know where else he would find paint in the village, but he did not want to fall prey to Mustafa's game.

Ask Ali. I cannot tell you what you want to know.

Tell me her name.

Adam shifted his eyes from the cans of paint to the shopkeeper's unshaven face.

Only Allah knows, Mustafa.

I don't believe you.

I know nothing about the rug.

Adam felt his jaw tightening. A small twitch in his cheek.

Mustafa lowered his head, pressed his thumb onto the counter, leaving a greasy fingerprint on the glass.

I didn't win the bid, did I?

His eyes had grown large, solemn.

Tell me, Adam. I know you know.

He spit on the ground.

Adam shook his head.

I'm sorry, Mustafa. Ali tells me nothing more than what I need to know to make his daughter well.

Mustafa searched Adam's face, detecting the lie.

He thinks I'm a poor man, doesn't he?

We're all poor men.

Shut up! You are a doctor. You live in the city. You have no idea what it's like to be poor. You come here twice a year to fix Ali's daughter and you think you're suddenly one of us. Ali's practically adopted you as his son. So don't you tell me he doesn't confide in you about the rugs.

Silence. The record ended. Only the scraping of the needle. The two men stared at each other.

Tell Ali that I am *not* a poor man.

Mustafa moved quickly into the darkness behind the counter and pulled out a box hidden by a stack of tattered clothes. He lifted the lid and pulled out a fistful of gold, watches, necklaces, rings, and bangles.

Adam eyed them suspiciously.

Where'd you get this?

It doesn't matter. It's for Ali.

The man thrust the gold under Adam's chin. He was verging on tears now, his hands trembling.

I will give it to him. If he lets my daughter have the rug.

Adam stared at the gold and swallowed. His throat had suddenly grown dry. His mind racing.

The bid has already been accepted, Mustafa.

He can change his mind. There's not a man in this village who has anything like this to offer him. You would know. You've probably been in every house. Nobody has gold here. You know this. Tell Ali! Tell him what treasure I have for him!

The shopkeeper shoved the gold into Adam's pockets, then got on his hands and knees and stared up at him, pleading.

Take it! Please! My daughter must have a son. She will marry into another village and will leave us on her wedding day. She will be a slave for her husband and his family until she bears a son. You know this. You have seen this. You have even been a part of this whether you like it or not because you are a man.

Adam nodded, swallowed again, sorry he understood the man's feeling of punishment for having a daughter.

She will be nothing without a son.

What makes you think the rug will bring her that?

The shopkeeper looked at him, appalled.

She will conceive a son on the rug. Like the others!

Adam pulled the jewelry from his pockets and laid it on the counter.

Thank you.

Let her womb rot.

What?

Whoever gets the rug. Let her carry a beast.

Adam said nothing, wishing not to offend the man further. He took the paint cans in his arms and walked out the door. The screen slammed behind him, and he stood outside in the searing heat of Mustafa's curse.

She sat alone on a rough karst stone and watched her reflection in the blue waters. Her hair draped her shoulders, the long black clumps absorbing the sun, hot on her skin. The metal skeleton of her braces lay beside her, her legs bare and bruised. She pulled her knees to her chest and inched forward to the edge of the rock, then dangled her feet in the water. It was colder than she remembered. Her ankles stung and quickly grew numb as she lowered herself into the river. She wondered if Mehmet had made a dam. The stillness disturbed her, and she had a strange sensation that she was being watched.

Mehmet?

A bite at her ankles. She looked down to find a school of trout swimming through her legs. Their scales iridescent in the light, like little rainbows. The fish were everywhere. She had never seen so many at once. She dove through them, her legs suddenly free and powerful. She kicked lightly and surfaced, wiped the hair from her face, and began to swim upstream. Her body gliding past the fish, their tails brushing against her arms and legs, tickling her back. She took long strokes, her arms lean and streamlined, elbows high above the water. She could move herself through the river unlike anywhere on land, and it was here she felt most free. In the water, under the water, she felt whole again and safe. The river twisted beyond the bridge and she could not see past the stones there. Then she heard his voice. Mehmet calling her name across the river.

Nurdane!

She sensed the urgency in his voice and swam faster. The current picked up, and she fought her way through the boiling water. The rocks scraped her knees.

Stay there, Nurdane!

His voice was higher now, clenched with panic. She kicked harder, pushing herself off the bottom, letting the current drag her to the surface. She choked as the water rushed into her mouth. Then everything blurred. Sounds. The panic in Mehmet's voice. He screamed something, but she could not make out the words. Her ears waterlogged, eyes burning from the silt. When she opened them, she saw a corpse. The skull had been shattered on the right side. She recognized the body immediately. It was the picker.

Let go, Nurdane!

Splashing around her. Arms on her shoulders, around her waist. She felt her hand being pried away from the dead man's fingers. Her nails dug deep into his flesh. She did not realize that in her panic she had grabbed the man's hands and locked her fingers around his wrist in the vicelike way he had taken hers. She squeezed as tight as she could until her body trembled and she fell back into the water, exhausted.

Mehmet grabbed her by the ankles, dragging her to shore. He covered her with his shirt, then jumped back into the water and pulled the dead body over the rocks. The current picked up, its eerie rush echoing along the canyon.

Mehmet sat down beside Nurdane, who had moved only her knees to her chest. His shirt hung loosely over her shoulders and she had done nothing more to cover herself. Her teeth chattered. Mehmet reached out to offer comfort with his hand, but she arched her back and turned away, praying that when she looked back, the corpse would have vanished.

Adam took longer than usual returning to the lodge, his mind heavy with thought, his arms tired. He set the cans of paint on the road and stopped by a stone pipe to wash the tears from his face. The water smelled of sage and stung his skin where he had shaved that morning. He spread his fingers over the back of his neck and dragged them across his throat, rubbing out the knots there. His body was stiff, his toes scrunched in the front of his shoe, his mind focused on them for a moment to release the tension. He ran the back of his wrists under the pipe, then drew his mouth to the water and drank.

He sat on the embankment to rest. The sun beat down, and he took his shirt off, twisting it around his head like an old Ottoman turban. He could understand now more than ever the pressure Ali felt, the weight he carried in his heart. He admired the man for his strength. How he endured the constant badgering of the villagers and entertained their desperate pleas for the rug. They were in this together. It would be easy to tell Nurdane the truth, to unburden themselves of the secret. They had become victims of their own conspiracy, and there was nothing to do but wait and hope that she would understand they had acted in her best interest. It was more, he thought, than Allah could ever offer the girl.

He felt a cigarette in his pocket and pulled it out, rolling it over his knee, leaving a trail of tobacco where the paper was torn. He rarely smoked, but needed something to do with his hands when they weren't fixing Nurdane's braces or massaging her calves. He wore the smell of her skin on his hands, and it kept him up at night, eager to know her more.

Where's your weaver?

He looked up to find Hennessey, pulling an oxcart toward him. Various shovels and picks filled the rickety transport. He wore his sunglasses and Panama hat, his cheeks sunburned, smeared with dirt. He set the cart down and drank from the bota tied around his waist, offering some ayran to Adam. He politely refused, jerking his chin.

Did you find what you needed? he asked.

Not yet. There's a lot to learn about this village.

Figured you'd know the secrets by now.

He grinned. Hennessey flashed him a smile, raised his eyebrows above the rim of his sunglasses.

I'm looking for Nurdane.

She's gone swimming.

Alone?

Her cousin took her to the river.

Doesn't she teach on Saturday?

Not with her hand the way it is. Why?

I need to ask her about the rug.

Adam sucked the loose tobacco from his teeth and sat up, anticipating.

I want to know when she'll be done, Hennessey said.

Adam let out a small huff and laughed.

Allah only knows.

But it should take only a few days.

Could take months, Hennessey.

Months?

It depends on her hand.

But it's almost done. The whole thing's there.

He spoke quickly. Adam detected his eagerness and a certain anxiety that defied his seemingly mellow demeanor.

She let you see it?

Hennessey dug his heel into the ground and dragged it through the stones. A dry wind blew across the road, and he wished it would sweep away his words. Shit. He nodded slowly.

You saw the hut?

Hennessey shook his head.

No. Muammer showed me.

What right does he think he . . .

He wanted to see it. He loves her work.

He knows better.

Yeah. I know.

Silence, save the bray of donkeys somewhere down the road.

Did anyone see you?

Only Nurdane. She caught us.

What?

Hennessey dug his hands in his pockets and lifted his eyes to meet the incredulous stare on Adam's face.

How was she?

Tired. I don't see how she can get anywhere with those braces.

Adam tossed the cigarette on the ground.

I'm not talking about the braces. How did she seem about you seeing the rug before it was finished?

Angry, of course. But I don't know who's more upset. She or Muammer. Does she have a habit of cursing?

What?

Hennessey laughed. Adam swallowed. He was not amused.

I'm kidding. She was angry, Adam. But not livid. It's not like we were trying to steal the rug.

Hennessey took off his sunglasses, his eyes, green glass in the light, bloodshot from the sun. He took another sip from the bota and spoke.

Today I started the surface scraping. The site covers the crest of the hill.

Adam leaned forward, reading him.

No.

What?

You think she's there?

Who?

The Goddess. You think the site is on the hill.

Hennessey shook his head.

No. I think it's under the hill.

Under. On. What's the difference?

Calculations.

Your calculations are wrong.

Adam shot him a dismissive glance and followed Hennessey's eyes to the hill that sat like a brown bell behind the village.

You're like the other diggers. They were always wrong, you know? Coming here with their chisels and picks, trying to excavate a wasteland. There's nothing up there, Hennessey. Trust me. You won't find your Goddess under Nurdane's hut.

Hennessey studied Adam's face, the tension in his jaw and in his eyes, the fear of an impending threat. He tried to allay his concerns and explained.

Nobody's ever thought of excavating the hill because it was detached from the ancient city. Like the Artemiseion at Ephesus. You know it?

Yes. Of course.

So you know the distance that separates it from the city. Probably took a half hour to walk.

Hennessey eyed the ravine separating the hill from the temple and theater ruins. A crow circled the agora.

Any geologist will tell you the fault line runs straight through that cleft there. An earthquake in the thirteenth century rocked the entire region. The mountains moved three feet to the west. . . . Kind of thing Rumi probably wrote about. Buildings collapsed. Villages crumbled. An entire civilization was destroyed. It devastated Asia Minor and the rest of the world. . . . You know this, right?

Adam shook his head. Hennessey continued.

Look, I'm not trying to ruin Mavisu, or Nurdane's livelihood for that matter. I'm trying to find the truth. There are so many secrets in the soil here. I can feel them slipping through my fingers.

What does an earthquake have to do with the Goddess?

Hennessey locked eyes with the doctor.

When land shifts, so does the culture. These brittle hills were green once, lush, when the nomads roamed. When they were forced to settle, there was no rotation for the livestock. The land became fallow, drought-stricken. Your people lost their culture.

I don't share their past. My family was not nomadic.

But you can see what happened. What's happening still. These people have lost so much of their culture. They've lost so much of themselves. They forget who they were. Men, women. The women suffer the most because there is almost no evidence they once ruled here. And that is what I've come to find for them. A little piece of their past to remind them of their power.

Adam leaned back into the dry grasses, elbows digging into the hill.

And you think this search is a good thing?

Hennessey nodded.

I know she's here, Adam.

Adam stood and stepped into Hennessey's shadow.

The hut has never been moved since Ali built it.

It's temporary. Until the surface scraping is done.

Adam threw his eyes on the ground, where a lizard snapped at a cicada and swallowed it in two gulps. Half a wing stuck to the outside of its lips.

Can you wait until the solstice?

That's a week from now.

It's her birthday.

Hennessey cocked his head, confused. Adam drew in a deep breath.

She's supposed to finish the rug before her birthday.

I understand, Hennessey said. I'm not asking her to stop. I need her to work somewhere else. For a few days.

A lot can happen in a few days.

Hennessey looked up to the band of storm clouds.

That depends on what you believe.

What's that?

Hennessey turned and faced him.

Do you believe in the virgin's knots?

Adam's face flattened. He moved his lips but said nothing, catching with his wrist the stream of sweat crawling down his

cheek. The buzzing crescendo of cicadas and the sputter of an engine broke the silence. Both men turned too see Mehmet's Jeep bar-
reling toward them under a canopy of dust. The Jeep pulled over
to the shoulder and Mehmet jumped out.

Mehmet? What is it?

We found him in the river.

He pointed to the body, and Hennessey and Adam walked over
to take a closer look. The skin was waterlogged and woodlike, de-
caying. The stab mark in his thigh had been split by the rock that
wedged there, but they recognized the body immediately. Adam
turned to Nurdane.

Where did you find the body?

Under the bridge, Nurdane said.

Mehmet interrupted.

Nurdane said she knew . . .

There were fish everywhere, she said, staring Mehmet into silence. Then she looked up and locked eyes with Adam.

It was a good day for fishing.

What did you know?

Adam searched her eyes for the secret.

What is it?

Nothing, she snapped.

Her silence consumed him, and he could feel her eyes turning
away for fear she might reveal what he suspected. He turned to
Mehmet, but Mehmet stepped back, his face red with rage. He was
angry with Nurdane for not telling him sooner. He spoke little on
the drive home, his mind spewing, heart pounding as she told him
the story about the picker. He glanced over at the body. Green flies
had already found the man's eyes and nose.

Don't bother burying him. He should be burned.

Mehmet hurled his keys at Adam, then chugged off down the
road, leaving Nurdane alone in the Jeep. She had folded her headscarf and pressed it against her nose and mouth to keep from
smelling the body, but the foul, acrid stench of death crawled over
her tongue.

Adam turned to her, his voice low.

I know what he did, he said, and reached out, taking her injured hand in his own. He felt her stiffen and wrapped his fingers around the pads of her palm, pressing gently where the bandage was thickest. He imagined how the picker had scared her, his misguided touch, aggressive and rough. He saw the knife slip from the picker's hand into her own, how it ripped across the flesh on the man's thigh. Two streams of blood flowing into one tributary of sin. Adam did not lift his eyes to meet hers, but instead spoke to her hand as if it were somehow separate from her now, as if it were the only vehicle of reason.

Nobody else will know, he said.

Know what?

Nurdane pressed the scarf against her mouth, her eyes wide, spooked. Her lips trembled beneath the cloth. Adam leaned in, whispering in her ear.

Your hand. I know about your hand.

Her eyes widened, pleading with him, but before she could beg him not to tell her father, he spoke.

Nobody has to know, as long as you finish the rug.

He watched her face for a while, how she held it perfectly still, until she dropped her chin to accept his offer.

Adam washed the body and wrapped it in the *kefen,* a seamless white cloth, then moved it to the mosque, where it lay strangely like a stillborn, the face blue and waxy under the flicker of oil lamps. Dressing the dead was not new to him, and although he prided himself on the few patients who had died under his care, he had learned the art through less fortunate doctors. In his younger days, he had bound many bodies in the *kefen*. Feeling like a student again, he stuffed the eyes, nose, and mouth with cotton to seal the corridors of intimacy with the world, and in his own way, to deny the picker any pleasure he may seek in the afterlife.

He agreed with Mehmet. The man did not deserve a proper burial, but the villagers would suspect his illegitimacy if he did not receive one. For Nurdane's sake, they did not need to know the truth. Why the man had no prayer beads. Why he was not circumcised. Why his clothes, even waterlogged, still smelled of anise. The funny language printed on the bills in his pockets. The stab mark. They did not need to know the answers to any of this. Adam performed the ritual, passing off the picker as a Turkish man who had somehow lost his way in the mountains. Under normal circumstances, the imam would have prepared the dead body, but he was in Antalya and would not be back for another week. The body was to be buried on the day of its death but, more important, before it raised questions.

The shuffle of feet. Adam stepped back to let the men pass in front of the corpse. A line had formed out the door, and he wondered why so many had come to pay their respects. Nobody knew the man, at least not that he was aware of. But here they were in their wool vests and knitted caps despite the heat, hands behind their backs, prayer beads looped through their fingers. They ambled forward in their stocking feet, heads bowed, a procession of moving lips reciting the *Yakin surasi,* the proclamation of faith in a second birth. *Glory be to him whose hand is the dominion of all things. Unto him ye will be brought back.* Over and over they repeated the verse, carrying it out the door and into the streets to the cemetery, where they stood waiting to bury the dead.

Only a few men remained to help Adam as pallbearers, and they stood milling about the coffin until he lowered the lid.

Don't lock it yet.

Adam looked up, surprised to see Mustafa standing in front of him, his trousers weighted by something in his pockets. He stood hunched over, eyes wandering up and down the coffin, hands moving nervously over each other as if he were washing them.

Can I see his face?

Adam straightened. He towered over the storekeeper's oily head, curious, suspicious.

Why?

I think I know him.

Mustafa shifted nervously, bit his lip as Adam lifted the lid slowly, his stare moving alongside Mustafa's eyes as he approached the coffin and looked down at the picker's face. His face suddenly pallid as if he, too, had died. He parted his lips as if he wanted to say something, but no words came.

You know him?

Mustafa nodded, fished the prayer beads through his fingers. He looked up. His sharp black eyes suddenly blank. He spoke softly, strangely apologetic.

He was coming to see me.

A fter the burial the men gathered outside the teahouse, where a small fire burned inside a ring of broken pediments. Odd shadows fell across the half-faces, remnants of a carnival long since abandoned. The crackle of fire broke the melancholic strain of two ney flutes that a shepherd and his son played on the roof. The smell of burning cedar in the air, and sage too, picked from the dead man's grave.

Adam poked at the fire with a stick. The wood splintered and a blue flame licked the air, then engulfed a piece of dried pine. The smoke burned his eyes, and when he got up to move, he noticed a glint of something metal on the ground. Small objects. He could make out a watch face and bracelet through the flames. Gold pieces strewn at the feet of the men standing before Mustafa.

The shopkeeper had kept his distance from Adam during the burial and had only then begun to speak to those who had come to pay their respects to him, the dead man's cousin. At least that's what they believed. He stood before them and emptied his pockets, stuffing the gold jewelry into the men's hands. It was a custom among the surviving family members to give alms for any unabsolved sins of the deceased.

Adam watched him curiously, studying the pieces of jewelry, the familiar way Mustafa held them in his fists, unwittingly giving them away. The sneer on his face, the puckered brow that Mustafa paused to wipe with the torn cloth from his pocket.

Adam crossed behind the fire and stood staring at the shopkeeper who had given away everything but the last piece of jewelry. A chain-link pocket watch dangled from his thick fingers, and he continued to caress it with his thumb. He turned to Adam, feeling his eyes on him, and hurled the watch at his feet.

Take it.

Adam glanced down but did not pick it up. Instead, he moved the heel of his boot over the watch face and crushed the glass.

All you had to do was ask.

I did.

For the rug.

What?

Adam shifted his eyes toward the cemetery, where votive candles burned in the grasses.

You hired him, he said in Russian.

I never met him, Mustafa snapped in Turkish.

Adam smiled. Mustafa had understood him, confirming his suspicions.

It's odd, isn't it? A Turk and a Russian in the same family. He's Armenian too.

Mustafa's jaw tightened. Adam dug into his pocket and pulled out a wallet. He opened it and shook the contents onto the ground.

Coins rolled out, lire and rubles. A license bearing the dead man's photo landed on bits of broken glass. Mustafa dropped to his knees and stared at the picture.

Sonofabitch, he whispered.

Let you down too?

Mustafa looked up. Adam leaned into him.

And he was the nice one. His brothers should be in that grave. But they got away.

You've seen them?

By the river. That's where I found him. Hurt. Stabbed.

Mustafa swallowed, stood frozen as Adam circled.

You know why?

Mustafa shook his head. Adam leaned down. He touched her, he whispered, grabbing the shopkeeper's wrist, squeezing as hard as he imagined the picker had done to Nurdane. Mustafa spoke quietly.

I told them not to touch her.

They forgot.

Adam stepped behind him and grabbed the back of his neck. He could feel the eyes of the men on him, but he did not care and wrapped his fingers around Mustafa's throat. With his other hand he grabbed a tuft of hair, jerking Mustafa's head back, his cheeks wet with tears.

Tell them what sins your cousin has committed.

Mustafa's eyes darted wildly from one man to the next. He pressed his lips together to keep from trembling. Adam kicked him hard against his right kidney.

Don't let his sins go unabsolved.

Please, Adam.

Mustafa lifted his eyes.

I'll give her the bracelets. I promise. I'll give her everything. Whatever you want. Whatever she wants.

She wants her hand back. Clean.

Adam looked down at the man's face and spit on the stones of his black eyes. The saliva slid down Mustafa's cheeks and mixed with the tears that ran black there. Adam pushed him forward until his face hit the ground, splinters of glass in his chin. Then he leaned close to his ashen face and hissed.

Kiss it.

The man's eyes grew wide, the whites glowing as he looked up at Adam.

You heard me.

He slapped his jaw.

Kiss the ground, Mustafa.

He waited, watching the man's mouth open, blood mixing with saliva. He coughed, trying to spit out the dirt, then pressed his lips to the soil. Adam held his mouth there, pushing his head farther into the earth.

Taste it.

The man groaned. Adam twisted his elbow farther, slapped his cheek with the back of his wrist. Mustafa wiggled his tongue, searching for the ground.

Taste it!

The man closed his mouth and swallowed, his nostrils flared in disgust.

Remember the taste, Mustafa. It is your soul.

Nurdane waited until the men had returned from the teahouse to make her way to the hut. A thick fog enshrouded the village and cast an ethereal haze on the buildings, rounding harsh lines, softening the austerity of cement and stone. The clay tiles, silver in the moonlight. She stepped carefully in her bare feet, the ground cool and clinging to her heels. She passed the *haman,* where steam clouded the air and men too old and tired to care about the funeral sat hunched over a hot spring. They turned when she passed but said nothing, heads bowed, reverent, the cherry embers of cigarettes the only light between them.

It was a strange evening, the air thick with rumors, the volume of the villagers reduced to mere whispers. Everyone had their theories about the dead man, but nobody had any facts. She could hear the hushed voices of the women between the clatter of pots and dishes. They were not invited to the ceremony but were told to cook, to fill the air with familiar smells to keep his spirit happy in its departure and honest in its questioning.

She wondered what the picker would say when Allah asked him about her hand. Was it her fault or his? She had no answers, the incident blurry now, thirteen days since. The picker's death was still a mystery. She wondered if he had drowned or if the wound on his leg eventually killed him, and, if so, was she to blame? *When Allah takes something from you, he gives you something in return.* She had no intention of taking anything from Allah, yet somehow she let a stranger take something from her— the purity of her hands, the vehicle for the knots that Allah made through her.

She paused at the fork in the road and looked up, hearing the flapping of wings. A stork perched itself on the roof of the hut as if to beckon her to the loom. She looked back at the *haman*. The men had deserted the hot springs and only the steam remained. She could turn back and sleep. Try to forget about the picker. Try to forget about the day. But she could feel it in her hands. The sensation in the pads where the doctor had touched her. The pulsing when the images came, the slow throb in her fingers, the dull ache and longing to tie the knots, to lose herself in the weft and warp. The numbers for the pattern flashed in her mind. She mumbled the equation, wondering if this was her test. Allah teasing her with desire, to let her know how much she needed the loom, how much she would miss it if He took it away.

She found the door unlocked, the ground raked. Stones had been removed from the walkway and stakes had been pounded

into the ground and strung together with red flags. A shallow
trench had been dug around the hut, bootprints everywhere. A
trowel stuck in the dirt.

She pushed open the door and found a white sheet draped over
the loom. The balls of wool that normally lay scattered on the
floor had been placed neatly in a large shallow bowl, the wooden
comb and tapestry bobbin on top. She took the lantern from the
wall, lit it, then shut the door and crossed to the loom, careful not
to knock into the pages of handprints. She held the lantern up with
her left hand, compared the lines on the pages with her right hand.

Her head line ran deep, transverse from the dip between her thumb
and index finger, then dropped into the center of her palm. The life-
line was long, frayed at the end like the tassels in her prayer rugs.
Nothing had changed. Even the feelings had come back, the nerves
awakening slowly each day from their temporary stupor. She cupped
her hand, folded her fingers, then spread them apart into a fan before
making a fist. She pressed it against her chest and felt her heart pounding. This time she was not as scared as she was relieved, realizing that
Allah had done nothing, yet, to punish her for breaking her vow.

She pulled the white sheet off the rug and sat down to face the
loom. She took the knife, a ball of wool, and fished the yarn between the weft and warp, tying a single knot. Her hands felt light,
strangely transparent. It felt good to weave, to speak again, the
language of the loom. She reached into the warp, fishing more
yarn through the weft, tying another knot. Slowly, she tied a third.
Then another and another until she filled the row, her fingers
plucking the woolen strands like strings on a harp. The percussive
thwap of the comb, hypnotic, pulling her further into the knots
until she tied three more, five, fifteen, thirty. Her lips mumbled
numbers, assuring the symmetry in the pattern. She tied forty
more, fifty, seventy, ninety, recalling the story of the Gordion knot.

Knots, her father had said, were powerful things, warning her
that in their innocence they could also be weapons. She had never
understood their power until then and wondered if they had been
a defense against the picker's touch, if the very thing Allah had

given her had prevented Him from taking it away. She had tied millions of knots in her lifetime, and she wondered if Allah had looked upon each knot like a good deed and testament of her faith. She trusted her role as the virgin weaver. She knew that her prayer rugs, if not sacred themselves, made sacred the mysteries of life. Consummation, conception. Love, death.

She paused, hearing a scrape on the roof. She lifted her eyes to the window and caught the tail of a stork before it swooped through the fog and disappeared.

She released the treadle and rotated the ratchet, rolling the rug farther into the lower cross beam. It had grown thick now, and her knees brushed against the edge. The rug was almost finished. She eyed the empty warp. Barely a quarter meter left. A day's work, really. She could finish it by morning if she worked through the night. She would have stayed under normal circumstances. The brides were waiting, eager for their weddings. But she wanted to wait this time. She wanted to know the truth of the virgin's knots.

A dam found her in the morning, sleeping with the knife in her hand. The bandages had been removed and lay in a pile of strips beside her face, a few had blown across the veranda. He set a tray of tea beside her and nudged her gently on the shoulder.

Günaydýn, Nurdane.

She blinked. Her face suddenly glowing when the light hit her eyes. She swallowed. Her throat was dry, her voice scratchy when she spoke.

What time is it?

Six-thirty.

She could hear her father murmuring prayers from the house,

the tinkle of goats' bells in the distance. Adam poured her a glass of tea. She set the knife down and sat up, taking the small glass from his hands. His fingers were dirty, the nails ground with soil from the grave site. He carried the smell of bleach and brine, death on his skin and his work-worn clothes. He looked fragile, disturbed by her hand.

You took the dressing off.

She nodded and spread her fingers.

It's been healed.

What?

There's only a scar now.

He set the pot of tea down and took the bifocals from the front pocket of his vest.

Can I see?

She nodded and offered her hand.

The skin was pink and tender where the scar was forming. Springy, too, when he touched it. He gave a curious laugh, then pressed her wrist with his fingers.

Do you feel this?

She nodded. He worked his way down her hand, massaging the muscles with his thumb.

This?

I feel everything.

Her voice was cheery this morning. It delighted him to hear her this way, to see the smile in her eyes, but today there was something else.

I couldn't sleep last night, she said. I kept seeing that man's face everywhere. In the clouds. In the moon. I even saw him in the sink when I washed my face. I needed to get my mind off him, so I went to the hut to work.

On the rug?

Yes.

She laughed as if this were a great surprise, then, reading his expectant eyes, continued.

I'm going to finish soon.

He smiled.

Your father will be pleased.

So will the bride, she said. I feel so bad that I've kept her waiting.

She'll understand.

She gave him a curious look, wondering how Adam knew the bride, but before she could ask him, her father walked toward them with a tray of tomatoes and bread so thin, the morning breeze carried it like paper to Nurdane. She reached up and caught it in her right hand. Ali stopped, incredulous.

Allah. Allah!

He rushed over and set the tray down beside her, then, kneeling, took her hand and studied it. A scar had formed around the stitches, sealing the wound completely. She had healed. He kissed her hand, then touched it slowly to his forehead, keeping it pressed against him longer than usual, knowing it was the last time he would honor her this way. He shifted his eyes to Adam and they exchanged a knowing look.

She says the rug will be finished soon.

Is it true, Nurdane?

She could feel their stares moving alongside her as she tilted her head, catching something in the distance. A flash of something shiny. Adam followed her gaze and saw Hennessey riding a rickety bike up the lane, a few loaves of bread stuffed in the front basket. He seemed hurried and set the bike down in the dirt, wiping his face with his sleeve.

John Hennessey, she said.

Who?

Hennessey, she repeated, pronouncing his name perfectly, as if she'd listened to a gramophone and imitated the intonation.

You know him? Adam asked.

She nodded, fixing her gaze on Hennessey as he carried the loaves of bread up the stairs, standing at the landing, shifting awkwardly in his boots.

Good morning, he said.

Ali sighed.

It's that fool for antiquities. The American, right?

Adam nodded, but it was Nurdane who spoke.

He's staying with the postman.

You met him?, Ali asked.

Nurdane looked over at Adam.

Muammer introduced us last week.

Ali gave her a disturbed look. Hennessey cleared his throat and offered an explanation.

He was showing me to the site.

What site?

The hut.

Nurdane nodded, making sense of it. The trench. The stakes in the ground. The flags and trowel she had found in the dirt.

Adam rubbed his forehead and groaned.

Now's not the time, Hennessey.

Hennessey crossed the deck, offering the bread to Nurdane. He looked only at her father and Adam.

There's a storm coming.

There's always a storm, Adam interrupted.

But I've been listening to the radio all morning. They predict flash floods. Even in the mountains. Every road to this village is going to be washed out. Who knows how long it will take to dry? The place is going to be a mud bath.

So what? You stay through the summer. Collect your samples when it dries.

Hennessey shook his head, desperate.

You don't understand. My research is due in two weeks. I've tried to collect samples here and there, where I could, but it's not enough. What I've come to find is under Nurdane's hut.

What?

Ali lifted his eyes, studying the tall man.

I have to take it down.

Ali looked over at Adam, who sat, shaking his head.

You can't just take it down.

I'll rebuild it, stone by stone. As it was.

Ali sliced through the tomato, the knife slipping in his hands. Hennessey could see Nurdane's hands in her father's. The long, thin fingers. The delicate wrists. But his hands were trembling, and despite the meticulous care he took to scrape away the seeds, he nicked himself, drawing blood.

What about the loom? he asked.

He can move it.

Ali shot a startled look at Nurdane.

I'm almost done. I can finish here, she said calmly, almost as if she had rehearsed the words in a dream.

Let him find what he needs.

V

Dawn bled into the horizon when the first stone fell. The ground shook and ravens exploded from the trees and everywhere the wind whispered a conspiracy of wings. Nurdane stood under the twisted cypress in the cemetery, where she could watch alone. She felt the hair rise on the back of her neck as the stones passed between Hennessey's hands. She was impressed by the way he handled them, so gently, as if he knew that even a stone could be fragile.

He wore his Panama hat and sunglasses and stood at the end of a long line of men who had come to help. Ali wanted to supervise but was too nervous to be of any use and paced the hill, smoking. Hennessey stopped to drink from the bota tied around his waist, his shirt riding up his wet stomach, his forearms already red from the heat. He tapped the last man in the assembly line. His command traveled to Muammer, who called out a number and whitewashed it on the stone before depositing it into a wagon hitched to a team of mules who shifted listlessly in the heat.

He dismantled the north wall first, exposing the loom on the inside. A white sheet had been draped over the rug and gave the appearance of a movie screen, silvery from dust motes sparkling in the light. A hot wind lifted the sheet and exposed the bottom cross-bar where the rug had been rolled. A few gasps from the brides who had gathered on the hill to watch. Hennessey quickly took a stone and set it down on the sheet to keep it weighted, respecting the superstition that it was bad luck to see the rug before it was finished. He had come early to remove the blue handprints and Nurdane's tattered copy of the Koran too. He didn't have the chance to tell her that these things were done in her best interest. He hoped she could trust him with their safekeeping. Hennessey knew that in taking down the hut, he had entered her life in a way no one had ever done before. It was not only an obligation, but also a duty to protect her now.

The south wall fell by midmorning and exposed both the front and back of the loom that stood adjacent to the remaining two walls, halfway between east and west. As the stones fell, Nurdane experienced an expansion in her heart, as if a great burden had been lifted, an obstacle removed, making room for a part of herself that had been hidden for so long. She remembered stories of the great sculptors, those who discovered life in stone. She wondered what Hennessey had discovered about her, if he, too, heard the murmurings, the voices locked in the rocks. She believed stones were the great keeper of secrets and was grateful for Hennessey's dismantling of them.

The sudden freedom made her dizzy. She sat down with her back to the tree, knees to chest, hands clasped around the braces on her legs. She saw clouds in the ground, grass in the sky. Everything was spinning, the world on a whorl. She felt a tingling in her wrist, a burning sensation, but when she looked down, there was nothing but a blue butterfly. She blinked once and it was gone, leaving only a trace of blue powder from its wings. The stork and the butterfly. The blind man who had come for tea. The young girl, too, she had seen weaving at the lodge. Everything appeared in a dream, then vanished like a breath on glass.

She blew the dust in the air and opened her eyes, feeling the cold nose of a goat nudging her elbow. Sitting up, she realized she had fallen asleep. The sky had grown lavender and black, only the flash of silver from a sunken sun and the glint of something in the goat's eye. She could see the east wall of the hut, curved like a spine, and the flutter of the sheet as the men carried the loom down the hill, women and children following, leaving a trail of red and white poppies in their wake.

Hennessey sat alone on a pile of stones and watched Nurdane prod through the grasses from the cemetery to the hill. She lunged between steps, compensating for the limp, letting her back foot catch up to the front foot before she lost her center. There was a certain choreography to her movements, a conscious coordination between her brain and the muscles moving her forward. He had never seen another person work so hard to keep their balance, yet despite the incapacity, she carried herself with a birdlike grace. Her determination reminded him of the orphan Demosthenes, the greatest orator of ancient Greece. Demosthenes had a speech impediment, a nervous stammer, and took to oratory to counterbalance his handicap. He filled his mouth with pebbles and performed ceaseless oratory exercises, learning to articulate his words around the stones. Legend has it the orator used to walk on the beach, his mouth full of pebbles, training his voice to rise above the crashing waves. In time, his speech was characterized by a tone of outrage, a vehemence, it seemed, to overcome himself. Nurdane operated under the same dynamic, her determination to stave off the advancing armies of her disease, her legs refusing to surrender despite their shackles. By the time she reached him, her headscarf was matted to her head, her upper lip beaded with sweat.

Hennessey stood and offered his bota. She took it and drank quickly, the two of them silhouettes on the hill. I'm surprised you stayed this long.

She wiped her lips with the back of her wrist, then shifted her eyes to the east wall.

I want to help you.

An awkward silence. Hennessey stared at her curiously. She

waited for an answer and lifted her eyes high enough to see how his mouth hung open, jaw shifting as he fumbled for the words.

The stones are heavy.

I'm strong, she said, and lifted her face again, feeling his eyes on her. And I work fast.

He nodded, glimpsing her forearms. The dip in her shoulders. The small mounds of muscle.

Can you write?

She turned, then crouched down and picked up a clump of fallen poppies.

Only my name.

I'll teach you the numbers.

She laughed.

You'll teach *me* how to write?

He smiled, taking a cigarette and lighter from his pocket, cupping his hand around the butt to keep the wind from blowing out the flame.

I'm not supposed to, you know.

No.

She stared at him incredulously.

I'm not supposed to write.

Funny, he said, and blew the smoke out of the side of his mouth. Looks to me like you write a lot.

She cocked her head, trying to follow him. He pointed across the hill to the old Ottoman house of her father, where the loom had been set under the veranda, sheet still draped over the rug.

What about the language in the knots?

What?

Seems far more sophisticated than anything I could ever write.

He watched her lips part in a smile. She immediately raised her hands over her mouth to keep him from seeing her teeth. It was so choreographed that it seemed rehearsed, not an involuntary response to a socially constructed behavior. He wondered if her joy had always been concealed, or if there were times she smiled with her hands at her sides.

If I teach you how to write, will you teach me how to read?

Read? I can't read.

You're wrong. You read your rugs, don't you?

She threw her eyes on the ground.

Shapes. Not letters.

Isn't a letter a shape?

But it's not complicated like that.

She lifted her eyes, watched his hands flick the ash from the cigarette. She was getting agitated and spoke sternly.

I don't think you understand. Anybody can identify a triangle or a square.

Maybe.

It's true, she protested.

Sure it is.

You don't believe me.

You don't believe *me*, he said. It's a simple task to understand shapes but a complex task to understand their relationships to each other. You see, not every literate man can read the rugs. You speak a very rare language. And that gives you power.

He watched her eyes narrow, considering.

I would be honored to learn even one word. Will you teach me?

She nodded slowly.

Just one?

Maybe two.

I can do that.

Good. Let's get started.

She followed him to the bucket of whitewash, where he took a small brush made of camel hair and dipped the ends into white paint. He wrote the numbers one through ten on his forearm, then asked her to do the same and handed her the brush.

Your turn.

She took the brush hesitantly, waiting for his arm. He pushed up the sleeve, his blond hair wet and matted like the fur of a baby bird, she thought. She wanted to touch it, the thick network of veins too, a map of rivers luring her to trace their course, along his shoulder, around his neck, down his chest. She propped her elbow on his knee to keep her hand steady, stealing a glimpse of his face, the furtive, inviting smile. Her hands shook, splattering paint on his skin.

Hold it steady.

I'm trying.

Don't try so hard.

He noticed she took the brush in her left hand, steadying it with her right as she stooped over his arm and wrote. The wet brush smooth and cool on his skin. She dragged the tip slowly, making long strokes.

Looks great so far.

She smiled, conscious of her teeth, a sign of vanity, but there was nothing she could do to cover them now, only lower her chin to keep him from seeing her.

They're beautiful, you know.

What?

It's a shame you keep them covered.

She paused, feeling her cheeks grow warm, then shook the excess paint off the brush and finished the numbers, working her way from his elbow to his wrist.

Very good. You're hired.

He handed her the notebook and a pencil.

Why didn't you give this to me in the first place?

Then I wouldn't have felt you on my arm.

She stared at him, dumbfounded, as he lifted the stones and set them on the ground, giving her no chance to respond. He began to call out the numbers and she took the notebook and pencil in her hand and recorded his words, watching the sweat stain his shirt as he worked. They spoke little, repeating numbers, confirming the order of things. When the last stone fell, they sat on the ground and drank goat milk from the bota. Hennessey reviewed the numbers in the notebook, flipping through the pages, pleased with her work.

What is that? she asked.

What?

Turn back.

He flipped the page back and Nurdane pointed at the symbol he had copied from the rug in Antalya.

You know her.

Who?

Cybelle, she said.

He nodded slowly and took the book from her. Their hands touched, but she did not move this time, the silver of his rings warm against her skin. He moved his hand over hers, his watch heavy on her wrist. The smell of musk on his skin, a raw sweetness. She felt a certain comfort beside him and closed her eyes, listening to the crescendo of cicadas in the grass. She could hear his breath join hers, heavy and slow, their bodies speaking in spite of the apparent silence.

She opened her eyes, feeling his stare, but instead of looking up, followed the contours of his arms where the hair glistened with his oils.

That's what you've come to find, she said.

The symbol?

She glanced over at the notebook.

Cybelle. She calls people here.

I know, he said.

She called you too. Didn't she?

She turned to him, tempted to lift her eyes, but fixed them instead on the minaret that pierced the sky over Mavisu. Hennessey laughed softly, then grew quiet and stared at her for a long time before he lifted her hands and kissed the insides of her wrists.

Adam stood by the window with a box in his hand, looking out at the empty hill, a black mound against the moonlight. He set the box on the sill and lifted the lid, revealing the red dress and a white poppy he had found on Nurdane's loom. He glanced at the calendar on the wall, where X's filled the days. June 20. Only a day until her birthday, the solstice. It seemed like years. He had never known such anticipation or exercised such patience wishing for the time to pass, pacing the room like a supplicant, listening to the ticking of the wall clock.

He waited for Nurdane while Ali, too tired to worry about his daughter's affairs, drifted off to sleep in the parlor. Adam tried praying, studying the diagram in the prayer rug, but it was too faded and he could read nothing from the knots there. He decided to eat and finished off the last of the *pekmez,* then the *helva.* His mouth was sore with ulcers now and his stomach ached. A cigarette, perhaps. Fresh air. Nothing seemed to settle his mind, so he picked up a book that Mehmet left on the table. Rumi's verses of bewilderment and love, truth and pain. The ways of teachers and mystics and saints. The pages were mildewed and marked with the stems of dried flowers. *The minute I heard my first love story I started looking for you, not knowing how blind that was. Lovers don't finally meet somewhere. They're in each other all along.*

The verse haunted him. He kept hearing it since his arrival, first in the song of a shepherd, then from the men in the tea-house, and, later, by the muhtar. He never read the verse before and wondered if seeing it now was an act of grace, as if it were the answer to a riddle. He had always been a rational man, yet he entertained a funny superstition. When he needed the answer to a deep personal question, he would simply focus on it, then open a book, a telephone directory, his medical reference guides, a novel, or poetry, and read the sentence he saw first, trying to unravel an answer from the words. He liked poetry best and found the verses more suitable to the kind of answers he needed most. The short, pithy phrases. A kind of economy of wisdom he could recall with ease.

He answered the first letter from Ali that way, debating whether or not to return to America or stay in Turkey and help the young girl "found paralyzed in a field of poppies," seventeen years ago, but always like yesterday. He kept the letter in his office, taped to the inside of his desk drawer, to remind him of his triumphs when he felt he had failed her. He wondered about the braces. They had been the very bond between them, but if he had fixed her, his work would have been done long ago. There would be no witnessing the woman she had become, no reason to help her now, and he realized that in helping her, he had helped himself. The more she needed him, the more he could love her, his love proportional to her disease. He had often found himself hoping that she would not heal as quickly as he had promised, and at times was even grateful for the postpolio syndrome that made his visits more frequent. He cursed himself now for this pitiless approach to the Hippocratic oath he had taken on her behalf.

He set the white poppy on the windowsill and lifted the dress out of the box. A cascade of material, the silk cool in his hands. He held the dress up and wrapped his arms around it, imagining how she would feel against him. Her long, glossy hair draped over his arms, laced between his fingers, smelling of rosemary and milkweed. How pleased she would be with the design. The way her eyes would shine, how she would cover her teeth with the back of her hand, half embarrassed by his gesture, half delighted by its surprise. Her voice light and cheery, like an angel's.

He had given her many things over the years. Better braces, improved medicine, exercises to make her stronger, ways to ease the pain. He had given her the greatest gift, movement, yet he believed it inadequate now as he held the dress and realized he had failed to give her a dance. He knew she was too self-conscious of the braces to try, but he had always imagined her dancing and could hear Rumi rousing her to the floor. *Dance, when you're broken open. Dance, if you've torn the bandage off. Dance in the middle of the fighting. Dance in your blood. Dance, when you're perfectly free.* He could see her thin arms swaying gracefully above her head, halos of gold in the bracelets stacked around her wrists.

In his dream, her legs were solid and strong and held the weight of her hips as she swayed against him. He took her to Antalya, to the harbor, where they danced along the pier and Gypsy girls tossed flowers at their feet. He would show her Olimpos and Phaselis, Termessos, Perge, Aspendos and Side. They would sit on the ancient steps and he would tell her stories of the warlike people who lived there. On hot days, he would take her to Duden Falls, where they would stroll through the park, then stop for tea and sweet cakes. He imagined the places he would show her, the things he would teach her. He imagined her with children and grandchildren, teaching them what she had learned from him, how different her life had become once she had left the village. He imagined her old, the way he would hold her hand and lead her to the weathered docks to dance again, slower this time, over the memories they had pressed upon the wood. He imagined this and all the ways he would love her.

He turned, hearing the door open, and quickly folded the dress, stuffing it back in the box. The creak of the braces. The shuffle of boots along the stone floor. Adam blew out the candle and stood as a silhouette against the window when she entered with Hennessey, her arm locked with his. His hand over her right, guiding her through the darkened doorway.

She stiffened when she saw Adam. Her smile quickly fading. She let go of Hennessey and raised her hand slightly over her face, carrying his smell on her fingers.

Nurdane? Hennessey said.

I'll see you tomorrow. Okay?

What is it?

She felt his eyes on her, heard the crack of the bones in his neck when he turned.

Nothing. Just go, she said, but he stepped toward her, searching her eyes for an explanation. She pulled her shoulders back, turning from him, shying toward the window where Adam sat watching. He got up and crossed the floor, hands behind his back, eyes fixed on Hennessey.

You kept her up all night.

She wanted to help.

We finished a long time ago, she said.

Then what?

Talking.

Talking? About what?

Nothing really.

Adam and Hennessey turned to Nurdane, who had unfastened the clasps on her braces and was taking the crutches from a wooden peg on the wall.

Where are you going?

To weave.

It's three o'clock in the morning.

I know.

It's late.

Why? The knots don't sleep.

She stole a glimpse of a smile on Hennessey's face that vanished when Adam turned to him.

Aren't you tired?

But before Hennessey could answer, Nurdane spoke.

Exhausted.

An awkward silence. Only the ticking of the wall clock. Hennessey studied her face, reading the contempt in her eyes, understanding neither its source nor target. He put on his Panama hat and excused himself.

Thanks for your help.

Anytime, she said.

Instead of lifting her eyes, she raised her right hand and waved good-bye. Hennessey studied her a moment longer, then moved into the hallway, letting himself into the courtyard to walk home. Adam turned to Nurdane.

You don't have to worry, he said.

About what?

His hand.

Nurdane tucked a wisp of loose hair behind her ear, her eyes shifting nervously.

Where's my knife?

I saw it.

It's not on the loom.

His hand, Nurdane. I saw you holding his hand.

She threw her gaze on the floor where he had abandoned the game of solitaire.

He's a good man, he said.

I know.

He's not like the picker.

She felt her body stiffen and drew in a deep breath.

You're right. The picker touched *me*.

She moved past him and felt her jaw tighten, trapping the words in her throat. She dropped to the floor, where a small bucket had been stuffed with various bobbins, combs. A drop spindle and random balls of wool collected from the floor of the hut. She dumped the bucket over and searched the contents, finding nothing, then slapped the floor with her hand. Adam walked over and crouched beside her.

What do you need? he asked.

I told you. My knife.

He put his hand over hers, trying to stop her.

Sleep.

What?

You need sleep.

Tomorrow, she said. Tonight I must weave.

In your condition . . .

Don't tell me about my condition.

She took a ball of wool and dug her nails into it. Adam extended his hand to her shoulder to offer comfort, but she jerked her body away and stood. He looked up, locking eyes with her. A stream of tears stained her cheeks. He reached out to wipe it with his hands, his fingers brushing her lips.

Help me find the knife, she said, speaking through her clenched teeth.

In the morning.

Now.

There's no light.

I need to find something, Adam. Your razor.

For what? Why?

The knots. I need anything that cuts.

He nodded once, standing, then walked past her to the corner where he stored his clothes and medical bag. He unzipped it, hearing her labored breaths as he rifled through the contents. Bandages, syringes, cold glass vials. A broken mirror. Stethoscope. Prayer beads. An envelope. He pulled out a razor. She approached him on the crutches.

It's sharp, he warned.

She nodded, taking it, and moved quickly into the hallway, where she popped the latch on the door to let herself outside, crossing the courtyard to the loom under the veranda.

Adam stood by the window and watched her pull the sheet off the rug. It wafted through the air and landed in a shapeless mass on the ground. Nurdane stepped around it and sat at the loom. She tucked her feet beneath her and emptied the contents she had wrapped in the flap of her skirt. The bobbin, comb, a ball of wool. She could feel Adam watching her and turned toward him, her eyes glowing in the light, warning him like a wild animal. She needed privacy now more than ever. She could see his pained expression, offended by her need to be alone. But she did not care, narrowing her eyes until he stepped away from the window. She laced her fingers between the weft and warp, and with the other hand threaded the yarn and tied the first knot. Then another until her fingers moved like spiders across the loom, tying the knots swiftly, without hesitation. Her heart pounding as she worked. Faster and faster. More knots. A hundred thoughts racing through her mind . . . *as long as you keep your hands pure, Allah will make the knots through you.*

Hennessey sat on the floor and ate spiced bulgur and chicken that the postman's wife had left for him in a clay pot, still warm from the fire. The flicker of a candle crossed his face, and Muammer stood behind the door, secretly watching him with uncertainty. Hennessey licked his fingers and wiped his hands on the bandanna around his neck, then carefully traced the lines on the series of blue handprints strewn about him.

He did not know why Nurdane had made the prints, but he tried to read them now in the winding wrinkles imprinted on her flesh. He read the lines as a scientist would, hypothesizing her potential, postulating the history of her craftsmanship. When it began, at birth and beyond to past lives, perhaps, through circumstance, happenstance, fate, or chance. He knew she carried a legacy in her hands and believed the prints to be a map of her soul. He was surprised that she had done nothing to hide the prints, and he suspected now that she wanted him to find them.

He rearranged the prints on the floor, trying to follow the pattern in the markings. She had taken a pen to each and circled strange places on the palm, slash marks on the fingers. Each one a successive series of circles until it appeared she had identified the deviant lines, the culprit being the leathery line crowning her wrist.

She circled it on the last print, marking it so hard with ink that she had ripped a hole through the paper.

Hennessey sat up and looked down, trying to connect the markings on the prints. Nothing made sense. The eerie blue dye. And the Arabic text. The verses from the Koran. He could not understand the correlation they had with her hand. The five fingers spread in vain over the words, clawing them like a cat, scratching its way through a screen.

He laid the prints beside each other and compared the fingers first. He knew the thumb disclosed self-discipline and the drive to manifest one's own potential. The index finger, which he had heard people call Zeus, was associated with leadership and the desire to influence others. Saturn, the middle finger, revealed the tendency to seek order. The ring finger, Apollo, showed creative talents, and the pinky, Mercury, encompassed the skill of communication and charm. Her fingers were long and lean, the pads of her palms, the Mars area, thick, revealing her creative impulses. But it was the triangle in the middle of her palm that intrigued him most. The triangle, the sign of a mystic or prophet. It appeared on the fifth and final print of the series, as a riddle he was summoned to answer but could not yet read.

He could read only fingerprints, working as a physical anthropologist in France, identifying the war dead. His study of forensics had taught him that every human receives a set of permanent fingerprints five months before birth. He knew fingerprints would always be a constant; however, the lines across the palm of the hands could change invariably throughout a lifetime, the changes as incremental as a few months, sometimes weeks, depending on the turn of events.

Hennessey knew, too, that the hand changes itself by doing. The hand learns from experience and remembers. He wondered what circumstance her right hand recalled to make the lines so distinct on each print, so different, it appeared that the handprint belonged to several people. He sensed in the disparate lines a certain frustration with her experiences, what her hand had touched, as if it had touched the wrong things or had not touched enough.

Hands had always held his interest, and in his own excavations he had found hands made of wood and ivory, obsidian and stone. He had studied only the fragments, piecing together fingers and wrists but had never been afforded the clues of prints and palms. He knew Chinese emperors had used their thumbprints to seal documents thousands of years before Christ and that the practice of palmistry had Eastern origins, purportedly dating back ten thousand years to India, where a piece of wood allegedly held the secret to the oldest ancient art. The laws and practices have passed through vedic scripts, the Bible, early Semitic writings. He read that Aristotle had discovered a treatise on palmistry on an altar to Hermes and claimed that a person's palm reveals their true nature, vices and virtues alike. Alexander the Great also practiced the art, Julius Caesar had used palmistry to judge his men, and he wondered how much of Nurdane had been revealed through her handprints.

He lay prone on the floor with his chin against the cold stone, watching the candle flame flicker to its death. In the silence, he listened to the dance of Nurdane's hand, and in the darkness read the words between the lines, trying to understand her conflicting pleasures.

She sat on the windowsill, looking out over the village in that fugitive hour where the light and land answer each other. She could see Hennessey through the front window of the postman's house. If she had the strength to walk only a quarter mile, close enough to smell him again, she could sleep. She waited until the sun rose and the village resumed its business, then took the bike from the woodshed and rode down to the fountain, where he stood, filling his bota with water. She rode up behind him unnoticed, until he turned, startled to see her.

You're up early.

I never went to bed, she said.

Hennessey smiled.

Me neither. I had a lot on my mind.

The dark will do that.

Yes, he said, noticing that she had changed. She wore a clean blue sweater the color of her eyes and a floral skirt instead of the familiar baggy trousers of the village women. Her hair had been tied into a single braid and draped her shoulder like a long black rope. Clogs hid her callused feet.

I hope you're not too tired to read.

He looked at her, suddenly self-conscious, as if she knew he had invaded her privacy, reading her handprints.

I've had more restful nights.

Trust me. The hardest part will be climbing to the lodge.

The lodge?

My students' rugs are there.

She pointed to the lodge on the hill that sat alone above the tip of the minaret.

You still want to learn my language?

Hennessey looked at her.

Absolutely.

He followed her through the village, past the spring-wheat field and storage sheds, where families were already threshing grain, stuffing it into woven sacs to be taken to the mill and ground into flour. They paused to watch the weaver and digger, resuming their work only when Nurdane lifted her head and nodded, obliging their curious stares. Hennessey waved and lifted his Panama hat and walked slowly behind the bike. Nurdane turned to him.

You should be in front of me.

Why?

Women follow men.

I'm not a very good man, he said, and stopped, letting her ride ahead of him even farther. When she was a good twenty meters, he turned, waving to the workers in the field, then jogged up behind her and put his hand on the back of her seat, pushing her up the hill to the lodge. She parked the bike in the generous shade of a walnut tree and dismounted. It was cool here, and she leaned against the trunk and caught her breath.

They'll talk, she said.

Good. It's a beautiful day for words.

Hennessey took the bota from his waist and handed it to her. She did not drink but rubbed her fingers over the initials engraved on the wooden neck.

A hook, she said, tracing the J.

John.

What?

It stands for John. My first name.

John, she said, and mimicked his American accent.

My friends call me Johnny.

Johnny.

The sound tickled her tongue, and she quickly covered her smile with the back of her hand. She raised the bota to her lips and took a drink, then handed it back to Hennessey.

We're not friends.

No?

Not yet, she said, raising her arm for him to guide her as he had done the night before.

When?

Soon enough.

He stood staring at her, watching the grin widen across her face. Instead of taking her by the elbow, Hennessey slid his hand into her own, pleasantly surprised that she did not protest, locking her fingers with his, allowing him to guide her to the lodge. He could feel her struggling to balance her weight. Together they shared the burden of her handicap, walking slowly, reverent in her pain, the creak of her braces punctuating the silence.

Nurdane stopped at the doorway, surprised to find the looms had been pushed against the walls to make room for the dozen wooden trunks that filled the space. Various sized paintbrushes lay strewn about the floor, and cans of paint were stacked beside the windowsills, some open, the smell of paint fumes in the air, but no reminder of the young weaver she had met the other day. She half hoped to find her here now, to see if Hennessey could understand the prophecy of poppies.

You work here?

I teach.

What are the trunks for?

The brides, she said. Dowry chests.

She broke away from him and moved between the wooden boxes that lay open and airing. They smelled of cedar and pine. She dragged the palm of her hand over the top, smooth and dusty from sanding. They reminded her of coffins, so raw.

Hennessey followed behind her and got down on his knees to inspect the workmanship. Intricate floral designs had been carved into the wood. There was not a single knot in the grain.

They must cost a fortune, he said.

Some do. The dowry is a lifetime of savings.

She wandered slowly this time and stopped, seeing that one of the chests had been filled with various household items, candlesticks, wooden spoons, and bowls, lace curtains, tablecloths, linens. The contents would have been enough to furnish five households, not one, and she wondered what other girls were getting married.

Is it yours?

She turned to find Hennessey standing before one of the looms, his face puckered in concentration as he studied the rug there. Nurdane closed the lid on the dowry chest and moved toward him.

Two sisters made it.

Hennessey stepped closer and pointed to the oversized treelike shapes recurring through a field festooned with flowers that were depicted by eight-pointed stars.

Are they minarets?

She laughed and ran her fingers over the knots.

This is a cemetery rug. Those are trees.

Hennessey pointed to a series of boxes woven in between the long poles of the trunks.

Mausoleums?

She nodded.

The rug is a gate to paradise, she said. If you pray for the departing soul, you can help guide them to heaven.

Seems like a heavy concept for a child.

Paradise?

No. Death.

There's no difference, is there?

She could feel his eyes on her, but she kept her own eyes fixed on the knots.

Two young sisters made it for their grandmother.

The whole thing?

Most of it.

The rest yours?

A little.

You're very generous.

Generous?

He stepped closer to her side to examine the rug.

The workmanship is perfect, he said.

She shrugged and turned from him.

Don't let beauty deceive you. There is no perfection.

She lifted the sheet off the next loom, exposing a prayer rug with the most simple pattern. A single niche composition. One blue tree in the center of a red field bordered by a series of deformed, stylized birds.

The weaver is blind.

Blind?

Those are birds. And that blue motif is a tree. The *tuba* tree.

The tree of paradise rooted in heaven and earth. You can see so much of the weaver here. You feel her. She wants you to know her. She's telling you she's survived.

What?

Death.

How can you see that?

Nurdane stepped forward and rubbed her fingers once again over the silken knots.

Read the knots. She's written the story of Anatolia. The women. She's recorded the history of our mothers and grand-mothers. The nomads. That's how the weaving started, you know. Tents first. It was out of necessity. The knots have always been about survival.

Hennessey nodded, listening intently.

What about the birds?

Ah, the birds.

She smiled.

My favorite symbol. I use it in my rugs.

What does it mean?

You see how deformed it is?

He nodded.

This blind girl understands it best. She knows there is no per-fection. Only Allah is perfect. You see, He gave all birds wings but not all birds can fly.

She poked through the weft where the knots had been tied loosely.

Nothing's perfect.

Except your own work.

She withdrew her fingers from the rug and lifted her chin slightly.

How would you know?

I've heard stories, he said.

She laughed.

That's all they are. Stories. Tales. Half-truths. Rumors mostly. People get bored here. They like to talk.

You should be proud.

Of the rumors?

Your hands. They've been blessed.

Sometimes, she said. Her voice was low, hollow.

Hennessey watched her eyes cloud as he spoke, as if each word were pitted against her, wedged deep within her heart.

They say Allah makes the rugs through you. That you must keep your hands pure if you want the gift.

She nodded slowly, drawing a breath. Hennessey could see her breasts rise through her blouse, and she looked as if the breath itself had suddenly filled her with courage.

They believe blue eyes are bad luck, she said. That a wound heals if you rub bread over it. They believe the mosque breathes answers to those who carry pure hearts. They believe many things. . . . We're superstitious, you know. Our blood runs with rumors.

Is it true?

She tilted her head, her cheeks, already rosy, shimmered in the early light as if they had been dabbed with glitter. She sat down on the lid of the dowry chest and pulled her knees to her chest.

I make dowry rugs. It's no rumor.

I know.

As long as I stay pure, keep my hands clean, Allah will continue to make the rugs through me, the rugs for the brides I'll never become.

It's ironic, isn't it?

Rumors often are, she said.

He stopped and looked at her face. The tears spilled down her cheeks, but she did not put her hand up to stop them or hide them from Hennessey. Instead, she let them fall into the palms of her hands.

I've always had a wish.

What?

It's foolish.

She wiped her face, sat up, mouth pinched, trying to compose herself.

I've never told anybody before.

Hennessey sat down on the trunk beside her, his shirt stained with salt. She shifted herself, and he moved slightly to the right, opening the space between them, making room for her words.

I don't know why I feel I can tell you these things.

You don't have to tell me anything, he said.

I want to. I just don't know how. I never spoke to the diggers. I was too young. I never understood them.

She shifted her eyes, dragged them down Hennessey's forearm into the palm of his hand, opened, it seemed, waiting to collect her secret.

You understand me? he asked.

You're the only person who understands me.

She drew in a deep breath.

My wish, she said, her voice trailing off.

What?

I wish I could give back the blessing in my hands.

She turned her head from him, fixed her eyes on the light coming in through the window.

Why would you want that?

She smiled.

My father.

He wants you to give it back?

No. He always told me that when Allah takes something from you, He gives you something in return.

Hennessey stared at her.

I don't understand, he said.

My legs, you see. Allah took them and gave me hands.

But he already gave you hands.

No, she said. Allah gave me a gift with my hands. He gave me weaving. He gave me the knots.

Did your father tell you that?

She nodded.

Don't you think you've given yourself the knots?

She stared at him, perplexed, drugged by his words. It was too much for her to accept without shedding years of teachings, inter-pretations of Islamic law she carried as naturally as her pride, the layers thick, entrenched in her being.

The knots are Allah's, she said with certainty. My gift is his. But I would give it back if it meant, only once, I would feel—

She stopped.

What? What do you want to feel?

She looked up at him, unsure of how to proceed, how much or how little she needed to say for him to understand.

I want to feel what it is to be the woman those brides become.

A hot wind lifted her skirt. Hennessey stared at her, catching a glimpse of the bruised and broken skin beneath the braces, realiz-ing that grief was the instrument by which Nurdane had come to grace. Pain and loss and grueling anxiety had been the pathway by which she had come to know herself, and she carried a certain dig-nity in her suffering. It was more than determination. It was duty, obligation. At her core, she embodied the strength of Anatolia, carrying the spirit of its Goddess past.

She reminded him of the Yekuana, the indigenous tribe of Venezuela who lived along the riverbanks of the Amazon rain for-est. They made baskets reminiscent of the Cherokee, with geomet-ric designs, abstract shapes much like those he had seen in her rug. The baskets functioned as a sort of cosmogram for the people, and like prayer rugs or Buddhist mandalas, represented a model for the heavens, a place for the spirit to travel. The Yekuana were shaman-istic in their craft, healers, traveling into other worlds with their hands. They believed that to weave was to conquer death, and he wondered if Nurdane knew she possessed the same power.

He watched her thinking. She seemed to be pacing herself. A million thoughts in her mind, each unfurled with the slow, shrewd look in her eyes. Her forehead had grown flushed, and he could see the tiny veins throbbing when she extended her hands and con-fessed.

You see, then, she said. That in their blessing, my hands are also cursed.

They spoke nothing more of her hands, of rumors or truths, and worked in silence through the day, the sun hot on their backs, necks white with salt. A truck honked, passing them, pulling a flatbed of tomatoes picked fresh from greenhouses in the valley. Village boys jockeyed for position on the back, clinging to the slated sides with their bare feet. They whistled at Nurdane, waving to her, blowing her kisses, but she was too absorbed in her work to respond. She sat back on her knees on a straw mat and sifted through the mounds of dirt she and Hennessey had unearthed, helping him search for clues of Mavisu's Goddess past. He wanted to find pieces of the ancient pottery vessels that had been used as tombs, simulating wombs, the skeletons folded into the fetal position. He told her the Phrygians were the first to introduce the tumuli burial custom, learning it first from the Cimmerian who passed through Anatolia seven hundred years before Christ. He wanted bones, but they found nothing but bits of broken plates and the rusted shells of bullets.

Are you sure you're looking in the right place?

Yes. Of course, he said.

You didn't consider any other spots?

This is it.

He looked up at her from the pit where he stood digging and wiped the sweat from his brow. He wore his sunglasses. She saw her reflection in the lenses.

We've been here all day.

I know. It takes time. We've only just begun. I could be here for years.

She brushed her hands together to shake off the dirt and

opened his notebook again, flipping through the pages until she saw the symbol of Cybelle.

Isn't this what you're looking for?

Not exactly that.

I thought that's why you're here.

I am. But it's only a symbol, Nurdane. I need hard evidence. I need bones.

Bones. Hmmm. That's all?

For now, yes.

Seems limiting, she said, wrapping her braid around her wrist like a coiled black snake.

Limiting? What do you suggest?

I don't know. I'm a weaver.

Hennessey shook his head and wiped the back of his neck, catching a fly between his fingers.

Look. It's been a long day. You didn't even sleep last night. I don't know how you can stand the heat.

You didn't sleep.

I'm not tired, he said.

Me neither.

I can take you home.

Do you want to take me home?

If you're tired.

I'm not.

Fine. Stay.

I wasn't leaving.

She wiped her face with the flap of her skirt.

I think you may be wasting your time.

What gives you that idea?

Hennessey scraped the side of the pit and filled the shovel with dry, rocky soil.

You're already pretty deep. Any deeper and you may hit a lake.

Doesn't matter. There could be layers and layers of sediment. Hundreds of years. Maybe thousands.

I don't think so.

Why not?

This is it. There's not even topsoil here.

I know that.

She cocked her head, curious.

Then you probably know that this is the windiest place in Mavisu, why my father built the hut of stone. It's hard to blow stones, you know, I'm sure.

More scraping. Hennessey was getting annoyed.

Maybe you'd like to contact the Ministry of Culture and tell them how I should do my job.

She bit her lip, trying not to smile.

I'm only trying to be helpful.

And I appreciate it, Nurdane. I really do.

You should.

Yes. Thank you.

That's what friends do.

Friends? I didn't think we were friends yet.

That was yesterday, she said.

Oh, so you get to say when.

Yes. Today we are friends.

Maybe I'm not ready to be your friend.

I think you are, she said, flashing him a smile, baring her teeth for the first time since they met. He stopped digging and leaned against the shovel, looking up at her, sitting on that straw mat as if it were a throne.

I want to show you something tomorrow, she said.

What?

I can't tell you until you see it. There's a chance you won't. And I don't think I can bear to see your face if you're disappointed.

Nurdane sat with the women in the kitchen of the muhtar's house, peeling eggplant. The brides and their sisters and mothers had gathered to clean vegetables, preparing food for the weddings. They hummed old folk songs but exchanged few words, the somber music filling the house, chasing laughter and idle chatter into closets and cracks. The preparation for the feast was a bittersweet reminder of not only their daughters' marriages, but also their separation from each other. Some of the brides would leave the village after the wedding and would not be seen for a year. They worked quietly, lips mumbling prayers for their daughters' safekeeping, only the tinkling of a spoon on glass punctuating the silence. They mixed honey with a special tea brewed from rose petals, offering Nurdane a cup.

Thank you.

We made it for you.

She looked at them curiously. They stared with expectant eyes, brides and mothers alike with their sugary smiles and pitiless winks.

You didn't have to go to any trouble.

You've been working hard.

She nodded, reading their faces.

Yes. I've been working.

The digger is lucky to have your help.

Ayse walked up behind her with a bowl of roasted pistachios, interrupting.

Fresh nuts? We picked them this morning.

The women dug their hands into the bowl, spilling shells that had already been split. Ayse exchanged a knowing look with Nurdane, noticing how she shifted on the floor, trying to find some comfort. But the women persisted.

He's a friendly man?

Nurdane nodded.

Yes. I enjoy his company.

We know.

Nurdane studied their faces, wondering why they threw their glances on the floor. Ayse passed the bowl again, hoping the gesture would at least divert their attention.

Is there enough salt?

What?

The nuts. Are they salty?

Yes, the women said, perturbed by Ayse's irrelvant questions. They focused again on Nurdane.

You have us biting our nails.

Why?

There's not much time. You have two days.

For what?

To finish the rug. *Allah. Allah.* You haven't forgotten.

Trust me. It will be done.

She stared at them, appalled by their incessant inquiries, doubting her. She got up and moved to the window with her crutches. Ayse followed.

Ignore them, she whispered, pulling back the curtain to see the grooms stomping grapes. Steam rose from the cast-iron vats where the juice boiled and turned slowly into a thick syrup called *pekmez,* to be poured over the sponge cakes baking in the outdoor oven. The smell of sugar and yeast came in through the window, and she closed her eyes, taking a deep breath.

What's the doctor doing there?

Who?

Nurdane opened her eyes, surprised to see him. He was busy washing his feet and did not see her from the window. The muhtar stood beside him, talking, joking, dousing him with lemon cologne before he stood and climbed into the large cubical container made of stone and joined the grooms. A flutist sat crouched on his heels and played for the young men while they crushed the grapes with their bare feet. A group of boys sat watching, envious, Muammer among them, ready to collect the juice from a small hole at the bottom of the container.

I didn't know Adam was getting married, Ayse said.

Nurdane could feel the bride's eyes on her, reading her response, but she offered nothing of the small lump she felt in her stomach.

He's not.

Then what's he doing in the grapes?

Trying to help. He does that. He's a doctor.

Nurdane moved away from the window toward the door and let herself outside. She stood in the shadow of a pomegranate tree and watched Adam, singing with the grooms as if he were one himself. He looked so silly, like a clown, arms flailing, drunk on his own delight. He looked so much older than the others, twice their age despite his childlike abandon. He was clapping now, slapping his knee, dancing on the grapes.

We should join them.

Nurdane turned to find Mehmet walking up behind her. He carried a basket of Turkish apricots.

Looks like fun, doesn't it?

He set the basket down and wiped his forehead with his sleeve. Nurdane kept her eyes fixed on Adam.

He shouldn't be dancing, she said.

He's celebrating.

What?

Your hand.

She turned to Adam.

Only grooms crush the grapes, she said.

Maybe he's getting married.

She rolled her eyes.

Right. To whom?

Mehmet picked out a ripe apricot and handed it to her.

Stranger things have happened here.

Nurdane bit into the apricot, the flesh soft and velvety against her tongue. The juice dripped along her chin, and Mehmet wiped it with his sleeve.

They're good, huh?

I've seen better dancers.

The apricots.

She looked at him, embarrassed.

Thank you.

I bet you wouldn't say the same if it were Hennessey.

What?

She turned to him, trying to read his brown eyes, the color of tea in the light. He leaned back against the tree.

There are rumors, Nurdane.

Rumors?

Everyone has an idea about you and the digger.

She turned to him.

All of them worthy, I'm sure.

None really, he said, biting into the apricot again. Except mine.

She smiled.

Everybody has an idea about you and Ayse too.

Mehmet stopped eating.

All of them worthy, he said.

She looked up at him, stealing his wink, then turned and moved back into the house to join the brides in the somber preparation of their parting.

Hennessey passed a small fire that had been burning outside the cemetery since the picker's burial. Groups of villagers had gathered around a stack of old tractor tires and fed cedar chips to the flames inside, lighting the way for the spirit. They believed in the power of light to guide a lost soul to safety, and although they did not know who the dead man had been, they entrusted their soil to him and felt obliged to guide him to heaven before he lost his soul to the dark.

They sat back on their bare heels, the whites of their eyes glowing, watching Hennessey come into the light, his large hands braced against the shovels and tools that were strapped to his back. Some boys ran up close to see his face, the man who had taken down the weaver's hut. And even in the late hour they carried tins of shoe polish and snapped rags around his ankles. He moved past them, through the gates of the village, past the teahouse and the mosque, where he sat on the steps to rest, his mind heavy with the burden of secrets.

He had never intended to know Nurdane. Her hut had been a small obstacle in his course, a blight on the map. How foolish for him to think this would have been like the rest. He laughed, thinking of Egypt and Venezuela. There had never been any consequences. The people whom he wished to know had died long before he uprooted their graves, his guilt absolved by the evidence he found there. More clues to anchor his theory that every culture in every nation had, at one point or other, revered women, that Goddess worship celebrated her journey, the ultimate hero, the giver of life. She had been an ancient force in South America and Asia, Europe, North America, Africa, and here in Asia Minor,

Anatolia, a place full of women, where she lived before Allah had a name, then died once he did.

Intimacy had never compromised Hennessey's work. He related to the dead, not the living. He was a child of Danu, the ancestral mother of the Irish Celts. Da Chich Anannan, County Kerry, the place of his birth where the famed twin conical hills rise from the green bogs of Ireland like giant breasts. Even as a boy he had the ability to listen to the voices of the dead, finding clues of their past in rocks, gleaning history from their bones. He was a lover of fragments, an alchemist of sorts who could make things whole again, piece together bits of the past. The legacy of the Goddess had been lost for so long that most people he knew were unaware it ever existed. His duty was to reacquaint the world with her ancient ways, which he believed held the truth to our spiritual existence. His reluctance to be intimate with the living allowed him to focus on the dead. But now he could think of nothing other than Nurdane, as if it were she, not the site, that he had come to find.

Everything had taken a turn. He suddenly found himself outside the safety of his own inhibitions, limited by the ethics of his profession. Nurdane embodied the spirit of the Goddess he had come to glean from the dead but had now found in the living. The irony unnerved him, and he felt frustrated. He knew that the closer a scientist got to the essence of the thing studied, the more he could alter its behavior. He considered the impurities he imposed on Nurdane by being in Mavisu, his attitudes and beliefs altering her, altering his perception of her. He knew Turkish village women were not encouraged to seek the friendship of males other than those in their immediate families. Brothers, uncles, cousins. That was the extent of their relationship, and anything else was frowned upon if not forbidden and strictly enforced. Outside the family, women were taught to keep their eyes on the ground and discourage any relationships with strangers. That's all Hennessey was to Nurdane. A man who had suddenly appeared in her life. A stranger now, whom she trusted.

A cool breeze hit his back, and he turned to find the muhtar standing in the door of the mosque. He held a bottle of lemon cologne and splashed his neck and face, then offered the same to Hennessey.

You're a mess.

I know, Hennessey said, outstretching his hands. The muhtar shook the bottle, dousing him with the fervor of a doctor delousing schoolchildren.

That's enough.

You'll want to be clean.

I'm going home.

The muhtar looked at him with a long face.

Already?

I'm exhausted. I've been working since dawn.

You'll miss the fun, he said, pointing to the lodge on the hill. Candlelight flickered from the inside, and he could see men painting something in the windows.

They were hoping you'd stop by.

Who?

Adam and Ali. They have a surprise.

Hennessey stood, leaving the tools on the steps, and followed the muhtar to the lodge. They stopped once to pick figs from a neighbor's tree. The muhtar stuffed a few in his mouth and spoke, chewing.

Can't get enough. They're so ripe.

Yes.

Tamam. Tamam. Take them.

He pressed the figs into Hennessey's hands and placed a finger over his lips as they crept past the house and turned down the path that led to the lodge. The windows were open for the heat, the air filled with paint fumes. Strains of a Turkish musician impersonating Benny Goodman played from a radio inside, where Adam and Ali finished painting the last of the twelve trunks they had unloaded the previous day. Oil lamps hung from the ceiling and cast shadows on the trunks. The raw wood had been transformed into a wash of color, green and yellow, red and blue. Intricate floral designs had been painted on the faces, still wet with paint and glistening in the light. The lids were open, the insides unfinished, filled with every conceivable household item.

Hennessey stood in the doorway and watched as Ali filled the last trunk with what appeared to be a trove of treasures from old fruit crates. Adam picked up a glossy magazine from the floor.

What's this?

He tried to piece together the front cover that had torn, Rita Hayworth's face split in half.

Nothing.

Somebody gave you a magazine for the rug?

Ali scoffed.

A city man. Came up from Antalya when he heard about the bidding.

Serious?

Ali nodded, rolled his eyes.

Said it would be a collector's item.

Adam laughed.

She's very famous.

Adam looked at Hennessey, who stood in the doorway. The muhtar had left him alone and was whistling somewhere down the path, his mouth still stuffed with figs.

Good evening, Hennessey said.

He lifted his Panama hat and stepped into the lodge, taking in the treasures that lined the trunks.

Thought the Pirate Coast was by the sea.

Adam laughed.

You know what it's for?

Hennessey nodded.

The brides. They're dowry chests.

Very good. But it's for one bride.

Only one?

Ali looked up and nodded, his chest puffy with pride.

She must be an angel.

She is, Adam said, walking down the line, closing the lids on the trunk with a finality of an undertaker shutting a coffin, the clap of wood as deafening as a gavel.

Hennessey stood outside the postman's house in the stone shower and washed the dirt and salt from his body, soaking his thoughts. The water was warm from the cistern on the roof, rainwater heated in the sun, fragrant too, naturally distilled with the blossoms of Lady's Fingers that had blown in from the wind. The smell reminded him of honeysuckle, and for a moment he felt like a boy, naked and exposed. He scrubbed his nails, scraping out the dirt with a toothpick, thinking about Nurdane's hands and handprints. He felt dishonest that he hadn't told her he still had them, had studied them, wondering why she hadn't asked, and what Nurdane would do to get what she wanted, sensing that what she wanted, she also feared. He could understand that if she believed the weaving was not her own, she could give it away, discard it like an old sweater, pass it along to a younger sibling who needed it more. But the weaving *was* her, embodied her, and there was no way she could give a part of it back without giving away a part of herself. Her beliefs disturbed him, the idea that the knots were Allah's work, that Allah compensates for human loss with talents and tricks.

He took a bar of olive oil soap, and scrubbing his hands, tilted his head back under the shower and opened his eyes, lifting them to the slit in the roof. He could feel the moon watching him, the strips of clouds like war paint on its face, challenging him, he thought, preparing him for a battle he had come to fight. He rinsed the soap from his hair and let the water run down his back, then turned off the shower until there was only the slow drip of water on his shoulder, his mind stepping away from itself.

He took a towel, stiff and crusted with salt, and dried his body, his raw skin stinging. He could hear rustling inside his room, the window open. He stepped out of the shower, slipped his feet into sandals, and crossed the yard into the house. The postman and his younger sons were still at the lodge with the other men, his wife with neighbors, making flat bread for the weddings. He had not heard from nor seen Muammer all day, and he wasn't surprised to find him now, rifling through his bags. Hennessey stepped into the room, the towel slung around his hips, his chest bare, skin pale in the moonlight.

What are you doing?

The boy jumped, startled. He looked up from the bed, his hand still stuck inside one of Hennessey's bags, the handprints strewn across the top sheet.

Gum.

Gum?

You never gave me the bubble gum.

You never asked.

Hennessey left his sandals at the door and walked barefoot, the soles of his feet slapping the stones. He collected the handprints from the bed.

Don't you know how to ask for anything?

Yes.

Muammer lowered his head.

Do you always have to snoop? Hennessey asked.

No.

You like invading people's privacy?

No. But you promised.

To invade your privacy? Tell me your secrets, Muammer. I'll scratch them into the door of the mosque next time I pop in.

Muammer scowled.

You promised me gum. You broke your promise.

Me? You said you would guide me.

I did.

You got me into trouble that day.

I got us both into trouble.

Why should I reward you for trouble?

I did what I said.

Lie?

I gave you a tour. I guided you.

If you call that guiding, let me get lost next time. Please.

Hennessey flipped through the handprints, noticing they had been marked with a pencil, the lines silver in the light. He could feel the boy watching him.

You got them all wrong, he said, his voice pinched with hurt.

Hennessey turned.

She didn't tell you? Muammer asked.

Hennessey knew better than to say anything. He just stared at him, waiting.

She won't tell you. But she wants you to know. That's why she left them hanging. Nobody knows.

Knows what?

About the handprints. Nobody saw them. You took them before you took down the hut.

Hennessey nodded, his expression revealing little as the boy spoke.

I was going to do it, but you got there before I did.

Why?

I wanted the same thing, Muammer said.

Hennessey locked eyes with him.

What's that?

I wanted to protect her. Like you.

Hennessey took in a deep breath, sitting down on the bed. He propped his elbow on his knee, holding his forehead in his hand. He lifted his eyes, fixing them on Muammer's face.

I'm sorry.

Muammer shifted on his feet, rubbed his shaven head with the backs of his hands. He pointed to the handprints.

Can you read them? he asked.

I'm no palmist.

The text. It's from the Koran.

I haven't translated it yet, Hennessey said.

It's the twenty-sixth sura.

Hennessey looked up, waiting. The boy lifted his eyes to the ceiling and spoke, reciting the proverb.

Have we not lifted up your heart and relieved you of the burden which weighed down your back? Have we not given you high renown? Every hardship is followed by ease. When your task is ended, resume your toil, and seek your Lord with all fervor.

Muammer lowered his eyes, fixing them on Hennessey, who was bent over, spreading the handprints on the floor.

She wants comfort, Hennessey said. Is that it?

She wants to touch Allah.

Hennessey looked up.

Muammer repeated himself, his voice self-assured.

Can't you see? She's trying to reach Allah.

He held up his hand, spreading his fingers, pressing them against the air, mimicking the gesture Nurdane had used to make the handprints. Then he turned and walked toward the door.

I didn't mean to snoop, he said.

Wait.

Hennessey dug into his bag and pulled out a pack of gum. He tossed it across the floor to Muammer.

You sure?

Hennessey nodded.

I'm sure.

You're not going to be mad at me?

Hennessey shook his head, gripped his knees with his hands to keep them from trembling in front of the boy.

You've been a great help. You have no idea.

Muammer bent down and picked up the gum.

I just see things. That's all.

Nurdane returned to an empty house, a triangle of paper tacked to the door knocker. She took it from the door, unfolding it, and a handful of fresh poppy petals fluttered to the steps. The door was slightly ajar and she could see candlelight flickering from inside. She pushed the door open and found, scattered on the floor, a trail of flower petals leading to her bedroom. She moved slowly through the hallway, hearing the thwap of Attila's tail on the stone floor in her room. She stood in the doorway, watching him sniff the box on her bed. He looked back at her and barked, his tail beating faster as she approached.

She was surprised to find even more poppies covered her bed. Hundreds of them were strewn over the mattress, the air fragrant and grassy. She cleared a space and sat down, taking the box in her lap. She shook it gently, hearing the rustle of paper. Something sliding. The box was wet with Attila's noseprints. The bow crushed. She untied it and pulled back the flaps to find a mass of red silk cloth folded neatly inside. Attila barked again and got down on his haunches, dropped his head between his paws, eyes staring up at her in anticipation.

She took the material out of the box and let it fall to the floor, revealing a dress. The sleeves were long, the bodice fitted, neckline high and embroidered with an intricate floral design. The same design she remembered from the box she found in the wall, the box her father had said was the postman's mistake. She stood and held the dress against her, let the material slide through her fingers. It was smooth and cool against her skin, a rare and coveted material, different from the coarse wool she was used to working with. She pressed the silk against her cheek, wondered if Allah had skin, would it feel like this?

She left the dress on the bed and went to the kitchen to get a rag and water, taking it back with her to the bedroom for a bath. She stripped in the dark, unwrapping the skirt from her hips, unbuttoning the soiled blouse, stained with her sweat. She let the clothing fall to the floor and unfastened her braces, then washed herself with the rag, letting the warm cross-breeze dry her body, the crush of cicadas serenading her. When she was clean, she took the dress from the bed, using the crutches to steady herself, and pulled it over her head, let the silk fall over her body. She smoothed out the wrinkles with the palms of her hands, delighted perhaps, for the first time, with the curves of her own body.

She turned and faced the window. Only the black face of the mountain watched her, her reflection exaggerated by candlelight. She looked taller in the glass, willowy in the flickering flame. The dress hugged her body. It was a perfect fit, and she knew that the pattern she had found, the measurements written there, had been her own. She ran her hands over her breasts, down her stomach, flat and tight beneath the silk. She took her hair out of the headscarf and let it fall down her back, like an ancient priestess, she thought. Gripping her crutches, she moved past the dog and into the parlor, then, taking her place by the bar on the wall, closed her eyes and imagined herself dancing.

Adam and her father told her the dress was for her birthday and said she could wear it for the occasion. She was anxious and thanked them, leaving without saying good-bye. There was not much time. She told Hennessey to meet her at the excavation site. She led him down a narrow goat path behind the agora, past the fallen columns of the temple and library to the opening of a small cave overgrown with weeds. A small votive candle burned at the entrance, the rocks splattered with wax. Nurdane pressed her fingers into it. It was still warm.

They've already come to visit.

Who?

The women, she said, taking the small knife from her pocket to hack through the rushes and thorns, clearing the entrance to the cave.

Nobody ever goes inside. The lakes are deep this time of year. Can you swim?

He nodded, intrigued by the color of the limestone, burnt ochre in the light. Beyond the entrance, blackness and the slow drip of water.

She turned, looking over her shoulder at the position of the sun, halfway between the horizon and the minaret.

Come quickly.

He stood and followed her through a narrow corridor, the cave walls pressed against him, the mosses soft and wet on his arms. The metallic cold of coins, too, pressed into the walls for good luck. They moved slowly through the darkness, the light from the entrance a pinhole in the distance. Soon he could see nothing and moved at the mercy of her braces, grateful for the slow creak to guide him.

The walls grew cooler the deeper they went into the cave. Hennessey slid his fingers against the rocks, where snails clung like small tumors, then nothing but space, the air damp and cool in the gaps. Suddenly the walls fell away and he felt the space grow wider, the blackness bigger. He raised his arms in the air, trying to feel the low ceiling, but there was nothing but space. He patted the ground with his hands and followed the lip of what felt like a small pool. The water surprisingly warm, like bathwater. The smell of sulfur. He could hear Nurdane's hand exploring, the drip of water from her hands.

We stop here. Take off your shoes.

Her voice echoed, amplified by the water so that it sounded as if there were a group of women instructing him. He could hear her unfastening the braces. Sliding them down her leg. Then something soft. Fingers against cloth. Rustling. Unbuttoning. The tumble of clothes.

He could feel his heart beating faster. Then a plunk of water as she entered it, one leg at a time. A shudder as the water hit her skin. It was warm, yet cooler than she remembered, the waters still chilled from the spring thaw. Then a deep breath and flutter of feet. Kicking. Splashing. Her breath disappearing under the water, then up for air, a quick gasp. The throw of damp hair against skin, draping her shoulders, he imagined. He turned back toward what he thought was the entrance. Only blackness. Direction inconsequential now. He was disoriented and had no way of knowing where they had come from. He suddenly felt lost and pawed the air with his hands. He licked his finger and held it up like a sailor, trying to detect the direction of the wind. Only a cool breeze, then nothing but the echo that slipped through his fingers.

Are you in yet?

Her voice echoed around the cave walls.

Not yet.

Hurry. We don't have much time.

He did not understand the rush, but he did as she instructed and balanced himself on either leg and took off his shoes and socks. His mind racing, wondering how many laws he would break if he entered the water with her, naked. He opened the top button of his shirt, then stopped. He stepped down into the lake, his feet light on the ground, searching for information, rocks, plants, moss. It was muddy and soft, like wet velvet, and he slid over it, releasing the smell of sulfur through the water.

This way. Closer to me.

He waded through the water, following her voice, then stopped suddenly when she told him to.

Okay. Stay there.

He stood still, not knowing where she was in relation to him, the gap of darkness between them.

Now lift your head. Right above you.

He raised his head, shifted his eyes in the dark. A small beam of light moved across the cave wall, and for a minute his heart jumped, thinking somebody had indeed followed them. But the light kept moving, slowly exposing layers of sediments, strips of marble and iron in the limestone. The light stopped and suddenly widened as if someone were spreading it across the cave. Brighter and brighter it grew, exposing the face of the rock and an oddly familiar figure painted there. The life-size head and body of a woman. Stacked diamonds for her torso, rounded as if she were pregnant. Cybelle. The same figure in his notebook. The same figure he had seen in the rug from Antalya.

Nurdane turned to him in the darkness, but the light was so far above them that she could not see him tremble, his fingers laced, pressed against his chest. After all this time, his evidence in ochre, hidden deep within a cave he never knew existed. He wished the merchant from Antalya could be there to see the origin of his prized rug, to meet the weaver who had made it, the girl he believed was not like us. Here she was, beside him, the living, breathing divinity, unaware of her power to make things whole again, weaving the past into the present through a series of knots. How simple it seemed. How obvious. His digging. His research. For what? A glimpse of a figure on a cave wall. He bit down hard on his lip, tasting the blood and the salt in his tears.

They stood there in the water, staring at the figure for what seemed like an interminable time. They said nothing, moved only their arms through the water to keep themselves warm but never once took their eyes off the Goddess until the light vanished and she was lost in the darkness once again.

There's no need to dig now.

He nodded, felt her step closer. The water moving between his legs. He laughed sadly at the irony, grateful for the revelation, wondering how everything had come to pass this way. Then, without warning, as if in a dream, she took his hands and placed them on her face. He held her, feeling her breath on his skin. It was warm and damp, pressing on him, the touch of her lips as she spoke.

What is it you feel?

He said nothing. His hands trembled, barely touching her until he spread his fingers over her cheeks, feeling her cheekbone with his thumb. Long and slender like split figs, he thought. Her flesh, smooth and dewy. He cupped the right side of her face, fingertips inching slowly along the edge of her jaw, then around her chin, feeling her move.

Do you feel anything?

Yes.

Then tell me, please. What is it? she asked, her voice naked in its frustration.

Hennessey rested his thumb along the edge of her nose and wiped the apple of her cheek and with his finger, traced the outline of her lips. The shape of a small heart. He did the same around her eyes, slowly, over the brow bone, then down around her sockets, wet now with tears.

She moved toward him and accidentally brushed his neck with her nose, lingering there for a moment, smelling him. The oils. The salt. A faint sweetness that reminded her of the sun. It was her intention to pull herself away. She hoped he would move too, but he remained as still as she, feeling her breath through his shirt. When he could no longer stand the stillness, he dropped his head to meet hers until their foreheads touched.

A woman, he whispered.

What?

I feel . . . a woman.

A warm breeze blew from the south that night, tropical winds from Cyprus and Egypt. Allah's breath, she thought. Winds of change. The clouds moved in over the village and she felt the pressure building in her lungs. She sat in the window overlooking the postman's house and watched Hennessey's shadow move across his room. The silhouette of shoulders, black hills against the walls like a giant mural painted by candlelight. The play of curtains in the breeze. Her mind, racing with thoughts of him, her skin carrying his smell.

She stepped down from the window and took the braces, propped against the sill, then slid them over her legs. Even in the moonlight she could see the dark bruises spread over her shin, like crushed plums, and she was careful not to pinch the skin when she fastened the buckles. The floor was cool beneath her feet, but she walked slowly, dragging her feet through the moonlight, careful not to wake her father and Adam, sleeping beside each other like two cats, snoring. She stepped around a tin of ashes and cigarette butts. Smoke and worry in the air.

She followed the hallway, feeling her way in the dark, the plaster walls cool and wet beneath her hands. She took the headscarf from the hook on the wall, then, opening the door, dropped it over the pool of moonlight on the threshold. She deliberately stepped on the scarf and the light, making peace with the final hours of the solstice.

She crossed to the veranda where the loom had been covered with the sheet, the cloth rustling in the hot wind, the tubular indentations like the intestines of a sheep, she thought. The loom looked bigger than she remembered. She pulled the sheet off as she had done before, but this time stuffed it into a large copper kettle used for dying the rugs. She set a match to it, starting a small fire to give her enough light as she worked. She added only two logs. She would not work for long.

She sat on the bench in front of the loom, her feet tucked beneath her, shoulders square. She breathed deeply, reciting in her mind old songs she had learned as a girl. Thoughts of her grandmother and mother, their voices echoing from the mountain. The words comforted her while she wove. She began a new row, and the knots came easily, as they always had, swiftly, without hesitation, filling the loom with symbols and song. Each knot had its intention, like a prayer or a curse, thoughts of Gordion in her mind, the legend repeating itself like a broken record, and her father's warning, that knots can be weapons.

Her head throbbed and her fingers were cramped. She paused to massage them, rubbing one against the other, searching the rug for something she forgot. She sensed an error in the symbols. Amulets, oleander trees, birds, rosettes, wheels of fortune and chance, protection, fertility, happiness, immortality. The bride would have everything she needed here. Arches to travel. The altar to rest. She reached out to the rug and traced each symbol with her finger, murmuring a prayer for each, then one last blessing for the bride. *Eksik olmayiniz.* May you want for nothing.

Her eyes had grown weary in the fading light as the sheet burned in the kettle. A soft hissing of gases. She cut the last knot and lay the knife on her lap to wipe the hair from her eyes. Her skin damp. Fingers cool, even in the heat. Her heart pounded.

She pushed herself off the bench and pulled the shed stick and lease rod from the warp. Raising her knife in the air, she slashed through the crossbars, severing the rug from the loom. She jumped out of the way as the knots tumbled forward like a weighted tongue, slapping the ground. Her own face stung and she felt dizzy, her legs suddenly weak. She grabbed the loom, turning her face into the hot wind. Dust clouds blew over the village like a spirit sent to disturb the dreams of sleepers. She stood there with her right hand outstretched, thanking Allah for the gift He had given her so long ago, for the blessings in the knots and the honor they had brought her. And yet at the same time, she felt nauseated. Her stomach, pitted with regret.

She shifted her eyes toward the mosque, where heat lighting split the sky and illuminated the tiles, squares of purple and green like fish scales. Her fingers trembled, her palms sticky and moist, fingertips cold. She drew her hands closer slowly, until at last she turned them palms-up to have the first look, then, confirming her suspicions, raised them to the sky for Allah to see what she had always suspected but was too afraid to know.

S he woke to the smell of roasted lamb, flesh and iron, blood. Marriage. She rolled over on her side and looked up to find a crowd of women standing around her in the dirt, hands outstretched with flowers and candles. They wore shiny black capes over checked trousers and quilted jackets, coins hanging from their headscarves. A flock of ravens, she thought, their voices as shrill, excited.

Get up, they said.

They lifted her off the ground and held her waist as she found her balance, her head groggy, neck pinched from sleeping on the rug. She looked down at the ground. Nothing but a square in the dirt where it lay. Older women sat on the ground and polished silverware from the ashes in the kettle.

Where's the rug?

Your father took it to the lodge.

She rubbed her eyes and yawned, the sun was already bright, high over the village. Her face, sunburned from sleeping outside.

Time for henna, they said, lifting her to a standing position. Having fastened her braces, they walked behind her in a slow procession and ushered her into the house. She was tired and her legs ached, buckling every few moments, but they did not offer to carry her and honored her simple dignity by letting her walk ahead of them, alone.

She stepped into the hallway, where the five village brides, red veils over their faces, waited with more flowers and bread they had baked in her honor. They stood in a line holding trays filled with her favorite foods. *Pekmez* and crushed pistachios, mulberries, ripe figs. A few young girls sat cross-legged, swatting at flies that landed on the blushing flesh of split pomegranates.

Nurdane moved passed them, into the parlor, where a group of older weavers rushed to kiss her hands, lifting them to their own foreheads to bless themselves. They caressed her face, the skin on their hands, oddly smooth, softened by years of lanolin, and oily too, like grape leaves. They touched her as they would an infant, delicately, slowly, trying to recover the part of their past that had been lost in the wrinkles and folds of their dying skin. Tears slid freely down their cheeks. They were too old to hold back. These were the women who believed in the myth, in the power of the virgin's knots. Their affection for Nurdane was not only for the rugs she made but for what they had inherited from her heart. Celebrating her was the least they could do to pay her respect.

They spread a red mohair blanket at her feet and offered plates of hard-boiled eggs, garlic, and peppers stuffed with lamb. She sat with them on the floor, backs against thick bolsters lining the walls, knees to chests, shoulders stuck to shoulders, the heat transferring from one woman to the next. The brides picked at the food, too nervous to eat. She could feel their stares, and when she looked up to drink tea, they met her with curious eyes, hands folded in their laps, pressing into each other. Their small muscles flexed in their arms, quivering with excitement. She suspected they were trying to tell her something in the silence. Hushed whispers between them. Then a burst of giggles until one of the older women stared them into silence again.

They offered coffee when she finished eating. The bitter grains usually made her stomach hurt, but they insisted it would bring her luck. She finished a cup and, against her better judgment, drank another and another until the brides emptied the samovar, pushing their cups to the center of the circle. Then, as if they had rehearsed it, the older women began to sing an old folk song as each of the five brides took off one of the gold bracelets they had received for their dowry and passed them around the circle for the women to bless. Then they passed them to Nurdane and slid them over her hand, stacking them on her thin wrist. They had never given her such gifts, and although she found it generous, the gesture disturbed her. She was struck silent for a minute and shifted uncomfortably on the floor. One of the older women spoke.

Don't you like them?

Nurdane lifted her face.

They're beautiful. Yes. Thank you.

She ran her fingers over the gold, still warm like Hennessey's watch on her wrist. She could feel them staring at her, trying to read her thoughts.

I don't understand.

The old woman placed a hand over the bracelets, turning to her.

You will. Don't forget us when you're gone.

The light from the teahouse spilled into the trees where five white flags had been tied to the branches, one for each of the brides. Hennessey noticed a sixth one above the door where he stood beyond the reach of light, watching the men dance. They were a raucous group, drunk on music and the distillate of good times. Young shepherds played flutes and schoolboys drummed for the dancers who traipsed clumsily across the floor, bumping into one another, braying like donkeys, laughing until their eyes grew wet. They wore skirts and headscarves, their thick arms waving awkwardly, trying to find the grace of the women they imitated with their bawdy charade. Hennessey was surprised to find Ali and Adam leading the group, their heads wrapped in silk brocade, with tassels braided from camel hair. They formed what appeared to be a conga line and snaked their way in and out of the bodies lumped on the floor, smoking hookahs. The smell of mint-flavored tobacco hung in the air.

Hennessey slipped inside undetected, and sat down beside a group of young men, the grooms, gathering to henna their hands. The muhtar crouched beside them with mortar and pestle, grinding the root into a fine green powder. He dumped it into a bowl then, pouring rosewater into the mix, formed a mudlike paste. He spread the mixture over five large coins, then pressed each one into the grooms' left palm, securing it with a cloth. He instructed them not to touch anything for twenty-four hours until the henna had dried.

Would you like one? the muhtar offered. The bowl still filled with henna.

Not if it means I'm getting married.

The muhtar flashed him a toothless smile.

Have you ever loved a woman?

Hennessey sat back and took a cigarette from his pocket. He winked.

All of them.

The muhtar's eyes grew wide. He poked Hennessey in jest, reclining against the wall beside him, the plaster cool on his head.

Why don't you dance? he asked.

I forgot my skirt.

We can help.

The muhtar waved his hand in the air and whistled, gesturing to a few of the dancers who had taken a break to drink *ayran* and honey.

The digger wants to dance.

It's okay, really. I'll watch.

Can you find him a skirt?

The muhtar shot a look at Hennessey, silencing him as the men crossed the floor shedding costumes, offering an array of fabrics and colors and mismatched patterns.

Take what you want.

Hennessey stared, overwhelmed at the selection, his cheeks flushed, trying to imagine dancing in a skirt. Crazy Turks, he thought. Anything for a good time.

The men jostled the skirts in front of him, but when he did not choose one, they dropped them in his lap, returning to their cushions on the floor.

Take the green one, the muhtar suggested. Matches your eyes.

Perfect, Hennessey grunted.

The muhtar looked at him with concern.

You can't dance. That it?

I can dance.

I don't think you can.

Not in a skirt.

He can't dance!

The men looked over and began to laugh, coughing clouds of smoke in the light. Hennessey grabbed the skirt and stepped into it, cinching it with his own belt.

Watch me, he said, and stormed across the teahouse, joining the circle of men, their shoes piled in a heap against the wall.

They whooped and hollered, cheering him into the ring, the shepherds and drummers picking up the tempo, the floor vibrating. The grooms, too, had gathered to watch, and stood in their best vests, stomping on the ground with their heels. Their clapping roused even the old men slumped in a cloud of hookah smoke, everyone anticipating Hennessey's performance.

He stood awkwardly in the center, eyeing each man around the circle, wishing for one of their cigarettes. He caught Muammer watching him, peeking out between his father's and Ali's legs, his black eyes wide, hands covering his mouth, quieting the sudden case of giggles. The muhtar, too, seemed quite amused by Hennessey's discomfort.

Dance, digger! Dance!

The men began to stomp louder until Hennessey lifted his arms above his head, his shirt riding up his belly, exposing his bronze, nearly hairless chest. They clapped and whistled as Hennessey began to wave his arms the way he had seen the belly dancers do. He closed his eyes and stepped back on his right foot, left hand in the air, then forward with his left, right hand in the air, until he could move in sync with the music. When he opened his eyes, the circle had broken apart and the men danced in pairs now, around him. Adam approached and took his hands, twirling him across the floor.

Well done, digger.

You guys always this crazy?

Before a wedding? Yes.

Adam squeezed his hand and looked up. His eyes were glassy, almost blazing. He possessed a levity that Hennessey had not seen since they met at the hospital.

You're in for a great surprise.

Am I?

A few men bumped into them, the space crowded now, filled with smoke. The music grew louder. Adam stepped closer to Hennessey and pressed his face against his, twirling him around and around as he spoke.

I'm getting married.

You? Who?

Adam pulled back, but only enough for Hennessey to see the finger he placed over his lips, still twirling him around the room.

Nurdane.

Nurdane?

I came back to marry her.

Hennessey felt his heart sink. He tried to force a smile. His mind was racing. A flash of images, puzzle pieces making the pic-

ture whole. The red dress. Adam's nervous energy since they're arrival. Even before, in Antalya. On the road. The anxiety. His need
to stop and pray for Nurdane after they had passed the wedding
party. His edginess, the way he spoke about her, protective, defensive, proud. Not as his patient, but as his bride. His future wife. It
made sense now.

Hennessey's head throbbed as if the stones in Nurdane's hut
had crushed his skull, grinding his thoughts to powder. She had
no idea. There was no way she knew she was getting married,
that the dowry on the loom was hers. She was the bride waiting for her own rug. His heart pounded. He felt dizzy. The
room grew suddenly hot and claustrophobic as Adam continued to twirl him through the mass of dancing men. He locked
eyes with Adam and found himself clutching his shoulder, trying to hold on.

You won the bid.

What?

Hennessey spoke louder.

You won the bid for her rug.

Adam nodded and spoke above the din.

Months ago, when I asked Ali to marry her.

Adam stepped back from Hennessey and opened his hands,
palms-up, where a henna stain formed a red circle in the shape of
the coin. The same he had seen on the grooms.

Hennessey felt his heart sink further, his throat tighten.

Does she know?

Of course not.

You didn't ask her?

What?

If that's what she wanted.

Adam flinched at the insult.

What do you mean?

Does she love you?

Adam laughed and slapped Hennessey gently on the back,
thinking it was a joke. But Hennessey shook his head.

You do love her.

I always have.

You love fixing her, he said, then pushed himself through the crowd, toward the door, and stepped into the darkness.

Nurdane picked her way through the skeleton of the temple. The night air was sweet with melting snow, the ground muddy. She sensed the promise in the poppies, careful not to crush them with the ax in her hand.

She had never been to the temple at night and thought the moon would be a better guide than it was. The path was difficult to follow in the dark, and she relied on gravity to keep from losing her balance.

When Allah takes something from you, He gives you something in return. Her lips parted as she mumbled the refrain over and over. *When Allah takes something from you, He gives you something in return.* Her father's voice. Her father's words, once a mounting surge of care and concern, had become swollen curses.

She moved closer to the altar of the temple, struggling to carry herself up the steps, the soles of her feet scraping the stone. She paused, leaning back onto her heels and crouched, catching her breath. She stood slowly and faced south, the first light of day on her left cheek, the crescent moon on her right. The ancient stare of the mountain at her back, warning her. But she could taste the bitter iron in her mouth, and spat on the ground. There was no turning back now. She had come to do what many had done before her. Only they had offered sheep and goats, apologies and praise. She offered none of these and instead rubbed her right hand along the altar.

Small pools had filled the holes in the stone and she could see herself in their reflection, the crease between her eyebrows, furrowed deep in concentration. She had never seen herself at the loom but imagined this was what she must have looked like, pursed lips, clenched jaw, tiny twitches in her cheeks, something stoic and unfriendly in her eyes. Fear. She had seen it in every bride she had known. She knew, now, that if it weren't for her legs, she would have been married, too.

She placed her left hand beside her right, remembering the tiny world they inhabited, the flowers they picked, the earth they dug, the bread kneaded, flesh touched, the billions of knots tied in her short life. She lifted her hands to her nose and smelled them, remembering everything she refused to forget, the sweet river, the woolen fibers, the damp cedar crossbars of her loom, the underground lake, the cave walls and the skin of a stranger. It was no longer her legs that troubled her most, but her hands, aching from years of weaving.

She pushed the gold bracelets away from her wrists and spread her long fingers, counting the five pillars of Islam on each. Shahadah. Salat. Zakat. Saum. Hajj. Professions of faith, prayer, almsgiving, fasting, the pilgrimage to Mecca. She knew she would never get there, but she had heard great stories of great men who had traveled thousands of miles to complete the duties of their faith. Her faith had been measured in a different way. She lowered her head and prayed to Allah for forgiveness.

Hennessey lay on his bed and played a game of solitaire with cards that had grown yellow from cigarette smoke. He shuffled the deck slowly, mulling over the news. The men from the teahouse were still dancing, drunk with laughter, their music louder as the night wore on. He stood, crossing the room to shut the window, pulling it halfway down, then stopped. He saw, sitting in the yard at the base of a lemon tree, Muammer sitting on a rolled-up rug, his cheeks wet with tears. Feeling Hennessey, the boy turned and quickly wiped his face.

You okay?

Muammer shook his head. Hennessey held up his finger, telling him to wait, then picked up the cards and walked through the hallway, passing the boy's mother and sisters, sleeping together on a single mat, their capes and elaborate headscarves hung on hooks, anticipating the wedding. Their faces were peaceful, mouths turned upward, grinning with excitement even as they slept. He walked past them, letting himself out the front door to the lemon tree where Muammer was resting. Hennessey sat down on the rug and offered the cards.

You play rummy?

Muammer lifted his eyes, his lashes wet. He shook his head and watched a group of drummers parading through the street. They chased each other in circles around the village fountain until they grew dizzy and collapsed.

You want to be with them?

No way.

Me neither.

Fools, Muammer muttered like an old man, wise enough not to regret the frivolity of his youth.

They wouldn't listen.

They're having fun. It's a big celebration. You must be thrilled she's getting married.

Who?

The boy turned to him, and Hennessey tried to read his eyes, detecting if he knew.

Nurdane.

He stiffened, wiped the tears from his cheeks.

What?

Nurdane's getting married.

Hennessey chuckled softly and shifted his eyes to the teahouse, where the flutist was climbing down from the roof.

No she's not.

She is. To the doctor.

No.

It's true. He told me tonight. Isn't it . . . wonderful?

The boy scowled, his eyes wide, glowing in the dark. He scratched his head, hands trembling, trying to make sense of the news.

She doesn't know? Muammer asked.

Not yet. The wedding's tomorrow.

Allah. Allah.

What is it?

The boy ran his hands along the rug.

Get up, he said. Get off!

Hennessey jumped to his feet.

Muammer.

Move.

The boy unrolled the rug, revealing the virgin's knots, Nur-dane's rug, the dowry for the bride in waiting. Hennessey felt his heart race. The boy fell on his knee and ran his fingers over the pile of knots he had consumed with his eyes only two weeks before.

What are you doing with it? Hennessey asked.

It's yours.

Mine?

She wanted you to have it.

Hennessey's mouth went dry, and he tried to swallow, felt only his eyes water.

But it's hers, he protested. She's the bride. Her rug is finally hers.

The boy shook his head, clenched his jaw so hard, he was grinding his teeth as he spoke.

I warned them.

Who?

Muammer dragged his finger through the dirt, making circles and spirals. He spoke through his teeth, seething.

Nobody would listen. They called me *kiz*. Girl. For the tears, you know, we're not supposed to . . .

He covered his face with his hands.

I don't understand, Muammer. Who called you?

They never listen to me. I told them about the ax!

Hennessey pulled the boy's hands off his face. He was trembling now, eyes darting nervously.

Who? I can't understand what you're saying.

I told her not to take it.

His eyebrows were knitted, the furrow deep between his eyes, the tears spilling uncontrollably now.

She wanted to borrow my father's ax.

Nurdane?

She said she was working.

On what? She finished the rug yesterday.

Muammer nodded, the words barely audible through his whisper.

I know. She said she forgave me for seeing it before it was done.

Hennessey listened intently, his heart racing.

What else? What else did she say?

To give you the rug. Then she gave me her hand.

What?

She gave me her hand, like this.

The boy stood and extended his right hand, palm-up, then

brought it slowly against his cheek and cradled himself, remembering her touch.

She told me to remember it.

Hennessey locked eyes with Muammer.

Where is she?

The boy spoke with bitterness.

At the temple. I followed her but she told me to go home.

Hennessey pushed himself off the ground and took hold of the lemon tree, his arms shaking. He tried to balance himself on the thin branches that reminded him of her arms. He lifted his eyes to the horizon, where the moon hung in the mooring. The first light of day swathed the rocks in pink. Then the muezzin's call and the heartrending strain of a woman's cry broke the vow of silence at dawn.

H er body lay calm, her cheek turned on the stones, ears pressed to the sky, listening. She could hear them running up the hill, their steps heavy, two at a time, racing to get to her. The brides found her first and dropped to the ground, their heads uncovered at this early hour, their hair blowing in the wind, so free.

She felt something wet on her arms. A paintbrush. She thought of Hennessey and the rocks, then realized it was the tips of the brides' hair absorbing her blood as they touched their forehead to her severed hand that lay at the base of the altar. She caught a glimpse of her frayed wrist and saw the tassles of her prayer rugs in the tendons and nerves. The gold bracelets had scattered on the stones. The brides spoke to her, but she could only see their lips move. She heard nothing but the dull thump of her heart slowing.

There were children, too, crouched before her, crowding her, waving their hands, clapping, trying to wake her. Muammer held them back, staving off their curiosity, trying to control his own. He picked up the ax, wielding it over her body, every muscle in his back and arms contracted, twitching, trying to keep the blade upright. The postman walked up behind him and took the ax from the boy, touching his hand to his son's shoulder, trying to comfort him, but the boy shrugged off the gesture and his father stepped away, unable to speak.

Muammer spread his fingers in the air, running them over the shaven bristles of his hair. He took a lemon out of his pocket and rolled it in the palm of his hand, the yellow skin spiraled with blood. He pressed it so hard, the skin burst open and the seeds spurted out, dropping into the open palm of the severed hand that received them. Nurdane could take anything into her right hand now and feel nothing.

Muammer took off his shirt and crouched at her feet, covering them from the stares of the brides who had moved closer to run their fingers through her hair, lifting it off the stones like a rope, wringing out the blood. She closed her eyes. She wanted to leave, to climb down from the altar and feel the cool stone beneath her feet, swim again in the river, go into the caves, and explore the hidden things of Mavisu. She could hear flutes and the kaval, a drum, the saz, each note speaking to her. The requiem lulled her further into the stones until she could no longer separate herself from the altar, from the rocks, from the brides.

They refused to leave. The grooms, too, had pushed themselves into the crowd and stood with their heads bowed, reverent in Nurdane's shame, the clicking of prayer beads in their nervous fingers. The soldier stood to the left of Ayse, Mehmet to her right. She was the only bride not staring down at the body on the stones, her head lifted, eyes on the stork that circled what she believed was the path of Nurdane's spirit. Her lips trembled, but it was Mehmet, not the soldier, who reached out, unnoticed by the others, to touch her, grazing the inside of her arm with his thumb.

There was a parting in the crowd. Ali approached slowly, cautiously, his hand clutching the Koran, the muhtar behind him. The muezzin followed with a vial of rosewater. Ali dropped to his knees, setting the Koran beside the severed hand. He looked up, searching the crowd for the postman, locking eyes on the ax. The postman passed it through the crowd, each hand touching the blade, wiping the blood on their hands, immortalizing what they could of Nurdane.

Ali said nothing of the gesture, waiting patiently for the ax. He laid it across his lap and took a small cloth from his vest pocket, carefully wiping the blade in one stroke, cleaning it with the skill of a surgeon. The scene was all too familiar, a reminder of his wife's death, Nurdane's birth. *When Allah takes something from you, He gives you something in return.* He twisted the ash-colored prayer beads in his hand, remembering the umbilical cord. He stared at Nurdane's face, seeing his wife look out through her blue eyes, looking through him, finding the truth.

It was too late for sentiment, he told himself, squeezing back the cry that swelled up in his throat. He turned to the muezzin and took the vial of rosewater, spraying Nurdane's forehead, the smell of blood and rose in the air. He took her left hand and kissed it once, touching it to his forehead, begging her forgiveness in silence, his tongue numb. There were no words he could say to bring her back, no words he could find to reverse what she had done, untie the virgin's knots he taught her to tie, slash through them, freeing herself from the warp of his lie. There were no words to comfort him, no hadith he could recite, so he told himself the only sura that he believed was true, deceiving himself again. *When Allah takes something from you, He gives you something in return.* But this time the words were only words, the truth a bitter taste in his mouth, the taste of blood and tears and rose, the taste of lies. He swallowed as he swallowed the prayer he wrote in the cemetery that night, a prayer for his daughter's health, a prayer for the woman he wanted her to become, a prayer for the bride she would never know she was, until today.

It was not his right to close her eyes, he thought, turning to the doctor who stood behind him, waiting, exhausting himself with worry. He carried the shadows of night on his face, unshaven and dark. He held a medical bag, setting it down quietly, an afterthought, the tools inside, symbols of everything he wanted to do to help her but couldn't. Her blood soaked into the seams of his shoes, turning the stitching black. He bent down beside her, moving the flaps of the silk dress that fell away to the stones, then took a large coin from his pocket. He dropped the coin in the pool of blood, taking her left hand, and pressed it on top of the coin. He held up his own hand, lifting hers, then matched the empty circle inside her palm to the coin-shaped henna stain in his hand, as he would on their wedding day. Her fingers, cold and stiff, refused him.

She could see his face, as if she looked through a dewy spiderweb, or stared up from the river at the sun in the trees. The shape of his face, a figure she had woven into her rugs, a playful addition without meaning. His lips trembled as he put his cheek against her and whispered, but his words were lost. She could hear only the beating of drums that pumped the sun into the sky, and recalled Hennessey's voice, her mouth still fragrant with his memory. A woman, he said. He felt a woman. He stood behind Muammer and the postman, the brides to his side, his hands full of poppies. She could see him more clearly than the others, his hair the color of wheat in the light. His eyes, too, broken bits of granite, had cast their spell in the trail they left for her to follow.

Hennessey returned her stare, fixing his gaze on her own eyes that seemed to look to him for an answer. But he realized her silence *was* her answer. Her actions did not confuse him, and he looked up, searching the appalled faces of those who called him digger, knowing he was the only one who understood what Nurdane had come to do. He was the only one who would ever understand the true intention of her handprints. Two hands had made her famous, but for what she wanted, one hand was enough. He touched the severed hand on the altar, one step closer to Allah. He recalled the rug, the series of steps leading to the invisible altar she intended to reach, and knew she had arrived. She had given back her hand, her gift, to Allah, reversing her spell. She had become the woman the brides would become.

Hennessey knelt beside Nurdane, her blue eyes watery like the river she was named after. He saw the dolor she still held, the light of her eyes outworn, dying in this early hour. He could not bear to see her eyes open any longer and took it upon himself to close them. He pressed his thumb on her right eye, his fingers on her left, gently pulling down the eyelids. He let his wrist brush her lips, parting them, letting the air mix with her final breath. He put the poppies in her hand, bowed his head, caressing the curve of her hips with his eyes, then unfastened the shackles from her legs and returned them to the doctor.

She could feel Hennessey but could no longer see him. She could see only women advancing toward her. Troops, it seemed, a colorful army of thousands ascended from the bare crags of the mountains, floating on the thick band of clouds that separated them from the ground. Others walked, marching from the road that led into Mavisu, from the valleys and hills and shallow fields. She could see their faces had been covered with ornate veils and silks, brocades and linens. Bejeweled tassels hung from the scarves instead of the traditional gold coins she was used to seeing. Some wore dresses too, dyed colors she had never used in the rugs, flowers she had never thought possible, pinks and lavenders and yellows so bright they made her squint. She knew the designs well, recognizing the abstract symbols from the patterns in her rugs, knowing that she shared a language with these women, reading their hopes and fears and dreams in the diadems they wore on their heads. Whether she had met them in this life or in the passing of the last, she extended her hand to them, welcoming them to the temple.

They formed a circle around her and stood shoulder to shoulder, holding up their hands stained red with henna. They turned their palms out, pressing them against the women beside them, then began to move around her, forming concentric circles that radiated from the temple and reached the farthest peak of the mountains. The women danced, slowly at first, faster when the drums picked up. Their bare feet glimmered with the jewels that were placed between their toes. They circled her, chanting, glowing rubbed-apple faces, glistening foreheads, dark, shining eyes of polished stone.

It was a dance in her honor. She watched the women move their legs and arms to the lyrical stutter of flutes, willows in the wind. She moved her arms in sync with theirs, trying to feel what her body could not. The circle uncoiled like a snake as the women danced between the broken columns and placed candles at her feet, in honor of the virgin's knots. But she did not need honor now. If there was one thing she wanted more than the light at her feet, it was to dance like the women before her. And although she was to pray for forgiveness, she could think of nothing but the dance she dreamed for herself in a field of poppies where the white bloomed with the red, and death was impossible.

ABOUT THE AUTHOR

Holly Payne teaches screenwriting at the Academy of Art College in San Francisco. She received her MFA from the USC Master of Professional Writing Program, Los Angeles. *The Virgin's Knot* is her first novel.